"Jocko, you've got plenty of long nights coming...

"...nobody knows what's going down for sure," said Chaz.

"So, why'd they set up Trip?" I asked.

"It seems they know your brother ain't long for this world. Anyways, he be gone soon enough. Buzz word going 'round my friend. Seems they may try an' help you along to your final resting place. May be no truth to it, but I wouldn't act that way."

A double jitter rush shot up my spine. I tried to act calm, like hey, no big deal, so hey, someone may try and kill me, like really no big deal. My insides felt like spastically shaking maracas.

"Ain't no rhyme or reason—your blood's been asked to dance."

BLOOD DANCE

21-3-34
1-26-25

BLOOD DANCE

DAVID MONROE

PAGEANT BOOKS

Publisher's Note: This is a work of fiction. The characters, incidents, and dialogues are products of the author's imagination and are not to be construed as real. Any resemblance to actual events or persons, living or dead, is entirely coincidental.

PAGEANT BOOKS
225 Park Avenue South
New York, New York 10003

PAGEANT and colophon are trademarks of the publisher

Cover artwork by Martin Hoffman

Printed in the U.S.A.

First Pageant Books printing: February, 1989

10 9 8 7 6 5 4 3 2 1

for my
father and mother

BLOOD DANCE

Chapter One

|||| |||| |||| |||| ||||

I KNOW A LOT about drug abuse, alcoholism, divorce, child abuse, teenage suicide. In the early seventies, after my parents died, when Nixon was still a good guy, my brother Trip became my legal guardian. We lived in our parents' house, and it became a halfway house of sorts. Someone was always sleeping in a spare room. Someone whose stepfather had tried to rape her. Someone whose mother had tried to stab him. Someone who had flipped out on LSD 25. Someone who was strung out on heroin. Someone who had drunk a quart of Jack Daniels and couldn't move. Someone who had dodged the draft and was hiding from the FBI. Someone who was suspected of selling mescaline to junior high school kids. Someone who had duct-taped a hose to his exhaust pipe, then strung the hose through the driver's window, then lay down

1

in the back seat to sleep—forever; that was Andy, my friend. Most of the others were friends of Trip's. It hasn't depressed me to know these things; somehow, it's bolstered my humor. The only thing I can't laugh at are my brother's dying jokes. Anyway, nightmares come to me in a police-man's uniform. And tonight I could feel the old fear knotting in my stomach. A detective was wait-ing at the bar, having a hamburger and coffee, wanting to talk to me, waiting for me to finish the last set.

I lead the band, The Armadillo Honkers. I know it's a stupid name, but I didn't pick it; the owner did, and he pays the bills—pays them nicely. I'm the lead singer and harmonica player. And tonight, we were kicking ass—people couldn't stop danc-ing. As the guitarist finished his solo, I looked out over the parquet dance floor. The lights changed colors—red, yellow, green, blue. I shook my head. I still couldn't get over it; people love to play cow-boy.

They come from all around southern Connecti-cut, southern New York, to the Armadillo's Armpit and play cowboy. Most people on the East Coast don't even know what an armadillo is. And I don't think there's ever been a "real" cowboy in this part of the country. But every week, especially every weekend, people flock to Old Orchard like ants to a catered picnic. People love to drink and dance and holler and sweat away the drudge of the week. It's a fluke there's even a bar in Old Orchard. Old Or-chard is a suburban hideaway—no commercial zoning—tucked off in serene Connecticut, 55 miles by commuter train, northeast of New York City. Most of the garages are big enough to be houses. I've lived most my life in Old Orchard. For the past

150 years there's been a bar in this building; the Armadillo's Armpit carries the tradition.

It was my turn to solo. I cupped my E-flat harmonica around the microphone and laid back for the first twelve bars. Then I started pumping. My throat was raw and sore from playing and singing all night. But now I was going to kick some butt, wop these dancers on the sides of their asses, and give them chorus after chorus of harmonica like they never had it before...

When the music stopped, suspended on the unresolved dominant chord, it felt like I'd fainted dizzy into the real world. People were stomping their feet and screaming "More! More! More! More!" But it was over. Two in the morning. Saturday night. Sunday's hangover only ten hours away. Monday's blues—always too soon.

My throat was burning. I needed something to drink. As I struggled to the bar, people kept grabbing me and shaking me and slapping me five and howling wolf cries in my ear and chanting my name, "Jocko! Jocko! Jocko!" like some ancient Indian chant. I just wanted something to drink. I wanted to sit outside and gulp some fresh air, not this sweat-drenched, cigarette-clogged bar air.

People were three deep at the bar desperately trying to get last-call drinks. I had to yell to the bartender who was mixing six vodka and tonics at once. When he saw me, he ducked down behind the bar and came up with a chilled bottle of Gatorade. As everyone watched, I felt a little stupid, but took it anyway. The detective finished his hamburger and pushed his plate toward the bartender. As everyone clambered around him for drinks, he sat there calm as a Buddha at the New York Stock Exchange. He got a refill for his coffee. I struggled

over to him, and he bent his head closer so he
could hear.

I almost had to yell. "I just want to change my
shirt. Then we can talk in the office."

He nodded his head slowly. "Fine."

It was only May. Already I could feel summer
heat and humidity coming. I hated summers in
Connecticut. The humidity blended with smog; it
was like taking a sauna in a parking garage. The
horizon was always a gray smear like a stain of
dead oyster juice. It wasn't bad now. May was a
nice but screwy month. Today it was in the high
seventies, and I'd spent the day on the beach with
Nicky—I hope she waited for me tonight. Tomorrow it was supposed to be in the forties with rain.

My van was parked in back of the bar by the
dumpster. I swung open the back doors. Funny,
things don't clean themselves. The back of the van
was a wreck, still cluttered with boxes of electrical
parts, guitar strings, beat harmonicas, tossed tee
shirts, tools and tool box, an old cooler. Someday
I'd clean it up. Now it was too convenient. If I
didn't know what to do with something, I'd throw
it in the back of the van. Other people felt it was
convenient, too; the back was knee-deep with junk
—mine, friends', even strangers'. I wondered if
parking next to the dumpster had anything to do
with it.

My ears were ringing like someone had crammed a tuning fork in them. I was getting too old
for this shit. This gig was rock-a-billy top-heavy,
not the gig I wanted really. But the money was
too good; the band would've dismantled my balls
with a bucking donkey if I turned it down. So I had
to take it. I could hear people leaving out the front,

whooping away. A couple of guys were kicking over their Harley motorcycles, trying to rumble their brains into scrambled eggs, I guess. I could hear clanking dishes from the kitchen. I unscrewed the top from the Gatorade, arched my head back, tilted the bottle up, and drank and drank. Stuff sure cured my thirst but had very little kick.

I could feel the sweat starting to stiffen on my tee shirt. The tee shirt was my trademark. It was black and had the face of a pink pig with sunglasses on it. The pig had a slobbering, deviant, hedonistic, desiring expression to him; a good time for this pig would be drugs, sex, rock and roll. I ordered the tee shirts from Blind Pig Records in Michigan. Then I cut the sleeves for good ventilation—for long nights of overdrive playing. I wear one every night with faded jeans. And I finally became part of the modern culture—I bought a pair of leather sneakers. Now I never take them off, except for sleeping and showering, of course. I pulled off the spent shirt and tossed it in the back. I pulled out a white tennis towel and mopped off the sweat, then grabbed a fresh tee shirt from a box and slipped into it. I finished the Gatorade. Now there was nothing to do but go talk to this detective and find out what he wanted. Oh well. Shit . . .

Chapter Two

IIII IIII IIII IIII IIII

As usual, the office was a mess. Invoice papers were piled all over the desk like used napkins. Pinup girls dangled from the walls. Phone books were left open to the Yellow Pages. Old coffee cups with mold growing in the bottom cluttered the desk and shelves. Cigarette butts overflowed from ashtrays. The office smelled like burned coffee and cigarette smoke and flat beer.

I had quit smoking a few days ago, a few days after I'd quit drinking and doing drugs. Now I drank Gatorade and did aspirin. It's about the hundredth time this year I've quit smoking and drinking and doing drugs. I fumbled through the cluttered desk drawers and finally found a pack of Marlboros. What the hell? I could quit again tomorrow.

When it came to police, I had a simple rule: never speak until spoken to. If I had to, I could sit in the office and not say a thing all night. I didn't have to.

"I'm Mike Stills, detective with Riverton Police." He reached out to shake my hand. My handshake had as much spunk as a dead fish.

"Nice to me' you," I said.

We were seated across from each other in office chairs. His horn-rimmed glasses were the size of halved grapefruits. He took off his dark blue suit coat and his arms poked out of a short-sleeved shirt. His knobby bones poked through his pale skin; his skin looked fresh patted with talcum powder. I guessed if he went to a suntanning clinic,

6

he'd lie under the fluorescent lamps. He had as much personality as a blank computer disk.

"Your music sounds good," he said.

"Thanks." Maybe I wasn't being fair.

He was so skinny. His arms hung limp like over-boiled spaghetti. I felt self-conscious. At one time I had nineteen-inch arms, able to bench 360 pounds; I'd built my five-foot-eight frame up to 195 pounds of muscle—my legs as solid as telephone poles, able to squat with 800 pounds. I stopped working out long ago—I wasn't big enough to kill folks as a professional football player. But I never shrank, really. People still kidded me about my coconut arms.

"Look," I said. "I'm glad you like the music. But I know you're not here to talk about it."

"No, not really." Bald eagles, frozen in flight, dotted Mike Stills's tie.

"So what can I do for you?"

"Well, how's your brother keeping?" he asked.

Damn it. I should've known. "He's okay."

Mike Stills looked at me, not saying anything. Then, "I understand he has cancer."

I shifted in my chair. Someday I'd be able to act normal when people asked me that. But what the hell was normal?

"Yeah," I said. "He does."

"I'm sorry, really." He sounded it, too—or was I just desperate for sympathy, understanding? "My father died of colon cancer," Mike Stills said.

"I'm sorry." Suddenly, I liked the guy. He knew what it was like. Maybe he was skinny for a reason; maybe he was a marathon runner. I shouldn't be hard on him. Give him a chance. Then a rush of panic seared through my insides—maybe Trip had died. I felt like I couldn't breathe. I stubbed out the cigarette. I started shaking. I acted like I was cold and started rubbing my arms. What would I do? He was only ten years older than I was, my only family. And I hated being with him—I knew he was going to die. And I hated not being with him—I knew he was going to die. I had to take it easy; they wouldn't send a detective to tell me Trip had died. A policeman, maybe. The ringing in my ears was shrill and faint. A dull pounding thudded at my temples. Trip had to be alive. I started rubbing my head and back.

"Was he under treatment?"

"He was, yeah. Then he stopped. He went on this special health food diet, all vegetables. He says it's better. I don't know."

"It must be pretty expensive," Mike Stills said.

"Where he buys vegetables, it sure as hell is."

"No, no. I mean cancer treatment."

"Well, you know. Anyway, Trip had insurance."

"That's what I understand."

I reached down to tie my sneaker. I noticed I could see myself in Mike Stills's shiny black shoes. It seemed Trip was alive.

"Have any idea where your brother might have been today?"

"Well, yeah. Probably lobster fishing."

"We know he was on his boat." He pulled out a super low-in-tar cigarette. He packed the tobacco by tapping the cigarette against the face of his old Timex watch. Well, I guess he wasn't a marathon runner.

"Ever go lobster fishing with him?"

"Sure," I said. "Couple of times. All he did was pull enough traps for himself and friends."

"So he didn't make any money to speak of?"

"No. He didn't have to."

He lit his cigarette with an old, silver Zippo lighter, then snapped the lid shut. I tried to think of what the hell Trip had done now. Maybe he'd been caught poaching lobster traps.

"I understand the insurance company was filing a law suit against your brother for falsifying records."

"They were just pissed they'd given him so much money. They wanted it back."

"I see," he said. He sucked on his cigarette like he was snorkling. He must have just switched to low-in-tar. I offered him a Marlboro.

He took it. "Thanks."

"No problem," I said. "They're not mine."

"I hate those low-in-tar things."

"Well, they're still better for you than New York City air."

He laughed. "I guess. I can't believe it. We both got cancer in the family and still smoke these things."

"Pretty stupid, huh?" I pulled out a cigarette for myself. He lit it for me.

"Damn stupid." He shook his head, disgusted with himself. "So. Anyway, your brother didn't need the money?"

"No."

"But," he said, "if the insurance company did win its suit, your brother would be in considerable debt. Right?"

"I guess." He didn't sound like other cops I'd known. He didn't have that brash, street smartass attitude. I was back to wondering about Trip. Someone had told him he could legally be shot for poaching lobster traps. Or maybe Trip had gotten into a riff with someone poaching his traps.

"So it's possible your brother would need a lot of money?"

I stubbed out the cigarette. It tasted hot. I didn't mind beating around the bush, but he was beating around the Amazon.

"I guess," I said. "Look, what is it you want to know?"

"Okay," he said as he exhaled. "You asked for it, plain and simple. Your brother's being held as the suspect in a double murder. He's also suspected of possessing six kilos of cocaine, close to 90 percent pure, with the intent to sell. There you have it. I'm glad you asked. There's no way to ease into it."

Here I was expecting a spat over lobsters. Now I was being told my brother was a murder suspect. I started coughing on cigarette smoke, the last drag from my stubbed-out cigarette. To ease the pain, I pounded the center of my chest with my fist.

"You're full of shit." Smoke sputtered out like bursts from a dying chainsaw.

"I wish. The Riverton police found him on his boat with two dead black men, both Haitian. They'd both been killed with your brother's shotgun. Well, the gun's at least registered to your brother."

I couldn't stop coughing. And now my eyes were watering. Mike Stills was a blur. I kept pounding my chest.

"When did you find him?" I couldn't believe it; leave it to Trip. I'd need the toes and fingers of a football team to count how many times I'd covered his ass. This time I wouldn't do anything. I couldn't—I had no idea what was going on.

"They found him about eight-thirty tonight. His boat ran aground on a private beach. Apparently, one of the two black men put up a fight and clobbered your brother with a baseball bat. Your brother's unconscious now. A concussion. Nothing serious. Right now he's our only witness and only suspect. We're not in the habit of arresting unconscious men."

"Jesus Christ!" I shook my head. "Good ol' Trip." I should've known the jerk was still alive. Now I wanted a drink.

Chapter Three

IIII IIII IIII IIII IIII

AFTER MIKE STILLS left I went to the bar. All the customers had cleared out. The waitresses, bartenders, cooks, and dishwashers cleaned up without looking at me. The band was loading up their cars; we struck the set on Saturdays. I sat on a bar stool and flashed two fingers at Pete. Automatically he fixed me a double fister—100 proof Absolut Vodka with a Beck's dark beer chaser. I took gulps of vodka followed by swigs of beer. The vodka tasted like water. I finished in less than a minute, lit a cigarette. Pete fixed me another round without asking. Out of nowhere, Nicky wrapped around me.

"What happened?" she asked.

"I don't want to talk about it."

Nicky's thick blond hair was cropped close on the sides and tufted out in a high fashion, new-wave style. She looked out of place in this fake cowboy bar, like she'd stepped out of a chic new-wave disco and stumbled in here accidentally.

"Is everything okay?" she asked with a moist tongue in my ear.

"Everything's fine." I finished my second round.

Nicky had only been around a couple of weeks, had kind of thrown herself on me, falling in love; she was so beautiful, it was hard to resist. Men often just gaped, their mouths hung open like garages for crows. Women got pissed off she was so pretty. But Nicky was bored with being beautiful. She'd decided going out with a blue-jeaned harmonica player was the twist her life needed. Honestly, I was uneasy with her being so in love so soon, but tonight I didn't want to be alone.

"You want me to massage your neck?"

"If you want."

She started kneading my shoulders. And I finished my second round. Good ol' me—when the going gets tough, the untough, like me, go and make things worse. Booze and drugs and bodily abuse, one love affair I could never end. Eddy, my mad Puerto Rican drummer, brought me some cocaine lines laid out on a pocket mirror. A nice gesture. The area was so coke dry, people were getting sinus headaches. If Trip did have cocaine, now would be the time to dump it. I did the lines and had another round. And snorted some more lines. And had another cigarette. And had another round. On and on and on . . .

At six in the morning I was in my bathroom, the hot white lights burning off the tile floor, hurting my eyes. I was throwing up, having one porcelain orgasm after another, tossing everything I'd eaten. My head pounded at the temples. My sinuses felt like they were expanding with rubber cement. After a spout of the dry heaves, it was finally over.

I lay on the cold floor and wrapped the damp bathmat around me, shivering.

Then I pulled myself up and started the shower and got in when the water was hot. I sat on the shower floor, letting hot water wash over me. I stayed as long as I could. Then there was too much steam, and I couldn't breathe. I killed the shower, got out, toweled off. I brushed to get the chalky film off my teeth, to get the sour chunky taste out of my mouth; I had to brush twice.

When I got back to bed, Nicky was sitting up waiting for me. I'd forgotten she'd come home with me. Then I remembered I'd lost count somewhere around the eighth round. And sometime after I'd lost count, everyone decided Nicky should drive me home. Nicky insisted.

"You all right?" she asked.

"Better, I guess."

I lay down. She wrapped close to me. I felt her hands massaging my back. She massaged me until I fell asleep. I slept fitfully, waking up off and on, dreaming about horses being slaughtered with shotguns.

Like so many other God-fearing Americans, I spent Sunday incapacitated with a hangover. Something was using my head for a gong, pounding over and over. Something was perplexed— why didn't I make any noise when hit? Something resolved I didn't make noise because I wasn't hit hard enough. Something decided to hit me harder and harder. All I could do was groan and groan.

I spent the day watching old Tarzan movies on channel 5 with Nicky. All day Nicky nursed me. All she wore was an oversized, red flannel shirt. She

walked around slow and lazy like a half-awake cat.
She fixed me her special hangover soup; I couldn't
eat. Fixed me her special hangover Bloody Mary; I
couldn't drink. With baby oil she massaged my
neck, my shoulders, my back, my waist. She
spread oil over my groin; the heat in my legs
spread like sunburn.

"Nicky, please. No."

"What's the matter?" Her pulsing hand stopped.

"I have a headache."

Most definitely hung over...

I tried not to think. It didn't work. Thoughts
were bumping in my brain like airport traffic,
blaring for movement. I couldn't get it in my
mind—Trip, a murderer. I couldn't imagine
murder. It made no sense to me. Murder was ab-
stract like a chalkboard filled with calculus scrib-
bles—I had no way to begin to make sense of it.
Murder always happens to someone else. Miami
was big on murder, New York City, too. But it
never happened to the girl next door. I couldn't
make it real.

Six kilos of cocaine was another story; that I
could make real. My limited math was enough for
estimating, especially when I used my calculator.
The street value was around $90,000. But no
dealer in his right mind would dump 90 percent
pure coke on the streets; he'd step on it good—eco-
nomic motives override considerations of quality.
Anyway, coke that good would give every Yuppy
on the East Coast a bloody nose; there'd be a rash
of bleeding Yuppies rushing to hospitals, not good
for a dealer's desired low profile. So, probably, the
coke was worth, when cut, well over a $100,000 for
Trip. Why did I think that? Trip hadn't done it. I
hoped.

But, no—none of it made sense. Trip had been straight, nothing, for three years, at least. He gave me shit about smoking and drinking coffee. He didn't need the money because the insurance company didn't have a case. Mostly, Trip didn't care if he died; Mike Stills felt Trip maybe wanted cash to start treatment again. I doubted it. I wouldn't mind if Trip went back to treatment. We had different views on cancer treatment; I believed in modern medicine, Trip in vitamin C and vegetables.

Chapter Four

IIII IIII IIII IIII IIII

TRIP HADN'T LIED to me, yet. I remembered his drug phases like most people remember the whims of hair fashion. He used to snort and smoke heroin, couldn't handle the needle; he promised me he couldn't become addicted that way. After detox at a $300-a-day hospital, he switched to reefer and made runs to New Mexico in a VW van and hauled back Acapulco Gold. Then he started dressing all in white, espoused the religion of peace and drugs —if everybody did the same drug we'd all think the same—and picked up the nickname "Johnny Acidseed." At fifteen I did some mean acid, some LSD 25, blotter, micro dot, orange and yellow sunshine. Then Trip went all natural, peddling mushrooms and peyote. He quit drugs, started tending bar, started drinking. Then it was back to drugs in combinations: quaaludes and angel dust, speed and booze, cocaine and reefer. For the first time I can remember, Trip was straight. He tells me, now that he's coming onto forty, he feels stoned all the time and doesn't need drugs.

During his hardest time he was living in the Everglades country in southern Florida, in a log cabin. He was strung out on speed—Black Beauties—and drank Boodles Gin to cut the jitters. He made a tax-free living by ripping off drug dealers. He wanted me to go in with him, gave me a rundown on why it was a perfect gig—you burn a dealer and usually get cash and drugs. And who can the dealer complain to? His biggest hit brought home $8,000 and four ounces of cocaine.

He'd stake out his victim in Miami, make his hit, then disappear in the boondocks—the swamp country where he learned a good recipe for raccoon, out to loving a black woman who couldn't read or write, but understood so fine the poetry of the body, Trip said. But his own body couldn't rhyme no poetry. The speed made him impotent. He grew paranoid; everyone was after him. So he kept himself on speed twenty-four hours a day. The speed and gin mixed with chronic insomnia and paranoia whittled him down to close to a hundred pounds. The black woman kicked him out.

Well, so far Trip hadn't lied to me. When our parents died, Trip made me promise I'd never lie to him; he promised he'd never lie to me. We were all we could trust, he said, and if we can't trust each other, we might as well be dead. So he hadn't lied. Maybe he got around lying by just not telling me.

I don't know when Trip started dreaming about lobster fishing. I guess it was the summer we drove up to Maine, still a family, in the old Dodge station wagon. I remember his head stuck out the window

most of the time, watching coast-life flick by like
flashing postcards. Well, the dream never left him.
When he found out he was dying, he told me he
was going to buy a boat and lobster fish. Liver
cancer. Maybe a year, maybe not, the doctor said.
Can't ever tell. But once it kicks in it moves fast.
Trip wanted to die on the boat. He wanted to be
cremated. He wanted his ashes spread over Bald
Mountain, in Maine, and I was to do that.

Trip found a boat listed in *Bargain News*. We
drove up to New London. The old man, maybe 85,
said he'd have to meet Trip before he sold him his
boat. We met for lunch. The old man was nick-
named Uncle Lee, everyone called him that. Uncle
Lee's hair looked like it'd been blown dry with a
vacuum cleaner. He shook and trembled like he
was lunching in a meat freezer. And when he
started eating, the mayo from his chicken salad
mixed with spit and leaked down his chin in
creaming drools. When the waitress saw, she just
wiped his chin clean. "Uncle Lee comes for lunch
all the time," she said. Uncle Lee had no family, no
friends but a black and white television, no control
over his chicken salad mayo. When we left, Trip
said he didn't know if dying young was so bad.
Another dying joke; I didn't laugh.

Trip paid cash for the boat, and it was in worse
shape than Uncle Lee. It was flecked with chipping
gray paint. The floor boards were rotting and soft
and swollen with water. Maybe the engine was
modern in WW II. Inside, the cabin air stunk of
mildew and hit you in the face like a wet rag. With
splotches all over it, the cabin mattress looked like
blue cheese—not a honeymoon haven. Uncle Lee
threw in the lobster traps for free.

Chapter Five

IIII IIII IIII IIII IIII

SUNDAY NIGHT NICKY brought me to see Trip. He was still slipping in and out of consciousness. A tangle of wires and tubes scrawled out from him like an angry child's doodle. His head was covered with bandages; it looked like he was wearing a 1920's football helmet. I watched him for an hour, hoping he'd wake. He woke once, looked at me glassy eyed, tried to say something, then fell off to sleep. Later in the week when he came to and was in a stable condition, he was transferred to a maximum-security prison hospital. After taking his statement, he was arrested for both counts of murder and possession of narcotics with intent to sell.

I talked to Trip before visiting him. He had strict instructions: I was to go to an organic foods market and buy a rainbow of vegetables, buy Deer Park bottled water to wash them; the food was terrible in the hospital. I bought yellow squash, purple cabbage, mushrooms, broccoli, radishes, sprouts, green and red and yellow peppers. It cost over 25 dollars for a salad.

Trip was still in a tangle of wires and tubes, in a room by himself, not a very cheery room. The cinderblock walls were painted flat gray. The window had bars on it. The door was two-inch steel with multiple locks and a wire and glass peep hole. The coldness from the floor seeped through my sneakers. Two video cameras were in the corners of the ceiling, both focused on Trip; the central nurse's desk monitored him on TV screens. I guess if he accidentally rolled out of bed, he'd hang himself with wires and tubes.

When I got there, Trip was relaxing, the week's newspapers spread all over his bed. I gave him the vegetables, and he started with the green pepper, slicing off wedges with a plastic butter knife—I wasn't allowed to bring in the serrated steak knife. Trip used to wear his thick, ash blond hair in a ponytail; now his head was shaved. He used to have a thick beard, which hung down like moss on the north side of southern trees; they'd shaved off his beard, too. They'd shaved off all his body hair. Looking at him I got a wrench of repulsion, like looking at a shaved, hairless cat. He was so ugly he was cute. His pajamas were made out of thin white paper, probably cheap toilet paper.

"Can you believe this shit?" He poked at the newspaper with the butter knife. "I mean, listen. They're making me into the 'lone cocaine pirate.' They think I've highjacked all this coke so I can sell it and get cured from cancer and pay off the insurance hounds. Hell, I'm not scared to die."

I thought of something Mike Stills had said— maybe Trip was scared but wouldn't let on. Trip shook his head, disgusted. He sliced off some more green pepper and chomped. The wet crunching sound filled the room. When he started refusing treatment, he'd gone on his special diet. He was convinced he'd live longer.

"They think I'm crazy or what? Shit, I had it with looting drug dealers years ago. Man, when you start coming on to forty, you feel like you're always stoned. So who needs drugs anyways?"

Trip was ten years older than I was. For some reason, I thought about our mother. In between

Trip and me were three miscarriages, the subject and controlling metaphor of reams of poetry written by our mother. She spent her mornings in the attic room—with a pot of coffee on the plug-in burner and a pack of True Green cigarettes—and wrote poetry longhand for two hours, then stopped. It was the only time she was sober. After writing she'd mix cognac with coffee to congratulate herself on a good day or to cheer herself on a bad day. By afternoon she'd switched over to gin and tonic with slices of orange.

"What the hell's the matter with you? You on drugs or what?"

I snapped out of it. "No, just thinking."

"About what?"

"Ah, nothing." Trip hated anything to do with our mother.

"Well," Trip said. "I hope I'm not interrupting anything."

"Fuck off, will you?"

"Sure, sure." He went back to eating green pepper and reading newspapers.

"So, what'd the cops think when you told them?"

"Well, they took my statement and everything. Then one of them asked if I lunched with Martians."

"They didn't believe you?

"Jocko, you're pretty smart. I didn't know that."

"Give me a break, huh? And what about Mike Stills?" It seemed to me Stills would've listened to anything.

"Man, that guy's a joke. He's a rookie narc. Look," he shuffled through the newspapers. "See?" He pointed to a blurb on Mike Stills's background. "He's done credit card scams, insurance frauds. If you gave him cocaine, he'd use it for Sweet & Low."

I lit a cigarette.

"Man, don't smoke that shit in here."

"What? I'm just having a cigarette."

"I know what you're 'just' doing. Come on, screw up your lungs fast and we can both go six feet under."

I stubbed out my cigarette—reformed smokers and people who've stopped eating hotdogs are zealots.

Trip drew a deep breath and leaned back his head and groaned. "Oh boy, dying sure is a tough life."

He looked at me to see if I'd crack a smile. Another dying joke; I didn't laugh. I looked away. He lifted his head back up, folded up all the newspapers, and flung them on the floor. They flopped down. A daddy longlegs spider high-tailed it away.

"Hey, look at that," Trip said. "A spider. Supposed to mean the place is clean."

"It's probably a mutant," I said.

I got up and walked over to the window. There was a beautiful view of a brick wall, a side of the building, just four feet away from me. When I strained my neck, I could barely see the flat gray clouds. It was raining. Now I knew where to go when I wanted to cheer up.

"I never thought I'd be a movie star," Trip said, gesturing toward the video cameras. "How 'bout you, Jocko?"

"Nah." I sat back down.

Trip started craning his head from side to side, adjusting his profiles for the video cameras. "I wonder which is really my best side?"

"They're both ugly with that hairdo."

"Ah, you're just jealous—even with a Hare Krishna haircut, I'm still better looking than you."

"Oh yeah, it really burns me."

"I knew it. I did."

"So anyway, what should I do?" I asked.

"What do you mean? Nothing. What can you do? I've been burned bad. And that's that. And I haven't done a fucking thing. Can you believe it?" He shook his head in disbelief; of all the things he'd done, he gets arrested for something he didn't do.

"Who do you think it was?"

He shrugged. "Who knows? Maybe someone in Miami's still pissed. I don't know."

"That was three years ago."

"I know it was, I know. But what can I tell you, Jocko? It's the only thing I can think of. Your past always catches up to you."

"Oh, how profound," I said. "I see you've been reading Chinese fortune cookies again."

"Fuck off, will you?"

He pulled out a yellow squash from the bag and started cutting off circles and popping them into his mouth like potato chips.

"So what'd they look like?"

He ignored me. "You sure you cleaned these?" He eyed the squash like it was a fake diamond.

"Positive."

"Bottled water or shit from the tap?"

"Bottled. Just like you asked, okay? Christ!"

"All right, all right. Take it easy. Don't get huffy." He went back to popping slices in his mouth.

"So what'd they look like?"

"I told you. One's a big southern boy, looks like a moose with blond hair. The other one's a shrimpy Spanish guy, looks like a horse jockey."

"Well, I'll ask around."

"And what're you going to do?" Trip threw out his hands.

"I don't know. Something. Anything?"

"Look, just let it ride, okay? When I die it'll be all wrapped up nice and neat." He went on chewing squash. "The only thing I'll miss is you. Far as I'm concerned, dying's a good way to flush this shit down the ultimate toilet." He motioned, meaning the world, life.

"If you're not scared of dying, how come you're on this granola diet?"

"Look, man, I may be dying, but that don't mean I'm into pain. Good food helps."

"Come on. You telling me yellow squash eases the pain of cancer? That's bullshit."

"Cram it, asshole." He finished his squash and brushed his hands. He pulled out the red pepper next.

Brothers...

He was always bigger, always faster, always better looking, always a better musician, always a hero—why couldn't I just wrap myself around him and cry and tell him I didn't want him to die? Sometimes I wondered if it wouldn't be easier with him gone. Trip pulled out the red pepper. After slicing it in two and cleaning out the middle, he offered me a quarter wedge. I took it and started munching. It wasn't so bad.

With a mouthful of red pepper, I said, "Trip, I feel I just got to do something. Anything."

"I know, man. But you mess with these guys, and you'll be dead before me. Just let it ride."

"I guess."

"Don't guess." He shook the butter knife at me. "Just let it ride. Let it ride."

Chapter Six

‖‖ ‖‖ ‖‖ ‖‖ ‖‖

IT SHOULD'VE BEEN just another day of pulling
traps. Late afternoon Trip had six lobsters, enough
for a small party. He called it quits. But a fancy ass
speed boat pulled up to him. A man with blond
hair, well over six feet, climbed on board and
thrust out his huge hand, greeted Trip in a warm,
southern manner. Said he wanted to buy Trip's
lobsters. They weren't for sale. Then a Spanish
man, no bigger than a horse jockey, climbed on
board too. Instead of shaking hands, he pulled out
a .45 and casually aimed it at Trip's balls; Trip
would be so kind as to follow, the southern man
explained.

The southerner climbed back into his boat and
pulled out. The Spanish man went with Trip,
making sure Trip went along with the southerner.
They took him to the back side of an island and
led his boat into a small cove. They loaded up
his boat with six kilos of cocaine, wrapped in
heavy-duty, black plastic garbage bags. They
loaded up the boat with two black men. Both
had their hands tied in back of them with yellow
nylon rope.

The southerner and Spanish man paced around
like they were blocking a scene for a play. When
they figured how things were to go down, the
Spanish man went below deck and came up with
Trip's shotgun—he knew it was there—and fixed
up the single barrel with a homemade silencer.
The Spanish man made Trip hold the gun.

The southerner positioned the first black man
then walked over and sat next to Trip. The black

man tried to make a break, but with his hands tied, he was awkward, like a three-legged dog. The Spanish man wrapped his hand around Trip's, crunched Trip's finger into the trigger. The black man burst into a shattering of blood and flesh, and slapped onto the deck like a slab of meat; then he started jittering and thrashing, finally settling calm. The southern man said, Tisch, tisch. He walked over to the dead black man and sliced off the yellow nylon rope. The southerner tiptoed through the pooling blood. It didn't do any good. His white canvas sneakers soaked up the blood like a Q-Tip.

The second black man was placed just in front of Trip; the shotgun nestled just under his ribcage. He was supposed to be a baseball bat's length away. Again the Spanish man's hand—sheathed in a rubber glove—wrapped around Trip's hand and made him pull the trigger. A torrent of human blood and flesh and splintered bones splattered over the deck like someone vomiting. Boy, the southerner said, that silencer sure works good, don't it? Sounds like someone fartin' in a bathtub. The southerner gave up on keeping his sneakers clean and sloshed through blood and sliced off the yellow nylon rope.

Now then, the southerner explained, just before the last fellow was killed, he's able to pop you one good in the head with this here Babe Ruth bat. The Spanish man demonstrated. He swung the 39 bat into Trip's left ear, lunged like he was going for a home run. Trip blacked out. Came to in a hospital. But this time there were no nuns. And he didn't find God.

I didn't sleep well after Trip told me that last night. I was only half-asleep all night. Every sound jolted me out of sleep, my heart rattling and sweat moistening my face. I spent the morning practicing my guitar. I didn't know I was going to be on TV until afternoon. I tried to nap. I wanted the whiteout of afternoon sleep to wash over me. But the phone started ringing.

The *New York Times, Daily Post, Stamford Advocate, Riverton Dispatch*, radio stations—ABC, NBC, CBS, and sister stations—all called. Questions flew at me like a drum roll. "What did I plan to do?" "Who in Miami was angry with my brother?" "What did I think of Mike Stills being assigned to the investigation?" "Was Trip lying or telling the truth?" I finally found out a videotape of me and Trip talking yesterday had been made public. "You didn't know that?" "Well, how does it feel to have private conversations being made public?" the reporter wanted to know.

At first I tried to answer the questions. Then my phone started bleeping in overdrive. Bleep: A reporter offered me $500 if I'd hang up on the *New York Times*. Bleep: "Please hold on a minute, someone's on the other line." Bleep: "It's me again, you just hung up on me." Bleep. Bleep. I felt like I was stuck in a video game. Someone was always holding the line. I was hanging up on everyone by accident. Everybody was calling back after I hung up, and I'd hang up on someone else. Bleep. Bleep. Finally I hung up and unplugged the phone.

When Nicky came over at night, we watched as many different newscasts as we could. It seemed everyone had had an exclusive telephone interview with me. There were news clips of my converted barn, Trip's boat, where I worked, my leaving the barn for groceries, Nicky coming over for the evening. Each station showed a different part of my afternoon with Trip. Every time we swore, there were censored bleeps. I had my doubts about being a media event.

Chapter Seven

THERE'S NO SCIENTIFIC proof, but it puts my mind at ease, and that's all the science I need. It's my own notion based on balance: if I exercise, I can offset all the bodily abuse I put myself through—offset the cigarettes, alcohol, and drugs. So every week I make myself run four miles, four times a week, make myself do a routine of 100 sit-ups, 100 push-ups, 100 side crunches, and 50 pull-ups before running. I also have a braking system. If I've been smoking too much, I'll quit for two weeks, assuring myself I can quit when I really feel like it. I put the brakes on the same way for cocaine, speed, reefer, alcohol, whatever. It's important to know I can quit when I really want to; it helps me enjoy the times I'm rocking through a bender. It's important not to be an addict. But, sometimes, I get the feeling my science has more hocus-pocus than I really want.

After Nicky left for work I got ready to work out. I live in a 100-year-old converted barn. My father had it rebuilt for better insulation and temperature control. Inside it's one big room—twenty-five feet to the main beam—with a pine step ladder leading up to the loft where my bedroom is. The walls are covered with rough-cut pine. My father had six skylights put in so natural light could wash through all day. It's sparsely furnished with two futon couches, a beanbag chair, Shaker rocker, and lobster-trap coffee table. The furniture can easily be pushed against the walls when the band rehearses. My father's Steinway grand piano never moves. I have an old farmhand kitchen table with bench seats. The kitchenette is small and looks fake, like a kindergarten's play set. The north wall is covered by a fireplace made out of gray rocks from stone walls. The barn used to be my father's music studio. He wrote hundreds of jingles, TV and film scores, Muzak arrangements, show tunes, anything. Music flowed out of him like the bourbon—over a quart a day—he made flow into him. Trip and my father used to jam every night. When I was three I joined them—my father stuck a harmonica in my mouth; it was the only thing I was big enough to play.

I did my routine of sit-ups, push-ups, and side crunches on the living room rug. On one side of the barn is a wood and tool shed where I have the chinning bar. After my chin-ups, I went running. I'd set up a course through the property so I wouldn't have to run on the road. My mother inherited the property when her parents died; Trip and I inherited the property when our parents died. It used to be our grandparents' horse farm.

I run through fields and crest over small cliffs; run through patches of pine, beech, oak, and maple; run past streams and small rivers, around a pond and past a waterfall; run up the highest rise in Old Orchard, 1500 feet, and jog in place and overlook a reservoir, the water banked with spruce and cedar and white birches, the view spreading for miles; run back through the rolling fields where horses used to graze. I love running in late spring. The earth completely thawed and cracking in chunks like chapped skin.

It took me thirty minutes to run four miles. Inside, I undressed and started the shower. When the water was hot enough, I got in. Trip was probably right. What the hell could I do? Maybe the guys would feel so guilty they'd confess? Sure. As the water washed over me I tried to remember who some of the bigger coke dealers were. Word had to be getting around. Showers are a good place to think.

A friend of mine ran a bar in Port Chester, New York. Chaz was an older black man. He played a mean baritone saxophone and sang the blues in a resonant baritone voice. He was soft with rolls of fat, the rolls blending in smooth with his large shoulders and frame. He loved to party and eat and drink. He was fifty but had more energy than a Sigma Chi fraternity member. He led Wednesday and Thursday night jam sessions that were a "Who's Who" of early rock and roll and Chicago blues. I used to go every week until I got the steady gig at the Armadillo. Chaz moved a lot of cocaine and laundered his money through his bar. The only honkies he trusted were athletes, musicians, and women. I never thought of him as a dealer; he used the coke money to put his children through college. Chaz would know something even if he'd only heard rumors.

I spent the afternoon playing my 1958—the year I was born—Telecaster guitar. It was a classic Fender electric with a nice, shrill, greasy and trebly tone, perfect for the blues, my favorite music, my father's, too. I felt funny saying I love the blues. But I did. I played for three hours, until my hands started to ache, until my fingers felt like mush, until my callouses felt like they were going to slice off and bleed. As I put my guitar away, I got the urge for a cigarette.

Last night I'd quit again. On the way back from seeing Trip, I bought a pack of Winstons. When I got home, I decided to quit, so I crushed the pack and threw them in the garbage. Now I wanted a cigarette. After putting away my guitar, I started going through the kitchen garbage. I pulled out the crushed pack and untangled it from a wad of brown and soft banana peels—Nicky was on some high potassium diet. I laid out the cigarettes on the cutting board and picked my most likely prospect. Then I doctored it up with Scotch tape. I did a fair job, but the cigarette still curved up like a dog's tail. I lit up and had to suck furiously; after I'd crushed the pack last night, I'd stabbed the pack with a sewing pin. I got a few pitiful drags, then started coughing from the hot, rancid taste of melting tape. I was dizzy from hyperventilating. I decided to hell with it. I stubbed out the cigarette. I'd just buy a pack on the way.

Before I got onto I–95, I stopped at a superette and bought a pack of Newports, then was off. It felt funny driving to Chaz's place so early. It was only 7:00. I'd never been there before 10:00. Hell, with daylight savings, the sun hadn't even gone down.

Gunning down the highway, I drove into the sunset. The sky was turning orange like sherbet. Dark, orange clouds splotched over the sun. Most cars had their parking lights on. I could see a stream of red taillights stretching in front of me, checkering against the orange-stained sky. As I drove seventy through Stamford—the fastest growing city in the country—the corporate building lights and mom-and-pop neon signs mixed with twilight. It was warm out. The air was thick with humidity. I had the window open with the stereo double loud to drown out the noise of the highway.

The first cigarette tasted good. The second, okay. Halfway through the third—time to quit again. I flicked the half-smoked cigarette out the window, took the pack and crushed it, and threw it out the window. Seventeen crushed cigarettes on the roadside. I imagined I felt healthy. After Stamford I passed over the Mianus bridge. It had been ten years—no, now thirteen—and every time I went over the bridge, the memory darkened over me like the splotchy clouds that were blotting out the setting sun. Shit, thirteen years ago; I wondered if it was bad luck now.

My parents had gone to a beach party on New Year's Eve. Friends had built an oversized sandbox in their basement and had infra-red heat lamps put in. My father dressed in his Hawaiian shorts, shirt, and golf hat. My mother dressed in her bikini and floppy Mexican siesta hat. I was only fifteen, but my father let me start the car. He told me to leave the heater on full blast. After the car idled for a half-hour, my parents ran through the snow in their flip-flops. Each had a bottle of Dom Perignon champagne; they'd already finished a bottle, celebrating themselves. After they left it started raining. And later it turned to freezing rain. And early New Year's morning my father hit ninety on the Mianus bridge and skidded through an ice patch and bucked over the guardrail and glided down 250 yards and splashed into the tidal river's 35—degree water. When they pulled them out four hours later, they were blue like robin eggs. The autopsy showed my parents were suffering from alcohol poisoning; both had overdosed on amphetamines, too. Speed and alcohol. The speed makes you feel so awake, but you're still way too drunk to drive. Late morning, when the state trooper stood out in the sleet storm knocking, my brother still hadn't gotten home. I was hung over from cheap champagne someone had stolen from his parents. After twenty minutes of listening to the pounding, I figured no one was going to answer the door but me.

Chapter Eight

|||| |||| |||| |||| ||||

THE SUN HAD set when I pulled into the parking lot across from Chaz's bar. Chaz had a real original name for his bar: CHAZ'S PLACE. The bar sign gleamed in neon above the door. It was across from the Port Chester train station and shared the same parking lot. I got out, locked up the van, and headed over.

Music was blaring out from the open door. Probably nobody was inside but the staff setting up for the late night coming. Tatters of late night party-

ing were strewn all over the parking lot—spent
joints, torn pages from magazines that were used
to wrap around grams of cocaine, broken beer bottles, cigarette butts, shriveled condoms, broken
glasses with swizzle sticks. A gust of wind sent an
old McDonald's bag scruffing by, the ghost of
someone's attempt to stave off the munchies. I
could hear the whirring of the highway off in the
distance.

Dole, the bouncer, was standing outside talking
with a local cop. People said Dole lied about
weighing 350—he really weighed more. His blond
hair was cut in a butch crew. You had to be six foot
nine to look him in the eye. When he found out he
wasn't going to be drafted into the pros, he tore
out every sink in every men's room in his ten-story
dormitory. It seemed Dole had grown up expecting
life to be as awesome as his size. So far it had been
quite uneventful; Dole hadn't gotten over it.

"Hey, Dole," I yelled out. "How's Mom's cook-
ing?"

He squinted to make out who I was, then didn't
look too happy.

"Dole, what's up?" I walked over to him and
stuck out my hand. He didn't shake.

"Chaz's no business with you. Just move on," he
said.

"What? Come on, just stopping by for a drink."

"Not open."

I looked in through the door. There were two people drinking at the bar while the bartender set up
for the night. I pointed to the two guys at the bar.

"Since when do you let the dishwashers drink on
duty?"

I tried to walk past Dole. He stopped me. He carried so much extra weight, just standing around

made him sweat. His baby face was wet and flushed red.

"Maybe you'd better leave," the cop said. He was middle-aged, the jolly sort, the sort who was cited in the local paper as a friendly, one-of-the-guys type cop. He had an oversized, ugly red nose; it looked like a plum tomato that had been stepped on with golf shoes.

"Just one beer. Then I'll go," I said.

I tried to push through. I felt it coming. It was too late. Dole put all his weight behind his fist and gutted me in the stomach below the ribs. I choked on a lungful of air and fell backwards. My head swirled dizzy. Everything went black. Then my eyes were open, the world out of focus, like trying to look at things under water. "Dole, take it easy," the cop was saying.

"No way. This juke box come here all the time."

Dole had a duh-duh-duh way of speaking. As I tried to focus my eyes, I wondered if his discontentment with life had anything to do with his intelligence.

Dole went on. "All the time I got to throw him, huh? Throw this slime back to the gutter. He don't listen. Chaz tells him to stay the fuck away."

Funny, last time I was here, Chaz carved out lines of cocaine all night, brought me breakfast, and promised he'd dump his DJ on his ass and hire my band. Dole heaved me up and started dragging me across the parking lot. As my sneakers scuffed over the asphalt, they felt soft as erasers. Suddenly things were in focus—Trip said one of them was a southern oaf: but no, Dole wasn't southern, and I doubted he could act. Also, Trip knew Dole.

The cop called out, "Need any help?"

"Nah," Dole called back. "Rest up. Be back soon as I know this dumb cluck's cruising."

I used to be able to call Dole a dumb Polack, not that he's Polish, and he'd laugh. I decided it was not the time to find out if we were friends deep down.

Dole started whispering and apologizing. "Sorry, man. When you came around it was show time. Boss's orders." Dole always tried to sound street smart, but it never quite worked, like a poodle trying to sound deadly.

He propped me up against the van. I fumbled around for my keys, found them, started unlocking the door. Then Dole grabbed my shirt and started jabbing my chest with a knife fist.

"You hear me? You dumb mother..." Dole was yelling. He kept darting his eyes over to the cop, making sure he heard and saw. Dole sucked up some snot through his nose and down his throat and coughed it up and spat at me. I gagged. Luckily, his wad flew by my ear and splatted on the van.

"Act like I hit you in the face," he whispered, not moving his lips. I wiped my face with my shirt. He kept poking me in the chest. Then he dropped something down my shirt.

"Twenty bucks for a car wash," he whispered, still not moving his lips. "On it's a phone number. Call Chaz tonight, three o'clock. You look pretty smart, but make sure you use a pay phone, huh?"

"Sure. Got a smoke?"

"Yeah." He turned his back so the cop couldn't see us. "I'm not so bad for a dumb Polack, huh?"

"Too bad you're not Polish."

"That's right." He slipped a pack of Marlboros in my shirt pocket, then started screaming: "And stay

the fuck away like we tell you!" He shoved me into
the van and slammed the door.

As Dole walked off he hitched up his pants. His
pants were big enough to make a canvas canoe.
His blubber sloshed around his waist like a water
bed.

When I'd driven far enough away, I pulled into
an empty parking lot. I flicked on the inside light
and pulled out the bill Dole had dropped down my
shirt. It was a twenty. Scrawled in red ink was a
phone number. I folded it and put it in my wallet. I
pulled out the Marlboros and lit one up. Mixed
with cigarettes were several joints. Nah, he wasn't
bad for a dumb Polack; I was relieved to know we
were friends deep down.

Chapter Nine

IIII IIII IIII IIII IIII

NOBODY WAS AT the Amoco station except the at-
tendant. He was scrawny, probably strung out on
NoDoz. He was bunched up in a too-big army
jacket; his mop hair sprigged out from a Yankees
hat. He sat smoking and drinking Pepsi and reading *Hustler*. All the glass on the outside phone
booth had been broken. I closed the door anyway;
the overhead light blipped on. I pulled out the
twenty and dialed the number.

"Hello?" Chaz answered on the first ring. I could
hear dishes banging in the background, sounded
like a diner.

"Chaz?"

"Yes, sir. Jocko, my friend?"

"Yeah, it's me. What's going on?"

"I'll explain later, my friend. Meet me at the McDonald's on I–95 outside New Haven, okay? Let's say, just around five, there abouts. Fine with you?" he crooned in his baritone voice. If he called selling used washing machines, I'd buy them from him. Anyone would.

"That'd be okay. Five?"

"Uh-huh. And don't be a dumb honkey. Don't come in your personal vehicle."

"All right."

"And make sure no one has a tailgate party with you."

"Okay."

"Dole tol' me he was a little rough, huh?"

"Not too friendly, no."

Chaz chuckled. "Aren't you glad he likes you deep down?"

"Oh yeah, makes me feel much better."

"Humm, well that's nice. So I'll see you round about five. Egg McMuffs on me. How's it sound?"

"Just dandy."

"Good, my friend. Later..."

"Later."

Chaz hung up.

Shit—where the hell could I find a car at three in the morning? I didn't want to, but I called Nicky anyway. I knew she had some straight nine-to-five job in advertising, in the city. She wouldn't be too happy to hear from me. The phone rang and rang.

"Hello?" Nicky was way away in never-never land.

"Nicky, it's me, Jocko."

"Yeah?" Still in the Disney Land of sleep.

"Look, sorry to call. But I got to borrow your car, if it's okay?"

"Sure. What's wrong?" Now she was waking. She seemed sparked about the hint of danger; she knew life with a harmonica player would be her kind of spice.

"Nothing's wrong. I just need a car that's not mine."

"Well, okay."

"I'll be over in a few minutes."

Nicky lived in a small, two-bedroom house tucked down a side street off the main road. When I pulled into her driveway, she got up from her front steps and walked over to me. She was wearing a long, white night shirt.

"What's wrong?" she asked.

"Nothing, really. Nothing." I got out of the van. "You sure it's all right?"

"Of course, here," she handed me the keys. I gave her my keys. Her eyes were puffy.

"I should be back. But if I'm not, just take my van to work."

"Okay."

Nicky had a BMW 2002 TI, maroon with gold spoked wheels. We walked over to it.

"Please be careful," she said.

"Don't worry. I used to have one of these."

I didn't tell her I got drunk and wrapped it around a tree at 100 mph. Why should I? It was way back, when I was sixteen, during my angry youth. I climbed into the car and adjusted the seat and mirrors. She had an excellent stereo, but no taste in music. I finally found a JJ Cale tape she must've gotten by accident. I started up the car—

it hummed in perfect tune—and slapped in the tape, eased into reverse.

"Thanks," I said. "I owe you."

"It's all right."

"I'll take you for dinner."

"That'd be great."

I pulled her to me and kissed her, then let her go. As I backed out, the headlights washed over Nicky. Then she was in darkness again, a white shadow with folded arms. A buzz of guilt came over me. She was falling in love. I wasn't. She'd be there when I needed something. I wouldn't. I could write poetry all day long. I could write music all day long. But I could never bring the two together in song. The only good tune I wrote, a blues, built up to two choruses. The first: I got the I-love-you-but-you-don't-love-me blues. The second: I got the you-love-me-but-I-don't-love-you blues. Love's always a muddle. As I drove off I saw headlights from another car. They didn't keep up with me.

I drove eighty to a hundred on the back roads. The only people I wanted on my tail were cops, them I could deal with. On the highway I drove with the window rolled, the stereo cranked to seven. I passed everything, gliding along at a steady 75 mph. Nicky had a fuzz buster that bleated shrill electronics whenever state troopers might have been lurking. I missed one radar trap, waved to a coffee-sipping trooper as I passed by.

The sun was just rising, glowing soft red, when I pulled into McDonald's. The parking lot was practically empty. A few cars were getting gas. I circled around looking for Chaz. He hadn't arrived. I went over into the rear of the lot and backed into a parking space. I could see everything coming and going.

I lit a cigarette and rolled down the window. The air was cool and damp. The fresh sprouts of weeds were wet with dew. There was a little traffic, mostly trucks; the sound of passing traffic was swallowed by lengths of silence. As I sat looking at all the asphalt, looking at highway weeds with soda cans cluttered about, I could hear birds; damn, if I could fly, I wouldn't live at a roadside McDonald's. I'm sure the birds stuck around to bum crumbs or score big and get sesame seeds. I had my doubts about a culture that turned birds into beggars. ·

Before I finished my cigarette, Chaz pulled into the rest stop in his white El Dorado. I couldn't see him behind the tinted windows. The spoked wheels splintered light as they swirled around. He circled around the parking lot, around back, around the gas pumps, stopped, then saw me, I guess. His car glided across the parking lot like an ice skater. He pulled next to me. Electronically, the window slid down.

Chapter Ten

|||| |||| |||| |||| ||||

"FINE MORNING, huh Jocko?"

"Sure is."

As usual, Chaz was groomed, manicured. He wore a white silk shirt under a black velour sports coat. A display of gold chains draped over his ex-

posed chest. On his left hand he had a gold watch
and three diamond rings, two on his ring finger
and one on his pinky. A pair of Porsche sunglasses
rested on top of his head. I could smell his Pierre
Cardin cologne. I'm sure he had on $200 shoes.

"How ya been, Jocko?"

"Not bad. Things seem to be weirding out,
though."

"Hummm."

Chaz had a friendly face, rounded from over-
weight, with a childlike glint of happiness, play-
fulness. He worked 18 hours a day but always
seemed relaxed, like he'd just returned from a
massage vacation in the Bahamas.

"Sorry 'bout your reception this afternoon."

I shrugged. "Well, it's the way it goes, I guess."

"Kind of had to, my friend. Hope you understand."

"Uh, not really."

"Humm." He fixed some hair around his ears,
looking in the rearview mirror. I knew he was
checking the parking lot, making sure things were
cool, his instinct for protection buried reflexively
into small, natural acts.

"See, now days," he went on, "anybody friendly
with you, well, could just be they're sizing up for
some cement shoes or some shit. That police fellow
just all a sudden showed up being friendly. Could
be he's keeping an eye out."

He offered me a Kool cigarette. I took it. He lit
my cigarette with a gold lighter. The lighter was
flecked with small diamonds. After he lit his cigarette he tore off the filter. He took a long drag,
rolled his tongue back over the roof of his mouth
as he inhaled. As he exhaled he blew three perfect

smoke rings that swayed like belly dancers as they dissolved in morning air.

"Used to make these things with no filters. Now everybody's scared. If you're going to smoke, might as well smoke. Right?"

"I guess."

"Humm. So how's Trip keeping?"

"All right, I guess. He doesn't seem to care."

"Humm. Well, he's been asked to dance with some pretty heavy dudes."

"Yeah, so I guessed. Any ideas?"

He shook his head. "That, my friend, is unclear. I had my sweet niche carved. Moved over five keys of goods a week, the blow coming up from New York way. Now? Thing's drier than a spayed bitch."

"So, you've heard nothing?"

"Oh no, I've heard lots."

"Like?"

"Well'p," he stubbed out his cigarette. "Seems the main dude's a fella named Raymond Broderick, a Russian cat, if you can believe that shit. Family owns a vodka import business. Brings in fancy ass shit from Russia, Sweden. I wonder why they so big on vodka?" He checked in his rearview mirror again.

"Must be the potatoes."

"Must be. Anyways, the Russian cat has a couple of gourmet food joints, too. Heard of him?"

"No. But I'm not big on vodka."

"Either am I, my friend, either am I."

I remembered Chaz always drank rum and coke, using a quarter of a lemon for a twist—the lemon wedge spreading in his drink like a forever smile. I took the last drag of my cigarette. Chaz offered me another and lit it for me when I accepted.

"So, the main guy's a Russian, huh?"

"Seems so. Understand, he's been here a while, sounds like any other American. Some other heavy buzz word going round."

"Like?"

"Well, it just may be the ol' high and mighty County Sheriff Scruggers may be on the take."

"Scruggers?!" So much good news. Once again I choked on cigarette smoke and started coughing. Smoke came out in quick bursts as I hack coughed.

"Yo, take it easy, my friend."

I caught my breath. "I'm all right. Just, all this good news; I'm not used to it."

"You all right?"

"Yeah, I'm fine."

"Understand, Jocko, nobody knows what's going down for sure. Everybody's guessing. Everybody knows it's funny."

"You're telling me." I scanned the parking lot. A few early risers were heading in for breakfast. Traffic on the highway was getting heavier, the first onslaught of commuters.

"So why'd they set up Trip?"

"Jocko, my friend, who knows? Only one thing's clear—some big dudes are trying to muscle in on some big dudes. When thou Titans bang swords, us little squirts get jerked around. Trip—your blood —has been asked to tango, like it or not."

"Leave it to Trip."

"Humm."

I stubbed out my cigarette and took another from Chaz. Shit, life is what happens to you when you've made other plans. I always wondered who said that. Maybe Confucius. Or was it Tom Smothers?

"Anyways, if I was you, my friend, I'd keep your

honkey ass double clean. Watch who's readin' your bumper stickers. Don't dial pretty Ma Bell from your home, understand?"

"I guess."

Chaz pulled out a thin slab of black marble. From a gold vial he tapped out some cocaine. He pulled out a gold razor and cut four six-inch lines. He passed the slab over to me. I took it. A gold tube lay on the slab. I snorted two lines and passed it back to Chaz. Maybe I was in a daze, but I swear Chaz melodiously snorted his lines; he had a swan's grace when sucking coke up his nose.

"Jocko, my friend, you've got plenty of long nights coming. This just may be handy."

He handed me a silver box. I opened it up. Inside was cocaine rolled tight in a plastic bag, lots. I took the plastic bag out and handed back the silver box. Chaz was gracefully sniffing the dust lining in his nose.

"Close to an ounce, my friend." He checked his hair in the mirror. "Had to dig way down in my private shoe box for that shit."

I mustered a flat, "Thanks."

"Yo, you still playing that hillbilly shit?"

"Yeah."

"Oh man, Jocko. Don't get me wrong now. Hillbilly jive's fine for a tune or two. But all night?"

"Yeah, I know."

"Then why you keeping on with it?"

"The money's too good."

"Ah, shit, my friend. Money don't mean a thing if you hate making it."

He sat shaking his head—when would my honkey ass learn?

"Anyway, that about does it for us, my friend. Now, hate to ask you, Jocko. But, please, don't call me until you've tidied up this mess. Understand, I'm not looking to be put on ice for nobody's business but my own."

"Don't worry. I don't blame you."

"When you get things straight, come on down and play some real music like you used to."

The coke was kicking in. Jitters shimmied up my spine. The back of my throat was numb. My sinuses were clear—never before could I breathe so much through my nose; I couldn't smell a thing.

Chaz was stalling. He had something else to say. "That's a nice machine. Where'd you come onto her at three in the morning."

"A girlfriend."

"Humm. She as pretty as her mobile?"

"Prettier."

"Humm. Send her on down sometime for drinks. I'd like to meet her. Send her alone." He chuckled, kidding.

I pulled out one of the joints Dole had given me, lit up, took a few tokes to soften the coke jitters. Chaz was tapping his fingers against the steering wheel.

"Now, Jocko, my friend. You watch your ass good, dig?"

"I'll do my best."

"I mean real good, okay? It seems they know your brother ain't long for this world. Anyways, he be gone soon enough. Buzz word going 'round my friend. Seems they may try an' help you along to your final resting place. May be no truth to it, but I wouldn't act that way."

A double jitter rush shot up my spine. I tried to act calm, like hey, no big deal, so hey, someone may try and kill me, like really no big deal. My insides felt like spastically shaking maracas.

"Now, my friend, when I say watch your ass, I mean watch your honkey ass but good."

"I will, believe me."

"Good. I like your honkey ass."

"Thanks for everything."

"Ah, I wouldn't want no news like that. Ain't no rhyme or reason—your blood's been asked to dance."

Chapter Eleven

THE COCAINE JANGLED my nerves. I felt like a violently plucked guitar string. I got out of the car and went into McDonalds. I had to try to come down. Inside I was assaulted by hot white fluorescent lights, pastel wood dividers, zombies in red uniforms bleeping, "May I help you? May I help you?" Assaulted by a swirl of half-awake people who were cranky, pissed about another day of work. And worst—someone had over-cranked the Muzak, and I was being blasted with a string and bassoon rendition of "Eleanor Rigby." Why did I think McDonalds would help bring me down? Maybe because it was so neutral, so normal, so homogenized. I ordered two Egg McMuffins with bacon—I craved salt— and a large orange juice. Back in the car I slapped in the JJ Cale tape, listened to a favorite song, "They Call Me The Breeze." I'd like to whisk away from life. I didn't whisk anywhere, so I chomped into an Egg McMuffin.

The only sort of funny thing was Scruggers. He

used to be chief detective, then commissioner of
Old Orchard's police force, not the biggest of jobs.
But he was smooth in public relations and got
elected into office as county sheriff. With Trip,
Scruggers was like a mutt driven by the fecund
smell of a bitch in heat, going bonkers, thrashing
wildly, doing anything, trying to bust, to arrest
Trip. Never did.

Once Scruggers pulled me in for questioning. Of
course, I didn't know anything. Scruggers asked
me if I knew anything about India. "Well, not
much," I said; I didn't expect a history quiz.
Scruggers asked if I knew millions of people were
starving over there? Well, I knew that. He asked if I
understood why they were starving? Well, I
guessed it had something to do with food. "No," he
said, "it had nothing to do with food, not at all.
Nothing to do with food. Those people in India," he
said, "are being punished by God—they are supposed to be starving. Did I know why God was
punishing them? Because they were sinners in past
lives. That's right," Scruggers said, "they sinned in
their former lives. We all live many lives," he said.
"And if we sin in this life, we come back to a life of
misery when we are reincarnated. Those people
were starving and suffering because they are supposed to. They deserve it. And I don't feel one
damn bit sorry for them, only a fool would,"
Scruggers said. "They were sent to India to starve
and live a miserable life. It was their own fault;
they shouldn't have sinned. They were suffering
hell on earth." He wanted to know if I knew what
it was like to starve slowly? "No," I said, "and I
doubt you do, because your blubber suggests
you're well fed." He ignored my wisecrack. He told
me if I was lying about Trip, I was sinning, and in

my next life I would come back to live a wretched
life in India or Africa—a life of misery, starvation.
"Well," I said, "that doesn't thrill me, but I still
don't know anything about Trip. But," I confessed,
"I once lied and wrenched two quarters from the
Tooth Fairy's good soul, and now I was scared:
Would God send me to India, or would Newark,
New Jersey be punishment enough?" He got dis-
gusted and scuffed out of the office.

That night I told the story over and over. Me,
Trip, and friends got soaringly high on opium-
treated reefer, the reefer Trip was accused of selling, the reefer I knew nothing about except that it
was the best fucking weed I'd ever smoked. We
blew joint after joint. And I told the story over and
over. We laughed so hard our stomachs hurt and
felt like we'd done hundreds of sit-ups. As I finished my second Egg McMuffin, I remembered the
night of laughing. We all decided Scruggers was
bullshitting. I'd have to tell Trip what Chaz had
said; he'd laugh so hard, the liquid in his IV
pouches would turn into club soda. I'm sure I'm
one of the select few who knew Scruggers's India
beliefs. Suddenly the cocaine pumped a surge of
adrenalin and fear—suppose Scruggers was serious? Then he was a serious nut. And maybe he'd
finally gotten Trip. I put it out of my mind. Impossible. He was just trying to scare the shit out of a
17-year-old kid.

When I got back to Nicky's, the sun was glaring.
Harsh slashes of light burned through open spaces
and clearings. The dew on the grass and weeds was
steaming into humidity. I pulled in next to my van.
Funny, both back doors were open. I got out of the
car and went over. The back of the van had been

ransacked. All the boxes were dumped. Guitar strings and stage lights and sheet music and music stands and electrical equipment were scattered and strewn like garbage—like the remnants of a raccoon's feast.

I looked over. Nicky's front door was open. Forgetting about the van, I went inside. Downstairs, lamps were knocked over, pictures torn down and ripped, furniture turned over and ripped. An ashtray filled with cigarette butts had been spread over the carpet like grass seed.

"Nicky?" I yelled.

No answer.

I went upstairs, slowly. I'd come down from the cocaine, but now adrenalin and fear pulled out one last speedy surge. My teeth chattered. In the kitchen all the plates and glasses from the cupboards had been broken on the tile floor.

"Nicky?!"

"Jocko?" A meek whine, like a kitten with still-closed eyes, came from the bathroom.

"Nicky! It's me. Jocko."

I went over to the bathroom. I heard Nicky unlocking the door. When she opened it she looked at me, then burst into tears and wrapped her arms around me. She'd been beaten. Her white night shirt was torn and looked like tattered,_ wine stained, party streamers; the dark stains were blood. Her right eye was swollen and black. A hairline slice under her chin went across her neck from one ear to the other. The blood had clotted and smeared dry on her neck. She buried her head into my chest, not letting me see her face....

I took Nicky home with me.

I got her an extra large tee shirt to sleep in and a clean wash rag with ice to put over her eye, hopefully to bring down the swelling. She lay down on my bed, the wash rag square over both eyes. After she told me what happened, it sounded like the same two: a southerner the size of an oak tree and a Spanish man no bigger than a horse jockey. The Spanish man drew hairline slices with a razor-sharp butterfly knife. Nicky had clotted, smeared lines of blood over her breast, across her neck, across her wrist, and over her legs. The Spanish man kept reminding her—if he slipped, his knife would slash a main artery, and she'd bleed to death. They were positive I was hiding in the house; the southerner ripped apart the house like he was looking for a magazine to go to the bathroom with. He told Nicky she'd better not call the police. If she did, she'd be resting before me, forever.

Shit.

I lay down next to Nicky. The drugs weren't doing me any good. I couldn't think. My brain felt like a stuck toilet, the flushing water only swirling and swirling, round and round, making me seasick. I lay down—Nicky was already asleep—keeping one foot on the floor. Sleep swelled over me like a hurricane ocean.

Chapter Twelve

|||| |||| |||| |||| ||||

TWO MINUTES LATER? Phone ringing. Over and over. Pick it up, out of reflex, to stop the ringing. Not thinking yet. Not anywhere near thinking.

"Jocko Miles, please."

"This is me. Who ... what?"

"This is Mike Stills, Riverton police. Remember? We met the other night."

I groaned. I was waking, from bad dreams to worse.

"Would you be able to come down to the station sometime today?" He sounded like he'd had a nice breakfast with fresh orange juice, plenty of time to read the papers, fresh coffee, and all in all a rather pleasant morning.

"Why?"

"Well, an interesting gentleman says he's a friend of your brother's. A good friend."

I groaned. Words were too much effort.

He continued: "I think you'd like to hear what he's saying. In fact, I know. When are you available?"

I looked at the clock—eleven, maybe two hours of sleep, so far. "About four?"

"Okay, fine." Mike Stills said. "I'll be waiting. I'm at the Riverton station on the corner of Adams and Main. Ask for me at the front desk. Need directions?"

"I'll find it."

I hung up.

I tried to go back to sleep. That didn't work too well. So, I sat up and took stock of my situation. I felt like shit. My lungs were clogged from smoking reefer and cigarettes. Behind my nose, from the cocaine, my head felt like a slimy, pulsing, jelly fish, and there was a dull pounding at my temples. I'd started smoking and drinking and doing drugs again. My brother was dying, accused of murder. My girlfriend—I guess she was my girlfriend— was beaten and sliced and told to keep quiet or she might end up dead. Chaz told me I was too healthy and might be nudged along to my final resting place. So, I lay back down, tired of taking stock. I wanted to sleep, curl up, and have the world go away. I closed my eyes, hoping. When I opened them, things were still the same. Oh well. Shit.

I decided to shower. A good thing about my barn is the hot water—it lasts forever. I got out of bed and went into the bathroom, turning on the shower. I climbed into the shower when the water was steaming. And I stayed under the hot water for a half-hour or more, wiping my face with a wet wash rag, kneading my neck and shoulders. I had a vague idea: if I cleaned up things, things would start to straighten out. To start, I'd clean out the van.

After toweling dry, I got dressed and went outside. Good old May. This morning it felt like it was going to be hot and humid. But a cold front had blown in, spreading a layer of thin, gray clouds. The wind blew steady. It was cool, too cool for a tee shirt. I went back inside and slipped into a sweatshirt. Back outside, I opened the van doors. Everything had been junked, overturned, broken. It looked like a drunk electrician's garbage can. I shuffled a few things about. My ambition sunk like a dead fish. I picked up my tool box—someone had put a padlock on it. Or maybe I did? Maybe someone was playing a joke on me. Who cares? I didn't. I closed the doors, decided to clean the van later. After quickly taking stock of my situation again, I decided I had more important things to do than clean out a van—what? I didn't know. Something would come to me. Back inside. I lay down next to Nicky, fell off to sleep.

* * *

Next I knew I was being awakened by the ringing phone. When I answered it, all I heard was a dial tone. It was almost four. I got up, half-asleep, and walked out into the living room where Nicky was watching soap operas. The swelling had gone down on her eye, but she still kept a wet cloth pressed against it.

I kissed her on the cheek. "I'll be back soon."

"Okay."

"When I leave, lock all the doors. If anyone comes up you don't know, call the police,...I guess." It sounded like a feeble, stupid plan.

"Okay." She adjusted the rag on her eye.

I wanted to say something, make everything all right. Nothing came. "This is what happens when you fall for harmonica players."

As I drove to Riverton, it rained, softly. There was a grayness to the world, like someone had spilled water on a charcoal drawing. I had no problem finding the police station, but I had a hell of a time finding a parking space. Finally, I parked in a no-parking zone, in a bus stop. I got out and locked up the van and walked over. The police station was a Roman-like building with pleated stone pillars the size of pregnant telephone poles.

Inside, everything seemed to be shiny marble, or at least a good imitation. It was quite a busy place. I guess law and order never stops. Everyone walked around quietly like they were in a library. I had my sneakers on, of course. If I squinched them just right, I'd get a high-pitched squeak, like a spinster math teacher scratching a chalkboard. After getting directions from information, I squeaked about; people looked at me like I was burping in front of the pope.

I didn't have to look hard for Mike Stills; he was

coming down the hall, looking for me. It looked like he was wearing the same suit. Maybe he'd bought five of the same kind. He came over to me and we shook hands.

"How are you? Come on, this way."

And he took off down the hallway, not really fast, but a lot faster than I wanted. I walked slowly, squeaking. He stopped and waited for me. The need for dominance manifests itself in strange ways—as I squeaked down the hallway, I felt an odd sense of control. I noticed he had a newspaper in his hand.

"By the way," he said as I walked up to him, "this your song?" He handed me the newspaper.

It was a free circulation newspaper patterned after the *Village Voice*. On the cover was a full-page spread on the Minor and Dutch case. Minor and Dutch were street artists—breakdancers, graffitiers, rap talkers, skateboarders—and one was a black man, the other white. They'd taken to repainting New York City police cars with graffiti. Well, one night six cops caught them. The police claimed Minor and Dutch had put up one hell of a fight. Minor's and Dutch's lawyers said the evidence didn't support the claim. Minor and Dutch couldn't say much of anything—they'd been beaten to death. The trial had been boiling in the South Bronx courts for months.

I'd written a long blues poem about it, "Skateboard Blues." True to form, I could never fit music to it. On the inside of the newspaper, where the articles continued, there was an insert with my blues poem, handwritten by me. My picture was in the insert with a blurb about who I was. I knew the editor, Russ Beardon. He was a friend of Trip's, an enflamed refugee from the sixties radicals. I handed the paper back to Mike Stills.

"Yeah, that's my song."

"Your handwriting, also?"

"Uh-huh. They made a reduction from my copy. The Xerox era, pretty amazing."

"I see."

I wondered why he had it anyway.

Mike Stills led me into a back office. We went from a Roman-like court to a modern motor-vehicle style—modern motor vehicle always ten years behind army surplus. Fluorescent lights, grouped off in squares, checkered the ceiling. Dull green metal desks and file cabinets angled in and about with cushioned dividers. Phones were always ringing. The only flare of modernism were clicking word processors. All I saw were middle-aged women with reading glasses and dyed hair looking up at us as we passed, taking drags off thin cigarettes, taking sips of coffee from lipstick-stained cups. Mike Stills led me into a back room.

The room was narrow. On one wall was a picture window, the back side of a two-way mirror. In the other room sat two men. One was an older man who looked like he owned an Italian deli. The other, a detective, probably my age, slicked his hair straight back over his head, a holdover from the golden era of Brillcream; his hair looked like a wet road. It looked like he bought his suits where Mike Stills did.

"Listen," Mike Stills said. He flicked on a switch, and their voices came through two small speakers, hissing. We sat in new, cushioned office chairs.

Chapter Thirteen

|||| |||| |||| |||| ||||

"NOW. AGAIN," the detective said. "Who were you informing?"

"I wasn't informing nobody," the older man said. He spoke with a thick Italian accent.

"I'm sorry. Wrong word. Who'd you share information with?"

"What's this? How many times I gotta say? I told the other a three already. Huh?"

"I know, sir. I know. It's just to get things in order."

"Ahhh!" The Italian man was disgusted.

"Please. Only once more. Who'd you tip off?"

"Like I already a said, Trip Miles. Okay?"

"And what did you share with him?"

"Ahh! You guys, huh? I hear a lots on the street. Okay? I say to Trip, 'I hear some a guys moving drugs to South Bronx.' That's all I say. Nothing more. Nothing."

"How did you come onto this information?"

"You listen or what? Huh?" He pulled out a Marlboro and lit up, dropping the spent match into the detective's half-drunk coffee. The Italian man's gray hair looked like steel wool, and his bald spot was dotted with moles like moldy pepperoni. His stomach had as much muscle tone as a slug. He crossed his legs, relaxed, like he was enjoying a cigarette and espresso after a Sunday dinner.

"Just explain it one more time, please."

"Okay, one more a time, for you numbskulls. But the last guy say a the same thing. Huh?" When he talked, his hands danced around like hyper puppies.

"Please?"

"Okay. Okay." He uncrossed his legs and shifted in his chair—Sunday story time. "I hear some rumors. Okay? Like I a say, I work in my own restaurant. I hear talking. From who? I no a remember. But I hear things. Lots. Okay?"

"How'd you decide to mention it to Trip Miles?"

"Hah! Trip Miles? Ahh, come on. Huh?" How could the detective be so stupid? "Trip Miles. His name as big as the a Brooklyn Bridge. Huh? People don't forget his kind. No way."

"What's in it for you?"

"Who knows. Maybe a good customer with some a good tips. Who knows?"

"So why'd you tip off Trip Miles?"

"What a you mean? Huh?" His anger surged like he was scolding a boy for stupidly shooting a .22. "Huh? These cuckoo Colombians. Huh? They ruin my a whole neighborhood. Okay? I see a little children, little children up to my knee, little children doing drugs. Huh? Understand? Think I want a drugs for my kids? Huh? And the cops? Huh? The cops don't do shit, not one fucking thing. Ahh, Christ." He spewed his words out, disgusted, like he'd found out his sister and mother and wife were whores.

"Okay," the detective said. "Now, let me ask you."

"What's this. Huh? How many a questions you going to ask anyways. Huh?"

I said to Mike Stills, "Turn it off."

He flicked the switch off. On the other side of the mirror their mouths kept moving.

"Things aren't looking good for Trip, Jocko."

"It's bullshit." I pulled out a cigarette. Mike Stills lit it for me, then lit one of his own. It felt good to exhale the thick smoke; I wished I could get rid of all this other shit so easily.

"Everything checks out," Mike Stills said.

"I don't care. All right? And who is this asshole?" I jerked my thumb at him.

"We picked him up the other day for DWI. He had a fourteen-year-old girl with him. She started screaming she'd been kidnapped, but we doubt it. He swore he didn't kidnap her or rape her. He offered to trade information. Now, this is the fifth time he's been questioned. Either he's fantastic at lying to pros who're trying to find out if he's lying, or he's telling the truth."

I pointed to the detective. "That guy's a pro?"

"Well, it was a practice round for him."

"And what about the others?"

"Myself and three others."

"Shit . . ." I was beginning to doubt—maybe Trip had lied, never told me, something. But who were those guys slicing Nicky. I stared at the Italian man. Maybe I should tell Mike Stills about last night.

"So this guy's a do-gooder, right? Cleaning up the streets. Beat the black market with the black market? Wasn't he porking a 14-year-old girl?!"

"We don't know that," Mike Stills said. "We do know the Bronx is a good area for narcotics. Possibly, the Italians and Colombians are vying for power. Maybe there'd be some kickbacks for this gentleman, for anybody who helped set back the Colombians' distribution. Who knows?" Mike Stills sounded like he was reading a manual on financial reporting.

"I'm telling you—Trip was set up."

"Well," Mike Stills delicately tapped his ash. "We've since found out that the two men your brother was with were suspected of ripping off drug dealers. Something similar to what people felt your brother was up to in Miami."

I ignored him. "He was set up."

"Set up? You think?" He scratched his head, thinking. "Approximately four o'clock. Saturday afternoon. One of the first hot days of spring. The beaches are crowded. Sailboats, motorboats— Long Island Sound's filled with boats. Kind of a strange time to set up a double murder, wouldn't you think?

"No. Four o'clock. And no one finds him until nine, right? Five hours later. Give me a break. It couldn't have been such a strange time."

That stumped Mike Stills. "Maybe."

I sensed he was thinking about it. I felt a little relieved—maybe I wasn't crazy. "Has anyone done anything about my brother's side of the story?"

"Like what?"

"Like find out who was on the boat with him?" I wanted to tell him about Nicky, but I believed they'd come back and kill her. No doubt. Also, they sauntered in and hung around, unconcerned if she could identify them—they felt securely insulated from any law threats. Scruggers?

"Well, there were no prints, and—"

"What do you expect them to do? Walk around on their hands?"

He didn't answer. He stubbed out his cigarette and lit another; he was as bad as me. I stubbed out mine, lit another, too. With my luck, we'd be in the same hospital room with black lung. On the other side of the two-way mirror their mouths kept moving; they looked like fish sucking for air. I decided to talk it over with Nicky, then maybe tell Mike Stills.

"Look," I said. I had to throw it out. "It's going around the streets that a Russian guy, Raymond Broderick, and Scruggers—you know Scruggers, right?—are behind this." It sounded ridiculous when I said it. Once I was caught playing doctor with the girl next door. She was six, I was seven, and we didn't have any clothes on when her mother walked in. I frantically explained to her mother: "the teacher said we had to go home and play doctor, the teacher made us do it, it's not our fault, it's homework"—her mother called the teacher. Even as a kid I sensed it was an absurd attempt to get out of trouble; that's how I felt now. It sounded so possible when Chaz had said it. And who were those two guys. But who was this Italian jerk? Shit.

Mike Stills smirked. "And where did you hear this?"

"Around, okay?" I felt stupid.

"Why would they do it?"

Well, good question. "Who knows?"

"Not me, for sure." Even when he was being a wise guy, he was polite.

"Shit ..."

"Look, I understand your frustration. But all the evidence—"

"It's bullshit."

"Well ..."

"Look," I said. "If I give you a lead on the two guys who set up my brother, will you follow it?"

"Of course." His interest perked. I knew if he heard Nicky's story, he'd burrow after them like a German shepherd digging for a porcupine.

"Let me see."

"You have something?"

"Maybe. I'm not sure."

Chapter Fourteen

‖‖ ‖‖ ‖‖ ‖‖ ‖‖

"COME ON, man."

"No. No way," I said. Eddy, the mad Puerto Rican drummer from my band, was drilling me with one of his insane ideas. Very insane.

"Come on, huh? Get me a quart of beer."

"I'm telling you, no way," I said again.

"Hey, man, tell you what. I get two quarts. Be good and ready with pinga juice."

"No way. All right? His house is a fort."

"What you mean, man?"

"He got some bomb threats or some shit."

"So? Man, you a pussy."

"A pussy? He's got a special security force around his house. Don't you watch the news?"

"The what, man?"

"The news."

"Ah, man, that's shit. Bunch of fairy ass gringos — what's it got to do with me?"

"Well . . ."

"He's scum, man. He don't deserve no mail."

"Look, Eddy, not tonight. It'd be fun, but not tonight."

He was thinking out loud again. "Yeah, man. Two quarts. Get me nice and juiced. Take me one minute, man."

"Eddy, you're fucking crazy."

"Well, I'll be over anyway, pinga head. Got some tequila, a little blow, little herb. You not home when I get there, I kick you balls if you got any."

Eddy hung up.

Hell—another night of keeping up with Eddy. Tomorrow I'd get nothing done. I probably

wouldn't be able to get out of bed. Eddy had this
insane idea: he wanted to chug some beer and
juice up his bladder, then he wanted me to drive
him to Scruggers's house so he could take a leak in
the mailbox. One of his favorite pranks. Eddy had
a simple philosophy about cops: they're all scum,
deserve to be treated so. When I told him what
Chaz said, he started screaming about what a
scum Scruggers was; scums had to be treated like
scums, so Eddy decided he'd take a leak in Scruggers's mailbox. Anyway, since I'd seen Mike Stills
—two days ago—Scruggers had gotten a bomb
threat; after, he assembled a special security force
for protection. Someone blamed Scruggers for
crashing the party, the cocaine pirating party.
Mike Stills called me, to make sure I'd heard, to
find out if anything had come up with my lead.
Actually, I heard about the bomb threats from
Mike Stills, not the news.

  I talked things over with Nicky. She said whatever I thought best. And I wasn't sure. I did convince her it was best, for safety, if she didn't stay
with me, really, I didn't want her to get hurt, so—
actually, I didn't want her moving in. I wasn't
ready for that. We decided it was best for her to
stay with her sister. I dropped her off this afternoon. On the way back I stopped and withdrew
1,500 dollars from the bank. The money was for
Nicky, for the damage to her house. But I didn't
know how to give it to her; I knew she'd fight me,
saying it was okay, don't worry. I had to figure out
a good approach. Tomorrow. After I talked to Trip
on Sunday, I called Randy, the manager of the Armadillo's Armpit, and called off the gig for the
week. So, I had nothing to do but wait for Eddy. I

pulled out my Telecaster and stretched my fingers into the blues—sweet and greasy, shrill and screaming, my Twin Reverb amplifier cranked to ten.

"Yeah, I be good and ready!"

Eddy was singing as he walked into my barn. He tilted his head back and finished a quart of Budweiser in one swig. Eddy had sharp features with skin the color of creamed coffee. He was big for a Puerto Rican, about 5 feet 10 inches. He loved to play the drums, but he loved boxing more; he worked out six days a week—his body symmetrically built, evenly proportioned, solid muscle. He never stopped talking, never stopped playing the drums, always singing and playing the drums. As a drummer in my band, he was a bonfire of musical energy. He opened a new bottle and started swigging his second quart of Budweiser. Under his arm were two bottles of Cuervo Especial and a plastic bag from Shopwell filled with lemons.

"Come on, man," he said. "Grab some salt."

I went over to the kitchenette and pulled out the salt shaker. I was never ready for Eddy. Nobody was. Trying to out-party him was like trying to out-hop and out-box a kangaroo. But it sure was fun trying to keep up. Especially tonight. I needed a good, roaring drunk to knock me out of my senses, to bury my troubles under six feet of numbed brain, to dull the pain.

"Oh yeah! Oh yeah!"

Eddy was singing some song he made up as he went along, half-English, half-Spanish. He was using the couch for his drum set. On the lobster-trap coffee table was a small mirror with a gram of cocaine and a couple of joints. Eddy cut lemon wedges, in rhythm to his song, with his black

Swiss army knife. Then he wiped the blade clean and dry and cut lines of cocaine. When he was through, he played and sang with his eyes closed, singing and pounding full volume.

"Hey, shut up for a minute," I yelled.

"Oh man, you ready already? Eddy ready."

I filled two shot glasses with tequila and set them on the table. Eddy salted his hand and licked it clean, threw down both shots, snorted a line of cocaine, bit into a lemon wedge, and went back to playing the drums. He kept the lemon wedge in his mouth and hummed his tune through the glowing yellow rind. I fixed myself one shot, salted my hand, and licked it, downed the shot, chomped into the lemon. Shivers rattled up my spine. I did a big line of cocaine.

Through all eight shots and eight lines, Eddy never stopped singing and playing the drums. Now he was standing, banging the kitchen table, doing some salsa shuffle dance, singing a bossa nova version of "New York, New York." He did a good, loud imitation of a big band's horn section. We'd finished the gram of coke Eddy had—he cut big lines, nice—so I grabbed what Chaz had given me, for the road; I couldn't believe I was going on the road. Fate. Somewhere around the sixth shot, I'd admitted Eddy had a good idea; it was downhill after.

I was drunk. My body felt like a Jell-O mold in a hot tub. But the cocaine gave me the distinct impression I was invincible. Why, I could do anything. Leap tall buildings. Stop trains. Catch bullets. Anything! Except roll a joint. When I finished, the joint's middle was swollen like a snake's belly after eating too big a frog. It was time to go. I grabbed the tequila. Because I was thinking lucidly, I decided it best to keep the $1500 I'd taken out for Nicky, not wanting anyone to happen upon it if they rooted through my place. Also, it was going to be a long night, and who knows where we'd end up. Maybe New York City. Boston'd be fun. Nashville was a hell of a city. I tried to explain how clearly I was thinking to Eddy. When I mentioned Nicky, all he could do was describe his porno-sexual fantasies he had about her. Definitely drunk—they didn't sound so bad. And then he started singing about them, real loud. With considerable difficulty, I climbed the pine wood ladder up to my loft. I grabbed the saddle of harmonicas; I'd decided to play a "Pissing in the Mailbox Blues" as Eddy relieved himself. I climbed back down.

I yelled, maybe not loud enough. "Let's go!"

Because he was the only other person in the room, Eddy realized I was talking to him. "Oh yeah, oh yeah!"

And he started singing about having to take a leak in the mailbox. Apparently, according to the song, the Virgin Mary had sent him on this holy mission. I lit the joint, headed outside. Eddy came out with his hands flying and playing everything for drums—the wall, chairs, door. Now he was singing in Spanish. Now he was imitating a rumba trumpet solo. Now he was singing about what would have happened if he'd known the Virgin Mary. I handed him the joint. He sucked on it. The end glowed and flared hot red like a taillight. He handed it back to me, the end all slobbered over. I wiped it off on my shirt. Eddy had few reefer manners. Oh well. It was cool out, dry. A thick layer of clouds blanketed the sky. With the open fields, there was enough light to see, enough to get in the van anyway—damn, still had to clean it out.

"Man, how you take these woods?" Eddy asked as he sucked on the joint. He lived in Stamford. I doubted he'd be able to sleep without honking horns.

"I like the quiet," I said.

"No way for me, man. Get humped by some maniac squirrel pack."

"Squirrels don't come in packs." Being drunk, it seemed an important zoological point.

"I know, pinga head. I know."

Now he was banging on the van and singing about rabid squirrels that humped gringos. As usual, he sang and pounded full volume, singing out to the open field so he could hear his echo. I got in the van and started it up. Eddy sashayed in and started banging on the dashboard, singing. And I thought my guitar was loud.

Chapter Fifteen

IIII IIII IIII IIII IIII

SCRUGGERS LIVED IN Riverton, by the ocean; as I drove the van, it felt like I was driving a boat through ocean swells. It was pretty taxing—I had to drive on winding roads and smoke a joint and snort the midget lines Eddy laid on his plastic driver's license. When I slammed on the brakes to avoid mushing a possum, Eddy shrieked in pain: his bladder was bursting, would I please be careful? And then he sang about his bursting bladder.

As we got close to Scruggers, I caught glimpses of the ocean through openings in trees; then I had a clear view of the ocean. A sea wall curved with the road for a quarter of a mile or more. The ocean was dark gray like ashes. Across the sound, Long Island was black like charred wood. I couldn't remember where Scruggers lived. Eddy rolled down his window—I finally had a good reason for him to shut up. But he still played the drums on his legs, gently. A soft wind was blowing. With the windows down I could hear ripple waves slapping against the sea wall.

First time by we missed the house. Eddy was leaning out the window trying to read the names on the mailboxes. Whether he could read English, I had no idea. When the sea wall curved with the road inland, I knew we'd passed his house. We doubled back and found it. I turned around and backed up to the mailbox, angled the van so the rear doors would open out to it.

Eddy climbed and clambered over all the junk, swearing in Spanish about what a slob I was. When he got to the back unharmed, he swung open the doors like he was welcoming himself to a Hilton Hotel. First, he kicked the mailbox so it tilted backwards. Then he pulled out a roll of duct tape and started taping the seams.

"What the hell you doing?" I asked in a choked whisper.

"Seal it up, man. Like a fishy bowl. Pinga juice still be in her mañana, man."

When he finished taping up the mailbox, he unzipped his fly and started relieving himself. I was giggling and coughing, trying to play a "Pissing in the Mailbox Blues" on my G harp. I could hear the wind and waves, and inland a few crickets and tree frogs were sounding off. And I could hear Eddy

taking a leak, whistling to himself, his free hand
rapping out rhythms on his leg.

Suddenly, something cracked through everything. Silence swallowed the sudden noise. Eddy
slapped back, flat onto the van's junk. My ears
were ringing. Eddy was groaning. In pain, he
rolled out of the van and onto the street, clutching
his midsection with both arms. Then there was
more, a fury like Fourth of July firecrackers. But
this wasn't kiddy show time. It was gunfire. Eddy
was groaning. Bullets ripped into the van, sounding like sprays of puncturing gravel. My heart
jolted into double time. I scrambled back to Eddy.
He was a shadow, doubled up.

"Eddy, come on." I reached out for him.

I grabbed him under both shoulders and started
pulling him up. Warm blood soaked into my shirt.
There was more gunfire. I pulled Eddy halfway
into the van.

"Drive, man! I hold on." He was screaming,
groaning.

"You got to get in." I pulled him in farther. And
there was more gunfire. Across Scruggers's yard,
flames from the firing guns flared in the dark. A
hot white bleached us; we were glowing ghosts,
centered in a spotlight. Someone was yelling over
a bullhorn.

"Drive, mother fucker!" Eddy screamed in my
ear.

I left Eddy sitting in the back, trying to close the
doors. I got into the driver's seat and pulled the
van into gear. The transmission clunked, felt like it
was going to fall out. I crammed the gas pedal to
the floor. The van spat forward, caught traction
then started fishtailing out of control. I could feel
the back swerving out from under me. I spun the

wheel to fix it straight. There was more gunfire. Someone yelling over the bullhorn for us to stop. I could hear everything in the back clanking out like garbage cans behind the newlyweds' car, the junk sucked out by the wild fishtailing. I looked back. Eddy was gone. I slammed on the brakes. The glaring spotlight bleached the road—for a hundred yards or more, there was a trail of junk, and all the way back I could see Eddy's shadow, hunched into · himself, trying to stand up. I crammed the van into reverse.

Then my eyes were blinded by orange and red flames. And the flames leaped up like snake tongues to the tops of the telephone poles, the blending of flames looking, for a second, like tulips. The explosion made my eardrums feel like they were being slammed into my brains with an air gun. I choked on my breath. A rush of hot air swelled into the van. Eddy was a shadow standing in flames, then falling.

I crunched the gas pedal to the floor and spat backwards, still in reverse. I yanked the transmission into drive. And the van shot forward. I was running into a tree. I turned the wheel hard. The van swerved and teetered off balance, then slapped flat onto the road. I kept the gas pedal smothered against the floor.

Chapter Sixteen

|||| |||| |||| |||| ||||

MY HEART WAS jittering ragged. My face wet, my
hands wet, my back wet, my body wet from sweat.
My chest wet from Eddy's blood. He had to be
dead. I guess. I hoped not. And I'd held him in my
arms, blood spreading from his chest to mine—I'd
brought him to take a leak in the mailbox—and
now he was dead. Dead. All his insane, drumming
energy laid to ashes. I guess. Maybe he was alive.
But how? I hoped. I should've gone back.

The parking lot looked like a spread of asphalt
football fields. Cars were parked in odd clusters. I
parked in the back. No one seemed to follow me.
And, like I'd hoped, a number of taxis were waiting
in front of the train station—the explosives had
probably been in my van for days, hidden among
the junk, buried. I bet they were in the tool box. I
bet they were planted the night Nicky was beaten.

I tried to catch my breath, tried to slow my
heart. Deep breathing, closing my eyes—Eddy taking a leak and gunfire and Eddy wrapped around
me, his chest flat against mine, his blood being
soaked up by my shirt. If I'd cleaned the van, I'd
have found the explosives, Eddy'd be alive. Maybe
he was. I should've gone back. Fucking coward.
Then I would've been shot, now lying dead next to
Eddy. I opened my eyes, turned on the inside light.
Blood was a dark smear over my chest.

I got up and scrounged around in the back. Almost everything had flown out. Stuck behind the
wheel well was one of my Blind Pig tee shirts,
dried stiff with sweat. I put it on after taking off
the blood-stained shirt. Still, my ears were ringing

70

from the explosion. I took what I had—tequila, cocaine, my leather saddle of fifteen harmonicas,
$1500 for Nicky, half-pack of cigarettes, few joints.
All with a sweat-stiff shirt, blood-stained jeans,
tennis shoes, a dead friend—maybe he lived, I
hoped, I prayed—and a dying brother, dead parents: what the hell was I living for? And the bomb
was for me, and the gunfire, for me—why'd they
miss? I got out, locked the van. Black holes dotted
the side, pock marks from gunfire. It was so peace-
ful outside; my insides were being gnawed like
meat at an alligator feeding. Riverton train station
was on the water. A soft salt breeze came off the
ocean. Lights across the harbor made squiggling
white and yellow and red lines across the water
like electric belly dancers. I saw Eddy as he tried
to stand up, his shadow falling to the ground
wrapped in flames—or was he behind the explosion? Maybe. I hoped. Neon light spilled from
overhead fixtures and blanched yellow taxis. Cocaine and booze—my mind felt clean and fluid
and awake and clear, and my body felt like a water
balloon rolling down the up-going escalator. One
neon light was flickering, off and on, a cheap
strobe light, jittering over the lead cab. I walked
up to it and leaned in the window.

"Need a fare?" Was I yelling? Screaming? Was I
ragged with fear and paranoia? I was. The pulsing
light was sending my mind bonkers.

"No, man." The cab driver was a skinny Puerto
Rican, working a cigarette and a toothpick at the
same time. Spanish music blared out from the
squawky speaker. I didn't leave.

"Hey, man, dig? No way. I waiting for someone,
see?" He looked away, trying to ignore me.

I pulled out a $100 bill, unrolled it in front of his

eyes. "Take me where I want, and you've never seen me."

"Hey," he said, soaking in the $100 bill. He had maroon, polyester pants on. His black leather cap had metal studs circling around it. "Hey," he said. "It's cool, dig? A C-note, man, brings you anywhere, almost, dig? Hop in, man."

I climbed in the back, lit a cigarette. I wanted him to drive me to the moon.

"Hey, man, most people I say: Cut the shit, huh, no smoking. Dig? This ain't no ashtray, I say. Know? But you, a C-note, it's cool. Dig. Anything you want. You want to pork a goose, hey man, get onto it. Dig?"

"Please. Just shut up."

Chapter Seventeen

IIII IIII IIII IIII IIII

I DIDN'T LIKE that the motel was on the main road, but I wouldn't have to use my real name. A choir of hookers used the place regularly; the registration book was filled with Bob Smiths, John Does. The cab driver let me off at the office. The meter read $10. I handed him the $100.

"Anybody asks, I went to New Haven."

"Okay. New Haven's a nice town. I dig. You enjoy, gringo." He drove off.

Dee's Diner was an old trailer in front of the motel. All I could see was a U-shaped bending of rooms strung together. The back of the rooms faced the diner; I knew the front of the rooms faced a pool that looked like a flattened urinal. When I was thirteen, Trip used to bring me here and pay for my nights with the women of my dreams—kinky whores who liked little boys, little boys being easy work. Now I was fighting to stay calm. I used an old trick Trip taught me: if you start freaking out on LSD, concentrate on things you know are real and harmless, and drink lots of orange juice. Well, I didn't have any orange juice. But I knew the cinderblocks were real, not going to hurt me. And I knew the pay phone was real, not going to hurt me. It didn't work—I'd go crazy being friends with cinderblocks and pay phones. And I wasn't high on LSD. I was wired with images and threats of death and dying. I had to keep calm until I got a room.

I walked into the office. A small, older woman sat behind the desk, flipping through a *Soap Opera Digest* as a commercial blared on her television. She had bleached blond hair with needles poking out of it. She looked like a truck driver's wife—a wife who'd ridden shotgun too many times, who'd spent too much time on speed, the speed aging her, giving her the wrinkles of a sixty-year-old, she being only forty, maybe—damn. Life passed her by. Nothing to look forward to, no fond memories, surrounded by dismal drudge. I felt sorry for her. I felt like I was going to cry. I was losing my mind.

"I'd like a room." Was I screaming?

She didn't look up from her magazine. "How long for?"

"The night."

She sighed and put away the magazine, looked at the television as the commercial ended and "Kojak" flashed on, looked at me. She looked at me a long time. She stared.

"Sure. Just sign in."

She spun the register book toward me, open. I signed, John Doe. I paid in advance, cash only. She made change for a $100 bill.

"Let's see, how 'bout room twenty-eight?"

"Anything."

"Well, they're all the same. Clean sheets, too."

She pulled the key off the rack behind her. She had so much makeup on in so many different colors, her face looked like a paint board sample. She shuffled out to me. Her blue jeans choked her legs like a wet suit; her ass flobbled in the seat like a flat beach ball. She was wearing slippers: aqua blue fuzzy puffs. They looked like punk-rock rabbits. Oh man, she's got the fuzzy, punk-rock rabbit slipper blues.

"Just follow me."

Stay calm, Jocko, stay calm.

She was at the door staring, licking her lips. I figured it was just her way to stare at people. I could care less. Then I figured out why she was staring at me. I think. I was staring at her—and who wouldn't—so I shook my eyes off her, made myself stare at her fuzzy blue slippers.

As we walked around the end of the building, I followed, staring at her slippers. The rooms faced a shut-down factory. How scenic. The urinal-like pool was being worked on. A light shone on the pool, and the water looked like an algae factory, someone being seriously into aquatic farming, I guess. The first time I ever got high, I skinny-dipped in that pool with two whores Trip had gotten for me. So long ago. So long. Stay calm, Jocko, stay calm. Cinderblocks are my friends, yes sir.

Room twenty-eight.

Like all the rooms, it had a single light bulb over

the door. Light washed over a peppering of fluttering moths, the moths spending their lives chasing a light that meant nothing, then dying. She unlocked the door for me, brushing away moths.

"Here you are," she said.

I stepped inside and found the light on the wall, clicked it on, then took the key from the door. She stared at me, licking her lips. She smiled. Her smile was so white, I thought she was turning on a flashlight. She reached up and tapped her teeth with her index finger.

"Dentures. Pop right out. Never have to worry about my teeth gettin' in the way of a good time."

"I'm sorry," I said, thinking fast and clear. "But I'm gay." I gave her my best I-hope-you-understand why I don't want your smile.

"Oh," she did a shivering, shaking, giggly-goo dance. "Why don't you call your lover boy, and we can all have a good time?"

"I don't think so. We're fighting." And I closed the door.

Alone...

The cocaine had kept me thinking clearly, sort of. Clear enough to get a cab. Clear enough to ditch the van. Clear enough to get here. But now, alone, it wasn't helping.

My teeth chattered. I started shaking like I was standing naked in a sleet storm. I flopped on the bed. A puff of dust floffed up from the cotton blanket. I sneezed. I closed my eyes. Tried to calm myself. With my eyes closed it was worse. I saw flames from the bomb. Heard gunfire. Saw Eddy, a shadow in flames—I should've gone back. I had to get up. Something. I flicked on the TV. A cat food commercial ended. Then, a news flash: Aborted bomb attack on the county sheriff, at eleven. Shit . . .

Now I'd hit the big times. Now I was going to be on TV. I went into the bathroom. Washed my face with cold water. Went back out and sat at the desk. Out with the cocaine—cut up six lines—and out with the tequila. I was going down. I had a whole bottle to go. How much did I need for poisoning? I'd already drunk half a bottle with Eddy. Eddy . . . I took a long, straight swig—straight, no chaser. Shivers rattled up from the small of my back. I did lines of cocaine. Shivers rattled from my nose to the small of my back. I leaned back, let them both kick in. "Kojak" was on TV. Next door some couple was fighting.

I lit another cigarette and tried to blow smoke rings, couldn't. I took another shot. Did some more lines. I couldn't go home and wake up in the morning and fix coffee, and practice my harmonicas, and go suntanning by the lake, and peel the clothes off Nicky, and fold into her sweet wetness, and go to work, and turn down the heat if it got too hot, and turn up the heat if it got too cold, and lie with Nicky under a layer of blankets, huddled together. I was supposed to be lying in a grave, next to Mom and Dad, waiting for Trip.

The news came on. Headline story: Attempted bomb assassination. Cameramen were at the scene. One man was in critical condition, first degree burns covering his body. And there was a shot of Eddy being slid into an ambulance, one arm poking out, looking like barbecued chicken. Eddy was screaming at the EMT: "Maricón, watch it!" He was alive. I never pray, but thank God he's alive. Swirling lights from the ambulance and cop cars washed over Scruggers's lawn. They had the make on my van, the reporter continued: the county sheriff had received a letter and handwriting analysis confirmed the letter had been written by the lone cocaine pirate's brother, Jocko Miles. They had a close-up of the letter; first time I'd ever seen it. In the letter I threatened to blow up Scruggers for busting my brother. Police speculated I'd goofed and accidentally set off the bomb. Nobody could explain the weird ritual of urinating in the mailbox. Like I would really write Scruggers a note in this age of reaching out and touching someone with the phone. Nobody uses the fucking mail! You are an idiot, Mr. Reporter. My handwriting was matched with a blues poem published in a local newspaper. "Skateboard Blues."

And then I was on TV, a picture lifted from a publicity shot. I was wanted for attempted murder. I was armed. I was deranged. Delirious. Dangerous. Willing to kill. A $25,000 reward for information leading to my arrest was offered. And suddenly Scruggers's wife filled the screen, crying, so thankful her husband was alive ... a commercial on how to mop floors.

I turned off the TV.

I did some more cocaine, lit another cigarette. I pulled my leather saddle of harmonicas. I pulled out the A-flat harp, a nice bass-tuned harp, good for slow, hobo blues. I played a couple choruses; it seemed I wasn't playing, sounded like someone else. I had no control over the world. Now I couldn't even control my harmonica. Shit. "Skateboard Blues."

Night passes ...

I keep doing cocaine. Keep taking shots of tequila. I stub out my cigarette, light another. I look around. The walls are pink. The ceiling is pale blue. The carpet is yellow and brown. The bedspread has green flowers. The sheets are clean. I have half a bottle left. I arch my head back and drink and drink. My body twitches as the swig kicks in. I lay me down. I hear Leadbelly singing: "I feel like walking mama, but I don't know which way to go." I close my eyes. A bottle of tequila. Maybe my heart will slow and stop. Maybe I'll choke on my puke. Images flash. I'm tending graves, picking up twigs, pulling out weeds, tossing dead flowers—only live flowers for the dead. Yes, Mom, I'm coming. Yes, Dad, Trip will be here soon, too. I clean graves. My father says, Son, will you bring your harmonica? I will, Dad. Good, he says, we so need music down here—pianos don't fit in the coffin. Guess not, Dad. My grave is dug and next to theirs. Trip's grave is being dug next to mine. May we all rest in peace. I smell incense. It's snowing, and freezing rain. I'm driving 90 on the highway. I read the sign: Bridge Freezes First. I wonder why. I don't care. I hit the frozen bridge and jerk the wheel and send myself flying. Smooth gliding, it takes so long to glide down. I splash into freezing water. If I dream I die, I'll never wake up; if I wake up, it'll be nightmares . . .

Chapter Eighteen

IIII IIII IIII IIII IIII

AND THEN I was waking. Slowly. Someone shaking me. My eyes opening, slowly. Hot white lights. People yelling. Someone shaking me, hard. And I had to throw up. Leaning over the bed, I did, over and over. And kept throwing up as someone dragged me into the bathroom, the cold nozzle of a gun stuck in my ear—how could I pull wise-guy stuff? And I kept throwing up until the dry heaves came. Over and over. Someone turned on the bathwater. Someone shoved my head under cold water. I was drowning. Choking on freezing water. Water soaking down my back, puddling on the floor. I was yanked out from under the water.

Two men jabbed their hands under my arm pits and hoisted me up. Things were coming into focus. These two guys looked worse than me—unshaven, bags hanging under their eyes like flat warts, their breath reeking of tobacco and gallons of thin, thermos coffee. They led me out of the bathroom, out of my room. I needed my harmonicas, my money, my cocaine, my cigarettes—bastards. And they dragged me outside. Headlights bleached my eyes.

The hotel clerk stood next to another undercover cop. She babbled on, still in her blue slippers, kept making sure the numbskull understood she was to get $25,000—she'd seen the rewards offered on TV —and boy, what she'd do with a wad of cash like that! The cop took everything down in a small scratch pad.

There were two unmarked cars. The rest of the lot was empty; all the John Does and John Smiths had sneaked home. The sun was rising, and a smear of orange light glowed over the broken-down motel. Out of one of the unmarked cars, a woman stepped out. Here I was, supposed to be dead, and about to go to jail—I guessed jail—and drunk, with only five or six hours to sleep off te-quila, and really, normally I would've been glad these fellas had awakened me, because now I was rested and had thrown up and was ready to enjoy that special tequila buzz; but, this woman stepped out, and like most men, I have two brains—one in my skull and one between my legs. Now the one in my skull weighs more, true, but the one between my legs is long and fat with opinions and usually wins out; and when this woman stepped out of the car, well, all I could think about was sex. She had dark, almost black hair, blue eyes, and her body was pure poetry, my favorite kind, with full breasts, a slim waist, curving hips, her body supplely toned. No, I wasn't greedy: three days in Tahiti would be long enough, as long as it snowed, as long as we *had* to stay inside, as long as I got to spread oil over her body and feel the sliding of my flesh against hers—nice thoughts for a dying man. Five hours ago I was burying myself deep, and now I had a pulsing hard-on—the emotions of a drunk-druggy are as predictable as a rabid mutt.

The two cops hoisted me into a walk. Their black overcoats were rumpled like plastic garbage bags. I noticed for a deranged psycho—me—they didn't have much manpower bring me in. It was a private party. Three undercover, no, four, cops. Anyway, I was being sexist: my Tahitian dream surely had a wonderful mind, but as I stood in front of the firing line, my last wish would not be a chess partner. I guessed I was going to die. Now I had one last wish. I went about sending telepathic waves, cosmic vibes, informing my Tahitian dream she'd never have a better lover—no sense being modest now. I guess my frequency was jammed; she didn't seem to pick up my cosmic vibes. She kept pacing.

I asked loud enough for everyone, "You going to try and barbecue me like Eddy?"

The cop who was taking notes for the babbling hotel clerk stopped, looked at me. "Throw him in my car."

The two cops brought me over to his car, opened the door; their fingers gripped my arms like over-inflated blood-pressure testers. The lady clerk kept talking, but the cop'd had enough. He closed his scratch pad. As he walked over to me, the clerk kept babbling away, staying right there behind him, telling him all the details—did he know I was gay? And there we stood, having a social gathering. Two cops gripping my arms, another squared off in front of me, a yapping hotel clerk; my Tahitian dream joined us and stood next to the cop I guessed was in charge. It looked like she was about to jump into the water from the highest cliff she'd ever been on—her eyes jittering, taking short deep breaths to get ready, almost, but can't, so she gathers more strength. What the hell. Her kettle was about to boil and whistle—nice old blues line.

"You plant the bomb the night your goons beat the shit out of Nicky?" I asked the big cheese.

He ignored me. "You have the right to remain silent."

First I thought I was hallucinating. But I wasn't. She was real. My Tahitian dream swung a karate fist into the cop's stomach, choking him off in mid-sentence. As he buckled forward, his note pad spilling out, she hammered him on the neck. He thudded flat onto the asphalt, the air bursting out of his lungs—he blacked out. Nobody believed it, including the two cops gripping me. Their mistake. She flung a roundhouse kick into the groin of the cop on my right, and he cuddled into himself in agony, his face flushed, red like thin tomato sauce. Another round-house kick, and she shattered the knee of the cop on my left; he squealed like a cat being run over by a car. Nobody had a grip on me. The hotel clerk caught on—she was next. So she took off running.

"Get her!"

"Me?"

"Move!" She pulled out a gun and held the three cops at bay.

I took off after the gumless wonder, her blue punk rock slippers floffing over the grounds as she tried to run. I grabbed her by the shirt collar. She went for my balls. In a drunkard's panic, I belted her on the side of the head. Her teeth flew out and clicked across the parking lot. She wobbled, then fell to the ground. This was one crazy night—bombing, arrest, busted arrest, suicide attempt, flaring sexual fantasies. Now I was kind of awake, and life didn't look so bad; it seemed my goddess had gotten my telepathic messages. I dragged the hotel clerk back as she groaned, coming to.

At gunpoint the injured cops climbed into the oversized trunk of the unmarked car. After all three had crammed in, she made the hotel clerk smush in, too. She started to close the trunk.

In an impotent threat, one cop said: "You'll never get away with this."

I was a tough guy. "Shut up, asshole. You want us to leave the car running?"

"You shut up. Just don't say anything, all right?" I started doubting her goddess status. I shut up.

She closed the trunk, leaning heavily on it for the last few inches. She held the gun in her hand.

"Come on, get in." She motioned with the gun for me to get in the other car.

"I got to get my stuff."

"Just hurry." Her teeth were chattering with fear.

I went into my room and grabbed the travel bag
—cocaine, harmonicas, money, cigarettes; they'd
all been put in a bag by the undercover cops. I
went back outside. She was in the second car,
starting it up. I climbed in with her. I had no idea
what was going on, where we were headed—I
didn't care. Her blue eyes told me all; with beautiful women I'm ga-ga dumb. We swung back in reverse. But suppose she's the one with the contract
to hit me? Suppose the others were the good guys?
I'm riding off to be blown away. She'd left the gun
on the seat. I grabbed it and tried to point it at her.

"What are you doing?" She yelled and tried to
look at me and the road and the gun at the same
time.

"What the hell you doing?" I yelled back. I tried
to point the gun straight, but my hand shook like
the tail of a happy, rabid dog.

"I just saved your life!" she screamed back; she
was only a car seat away.

I yelled back, "How do I know?"

"You know how to use that thing?"

"Of course." My hand started shaking worse.

"Put it down!" she screamed. Then, she forced
herself to stop yelling, to be calm, sort of. "Please,
keep it. But please, just don't point it at me.
Please, put it down."

"All right." I forced myself to be calm, too. "All
right." I put the gun between my legs. "There."

She slammed on the brakes to catch a red light.
My nerves were jangling like an overslammed
gong. I lit a cigarette.

"Do you have to smoke?"

"What?"

"I hate cigarette smoke."

"Jesus," I said. I rolled down the window and blew the smoke outside. "There."

Then someone in back of us blared his horn. The light was green. She punched the gas and the car jerked forward. I was jolted and dropped my cigarette on the matting.

"Get that thing out!" she demanded.

"I'm trying. God damn it, I'm trying." The car kept sputtering, and I kept banging my head against the dashboard. Finally I got the cigarette. I threw it out the window. She settled the car into a smooth thirty. I lit another cigarette. She stared straight ahead, eyes fixed on the stream of green lights stretching a mile or more in front of us. I pulled out the bag of cocaine; I needed to clear my head. I blew on my thumb and first finger to moisten them, then jabbed them into the bag. White dust powdered my thumb and first finger. In a spastic motion, I snorted everything.

I flipped down the sun visor and looked in the small mirror. I had white powder all under my nostrils. I rubbed under my nose, getting most of it; what I couldn't get in my nose I rubbed against the gums of my front teeth. The nerves in my spine started twitching as the cocaine kicked. I jabbed my finger and thumb in for another round. She glanced over at me.

"Are you crazy?! Don't do that here!" She had to jerk the car away from a sidewalk.

"All right, pull over. I'll do it in the back seat."

"I said, don't do that here. Some punk cop'll pull us over because you have to snort coke. Put it away, now!"

"All right, give me a fucking break." I rolled the bag of cocaine up and put it in one of my empty harmonica cases, put the case in my leather saddle. Christ. The string of green lights changed to yellows. She slowed and stopped. At the red light she nervously tapped her fingers against the steering wheel.

"Look," she said. "Do you have to swear?"

"What?" I couldn't believe it. I looked at her; she was serious. Well, if we got to Tahiti, I didn't know if it'd be worth it.

Chapter Nineteen

IIII IIII IIII IIII IIII

WE DROVE ALONG Route 1, scuttled through Norwalk, picked up Route 7, and followed it through Wilton, Ridgefield, then cut over to New York, headed north. She pulled into a Dunkin' Donuts for me. My stomach was knotting from the cocaine, but I had to put some food in it. I got a dozen glazed doughnuts and three large cups of regular coffee. I knew I'd quit drinking. And to start, I'd stop drinking tequila. The sight of it—even worse, the smell—would make me sick. I was on my second doughnut when I climbed into the car. Before, I took the car keys and locked the gun in the trunk. I handed her back the keys. She started up the car.

I ate seven doughnuts; the sugar felt good. She didn't want any, couldn't understand how I could eat such junk; again, I was having doubts about being in love with her. I drank all three cups of coffee. Then I lit a cigarette, carefully blowing all the smoke out the window. She told me she was allergic to cigarette smoke. Also, with the window down, she was getting cold. If I had the gun, I'd ask her to please shut up.

As we headed north we kept weaving back and forth across the Connecticut and New York border. Then we were weaving back and forth across the New York and Massachusetts border. I felt like a drunken ant.

"Where're we going?"

"It doesn't matter," she said.

"Oh."

About an hour later we pulled into a dirt driveway; it curved through a snarl of sapling oaks, maples, and birches. The birches had just been planted, and wires stretched out from their trunks like tent lines. After a half-mile we pulled into a new parking lot. The asphalt was shiny black, like motor oil, and fluorescent yellow lines slashed the blacktop into orderly parking slots. The lot surrounded a new, two-story, unpainted cinderblock building. It looked like it had been made by a bored child with Legos.

"Where are we?"

"We're not staying," she said.

"Oh."

We pulled around back and parked in a four-car garage.

"Come on," she said.

We got out and I followed her through a hallway, passed through a large room with fifty or more chairs facing a movie screen and acting stage.

"Where are we?"

"Shh! We're not staying. Come on."

She led me into a large, open room. Everything was in muted shades of gray, the only light blurring through frosted windows. It was like being backstage at a Broadway play. Work benches with mirrored walls were cluttered with open makeup kits and mannequins' heads with wigs. On cork boards hung pictures of America's melting pot— punk rockers, football players, Wall Street executives, fashion models, whores, bag ladies, street bums, Puerto Rican youth gangs, suburban housewives, blue collar workers; a magazine rack had been assaulted with a knife. The room was L-shaped. Where it turned to the right, there were racks of clothes. She started pulling clothes off the racks like she was pulling silk blouses off a clothesline before a thunder storm.

"What size pants you wear?" Five shirts hung over her left arm.

"Uh, 30, 32."

"Okay. Shirt?"

"Large."

"Okay."

She stopped pulling clothes off racks and hustled over to a chest of drawers. She pulled out a pair of Levi's jeans and threw them to me. A Yale sweatshirt followed.

"There's a shower over there," she pointed behind the racks.

I guess I needed a shower. "Any socks?"

"Yes. Just a second." She pulled out a pair of socks and tossed them to me, then went back to work.

I stood around. Two seconds ago she threw me socks; now I felt like she didn't even know I existed. My mind felt like a blob of creamed spinach.

"Come on, hurry up. Take a shower."

"Uh, right." I'm always one for intelligent re-marks.

After wandering through the maze of clothes, I finally found the bathroom. Next to it was a barber shop. I went into the bathroom and peeled off my clothes, started the shower. When it was hot enough I stepped inside. I soaked my hair. I let water wash over me, streams pouring over my chest. Then I sat down and let the water and steam cleanse me. I was feeling all right. But the morning after was coming. The morning after too much coke, too much booze, too much smoking. I could feel it coming. The long, hot shower stalled. I could relax. It was nice being away from this woman. Being around her made me feel like I was in Grand Central Station during rush hour, my insides rat-tling, my armpits soaked with coffee-reeking sweat. I'd had a long night; I needed to take it easy. And where the hell was I? An acting studio? Was she an actress? Well, for now, I'd just relax.

She started banging on the door. "Come on, let's go."

"Hold on." I turned off the shower.

I climbed out, toweled off, slipped into a new pair of jeans—forgetting the old underwear—put on the sweatshirt, new socks, old sneakers. I felt I was clipping along at a good pace. She started banging on the door again.

I flung open the door. "I'm ready, all right?"

"Come on. Hurry up."

"What should I do with these?" I held out the pile of spent clothes.

She turned her nose away. "Anything. Just throw them away."

"I'll keep the shirt."

"Fine. Come on."

I followed her back out into the middle of the dressing room. She had two large trunks filled with clothes and shoes. She started closing one. I poked around for a garbage can.

"There's a dirty clothes basket in the corner. It'd be better to put them in there."

"Okay." I tossed the clothes into the basket. It was full. "Got any underwear?"

She pointed. "Check in that chest of drawers."

I rummaged through and found a drawer filled with Hawaiian print boxer shorts, all extra large. Well, they'd have to do. I took three packs of three and walked over to where she was working on the trunks. I tossed my tee shirt into the open trunk, threw in the underwear, too, and started closing the trunk. Then, working together, one trunk at a time, we brought both to the garage and loaded them into a blue Volvo station wagon, turbo, new.

I noticed she'd changed—khaki pants and Topsider shoes, Izod shirt, pink with green alligator. And here I was in Levi's jeans, Yale sweatshirt. Both of us climbing into a Volvo. My God! A couple of Yuppies off for the weekend, perhaps to Maine, to L.L. Bean to buy some gum boots. I wanted to put on my deviant pig shirt. My life was changing big time—my creamed spinach brain was in overdrive with shattering realizations. But I felt out of sorts in these clothes, like I'd have to wear these Hawaiian shorts—nothing else—to the opera. Ugh...

Without saying anything, she got into the car. I did too. She backed out, put the car into neutral, crunched up the emergency brake, hopped out, and closed the garage, then appeared at the back

door where she typed in a series of numbers into
an alarm panel and then closed the door. She got
back in the car, popped in a Jackson Brown tape,
eased the car into reverse, arched back and
around, and started off down the dirt road. Her
methodical efficiency was making me nauseous.

Chapter Twenty

|||| ||||· |||| |||| ||||

"MIND IF I ask you a question?" I lit a cigarette and
rolled down the window.

"Depends."

"Who are you?"

"Michele. Michele Swan."

"Humm, nice name. I'm Jocko, Jocko Miles."

"I know."

As we drove down the dirt road in second gear,
she tapped her fingers on the steering wheel. Her
eyes were straining from concentration, like she
was reading the pinhead, microfine print of an insurance contract.

"When do I get filled in?"

She didn't answer. Maybe I was wrong about her
squinting. Maybe she couldn't see. No, it was concentration, her mind not on me. She realized I was
talking to her.

"I'm sorry, what?"

"When do I get filled in?"

"Soon as you sober up."

"Well, it may be a few weeks."

"Well, you may not live that long."

Ideas like that certainly would cure an ulcer. She was back to thinking. Trying to pull her out of her thoughts was like pulling a mud-filled tire out of a pond with dental floss.

She sneezed, then coughed. "Do you have to smoke?"

"No. But I enjoy it, really."

She sighed. I smoked.

We headed south, winding back and forth across the New York and Massachusetts border. Every time we crossed the border, a sign would greet us: Welcome to New York, or Welcome to Massachusetts. And every sign also blurbed: We Enforce Our Laws. I dreamed of a perfect sign: Welcome, and Hey, Don't Worry: We Don't Enforce Our Laws. That kind of policy would bolster tourism.

Michele was spinning through the radio, stopping at every news break. There were plenty. We were the headline story: After a dramatic bombing attempt, the delirious killer was found holed out in a slum motel, drunk as a skunk. During the quiet arrest, a special security officer, Christy Thomas, who'd been hired for special operations by Scruggers, had, at gunpoint, forced the arresting officers into the trunk of their car and drove off with the drunk maniac bomber who'd even stooped so low as to beat old women. Eddy was alive and well and driving the nurses crazy at Riverton Hospital.

"I didn't know you were a cop, Christy."

"I'm not a cop. And my name is Michele."

"So what were you doing?"

"Working undercover."

"For who?"

She found a fresh news cast. "FBI. I'll tell you later, okay? Not now."

I lit another cigarette. She groaned.

I didn't feel like a maniac bomber who beat old ladies. I felt like someone coming down from too much cocaine and booze and reefer. Someone whose brother had been set up for murder. Someone who had a bomb planted on him. Someone who was supposed to be dead, lying underground, waiting for his brother. Someone sleeping, forever, with his parents. I tried to stop thinking. I tried to focus on this Turbo Volvo with only 10,000 miles. I tried to melt into the comfort of the nice roads, the clean clothes, the serene clouds in the thin blue sky. Yes, this was reality. I was in a car. If it got too hot, I could make it cooler; and if it got too cold, I could make it warmer—an environment unto itself: alterable, adjustable, giving me push-button control and mastery over the haywire, chaotic world—the promise of the microwave age. Yes, things were fine. But my stomach would start jittering. I'd feel nauseous and ready for a bout of the dry heaves. My hands would shake. Anxiety would rattle through me like a slow-breaking, deep-digging dentist drill. Nice car, nice clothes, nice day —none of it meant shit. I was going to be hunted. Wanted Dead or Alive. And I guessed dead; dead men don't talk. Hell, I had to stop; I was being paranoid. Here I was being chauffeured around by the FBI. I had to take it easy. Hell, few days I'd be home. In a week I'd be calling Michele, asking her for a date—humm, that'd be nice. Relax, Jocko, relax...Suddenly I heard Eddy's voice on the radio; he was being interviewed. He accused the maricóns of shooting first and throwing the bomb at us. The reporter wanted to know how Eddy ex-

plained the guns in my van. Hell, Eddy said, all
maricóns are interior decorators. What? the reporter asked.

I said, "You know that bomb was planted on
me?"

"I know. The men who were arresting you
weren't supposed to make any more mistakes."

"I guess they didn't know about you."

She glanced at me. "I didn't even know about
me."

We'd crossed the borders so many times I didn't
know where we were. Then a sign flashed: Connecticut Enforces Its Laws. We were on Route 7,
heading north. Another sign flashed by: Massachusetts was only fifteen miles away; New York, four.
We pulled off Route 7 onto a squinched road of
broken asphalt. The road sloped sharply down and
to the left. Michele stopped the car, got out, and
unlocked a rusting red metal gate. She pulled the
gate back and got into the car, drove just past the
gate, then climbed back out of the car, closing and
locking the gate. As I tried to remember what she'd
just done, I got tired. Back in the car I noticed
she'd worked up a little sweat.

"Where are we?" Even I was getting tired of my
questions.

"It's an abandoned artists' colony."

After curving left, the road curved right. It was
barely wide enough for one car. It was flanked by
pines, the bottom branches dried and dead and
brittle. The middle of the road buckled; Michele
drove slowly so she wouldn't dent the muffler. All I
wanted was sleep. Where the asphalt stopped, dirt
roads split to the right and left. In front of us was a
string of one-room cabins, the red paint peeling off
in slices large as potato chips. A warped porch

loped across the cabins. Like coffee-stained cheese cloth, each cabin had a rusting screen door, the screening broken and torn.

"This home?" I opened my door.

"For a while."

We clambered out of the car like wounded, scarred old mutts. We left everything in the car. I went in the first cabin and flopped down on a cot. I guess Michele took another cabin. She didn't come in behind me. The sheets on the cot were musty, clammy. It didn't matter. As soon as I lay down, I fell asleep faster than a drunk falls off the wagon.

Chapter Twenty-one

IIII IIII IIII IIII IIII

IT WAS LATE morning when I went to sleep, late morning when I woke the next day. The first hours of sleep were fine. Then I kept waking. My whole head ached. My neck was stiff as fiberglass. If I moved too fast, my head would pound—a slow, deep throbbing. My only escape was sleep. And even then my head pounded. Then I'd be half-awake, my head pulsing at my temples and neck like too much blood was pumping through, like my veins were swelling and stretching and about to split and let my blood gush—I wanted the relief. From sleep to half-sleep. From being too cold, then too hot. From being awake and wanting to sleep to being asleep and wanting to be awake. I tried to keep the pounding—always pounding—to a dull thud.

Finally, I forced myself up. I had to walk slowly. I shuffled along the floor. I guessed Michele was gone. I found a bathroom, my face in the mirror. My hair was stringy, oily, uncombed. My face was chalk white. Black circles hung under my eyes like dried, dead lizards. I felt like shit. Alcoholic poisoning might be a good, fun way to go, but it sure as hell was a bad way to goof.

I shuffled back to my cot, lay down, and held my head in my palms. It was hard to breathe. The pounding swelled. The thought of a drink made me sick. The thought of cigarettes made me sick. I was going to eat a pile of bean sprouts the size of a hay bale. Get my health back. I was going to quit drinking. I was going to quit drugs. I was going to quit smoking. I was going to make the cover of *Prevention Magazine*. I could see myself smiling on the front cover, the magazine on coffee tables in doctors' offices, my teeth white as soap, my skin bronzed, sparkling eyes saying I always felt happy and awake and glad a new day came my way....I fell back to sleep, groaning. The pounding...

For the first sober time I looked around my new home. My room was a perfect square, about fifteen by fifteen. The walls were painted white and chipping. I could see the two-by-four framing, the walls nailed directly to the studs with no insulation—summer place. The ceiling was made of rippled cement. One bare bulb poked out from the center of the ceiling. A chain dangled. The light came on, a weak 25-watt bulb. Well, we had electricity. A white room with white walls and white ceiling—this place was as exciting as an overwashed hospital sheet. I thought of Trip: now that I couldn't see him when I wanted, I had to see him.

I went into the bathroom. A white tin casement housed the shower head, a white shower curtain dangled on white rings. The shower floor was cement. I turned on the shower and waited. Well, we had hot water. And there was a clean, white towel I guessed Michele had put out. I undressed and showered. There was no shampoo, so I used—damn it—a white bar of soap. I expected the water to be white. I let water wash over me until it started cooling.

I felt like I'd never dry off. The towel was teeny, the size of a double wash cloth. Oh well. Still damp with beads of moisture over my skin, I slipped into my jeans and sweat shirt, socks and sneakers. I rubbed a clearing in the mirror and combed my hair with my fingers. Back out in my room I went through a door and into another room.

The cabins were connected, nailed together, wall to wall. This room was darker, with windows only in the front and back, none on the sides. It was a kitchen. I never thought I'd be glad to see a yellow kitchen table with red, vinyl chairs; but after all the whiteness, I was. The stove, fridge and freezer, sink and cabinets looked like they came from a kindergarten's playhouse; it reminded me of home.

Another door, another room. Michele had set up here. I could see her cot. And the trunks we'd loaded, she'd unloaded them all. Clothes hung from makeshift racks. All my stuff was piled on top of a closed trunk, neatly. I pulled out my harmonicas. I found my cigarettes, lit one up, then remembered I'd quit smoking. So I stubbed it out on the floor. Then decided I shouldn't try to do everything at once. So I lit another. I checked through my harmonica cases. Inside the empty ones were plastic bags rolled tight with cocaine. Good. I'd quit doing coke soon as I ran out. I judged I had three quarters of an ounce left—judiciously rationed, I figured I could ease out of my habit in a month, not too fast, and it wasn't a habit really. With my fourteen harmonicas, I walked back through the rooms and outside to the porch. Michele was sitting on the porch, leaning against a post. I sat across from her, leaned against a post, not saying anything. I stubbed out my cigarette.

The air was sweet smelling, cool and fresh with the feel of heavy rain. There were two layers of clouds. One layer was thick and even, spread high and flat like slate in the sky. The other layer was swirling and boiling like wind-churned fog and moved low to the ground. The tops of pine trees were muted in low, misting clouds. Lightning, in veinlike streaks, ripped through the sky in flashes of hot white. The rain was soft at first. But thunder was sounding off to our right and left, in back of us and in front of us, close and far.

Then it let loose. The rain gushed. On the rippled cement roof, we could hear the frantic spattering of rain. The thunder pounded—a relieved pounding—like the bass drums of Sioux Indians. The rain fell fast. The ground couldn't absorb it. Small rain water rivers formed everywhere. A rain stream rushed past us, under the porch and our feet, with swirls of white froth floating on top. The winds gusted to the right, then left, spastically. Over the open field, wind gusted against slashing rain and made puffs of mist-clouds that vanished like ghosts. The tops of trees swayed back and forth; it was dark, the trees now only shapes in

black and grays and muted greens. It rained and
rained. I wanted to get naked and lie in the rain,
have Michele, naked, lie next to me in the fresh
rain water...when the rain stopped, the sun broke
through and spread a soft pink light on the underside of drifting clouds.

Chapter Twenty-two

IIII IIII IIII IIII IIII

EARLY EVENING MICHELE was still sitting on the
porch, leaning against the post; it seemed she
hadn't moved all day. I sat across from her, leaning
against a post, too.

"I need a notebook," I said.

She looked at me. "What for?"

"Well, might as well do some work."

"I'm sorry?"

"I'm a song writer." I started cleaning my B-flat
harmonica. I wetted the metal casing that housed
the wooden reeds, then wiped it clean with a bandana. With a toothpick I etched the dried flecks of
skin—from my lips—out from the grooves.

"I like to think of myself as a blues poet." I was
half-kidding, but she didn't notice.

I finished the B-flat harmonica and moved on to
the F harp. Michele was gazing across the field toward the trees. I doubted she knew how beautiful
she was. I thought of Nicky, Nicky being bored
with her looks—what had they gotten her but a
bunch of drooling drunks. Well, me anyway. Big

deal. Michele probably felt her looks got in the way of people taking her seriously. Who knows? I wasn't made to speculate.

After a long silence I asked, "You going to fill me in?"

"Another night of rest'll do you good. Besides, we're not going anywhere soon."

"Got anything to drink?"

"You don't need alcohol."

"No, no. I quit drinking. I mean anything. I'm dying of thirst."

"I'll get it for you." She got up and went inside.

I started playing my C harp, playing anything. Out came a long, slow, and painful blues. I was moaning through my harp. Drawing my tongue slow and hard along the bottom of my mouth, bending the notes flat and blue. Crying through my harp. Wailing tears as music. Growling through my harp. Groaning. I couldn't moan long or hard or loud enough. Oh man, did anybody hear me? I never knew...

I don't know how long I played for. When I stopped, Michele was across from me, listening.

She said, "You sound so sad."

"Guess I am."

"Here," she handed me the glass. The sides were sweating with moisture. It was filled with a red, pulpy drink.

"What is it?"

"Cranberry juice."

"Really?" I looked at the glass again, held it up for both of us to see.

"It's real cranberry juice."

"Oh." I was into that. Real cranberry juice. Tomorrow I'd eat bean sprouts. Playing the harmonica had dried the back of my throat. I arched my head back and took a swig. The juice was mushy and pulpy and tasted like lemon juice with vinegar. When the first gulp was halfway down my throat, I sputtered and choked and gargled and sprayed real cranberry juice all over the porch.

Michele jolted back, shrieking. "What are you doing?"

"What is this shit?" I was gasping like someone who'd been held underwater too long.

"Cranberry juice. I told you."

"This ain't like no cranberry juice I ever tasted."

"It's real. They don't add sugar." Michele started wiping juice off her arm.

"Well, they should. It's terrible."

"You need it."

"For what? Epileptic fits?"

"It'll clean out your liver."

"What?"

"Go look at yourself in the mirror. You're yellow."

"Yellow? You crazy? I'm pale white."

"You're yellow."

"Bullshit."

She started wiping juice off her other arm. "It's from alcohol poisoning."

"I'm not an alcoholic."

"I didn't say you were. You did."

"I said, I'm not."

"Fine. But cranberry juice will clean out your liver. It's good for drying out." She was as forgiving as a cinderblock.

"Personally, I'd rather be drunk."

She glared at me. "You get drunk one more time and I'm dumping you at a local police station and collecting the reward. And they'll kill you before you sober up."

I hated people who had all the aces. "All right, all right. You could've warned me."

"It's good for you."

She wouldn't let up. Damn. "Isn't there anything else?"

She took the glass from my hand. "I'm surprised this tastes worse than all the junk you drink." She got up and went inside.

When she came back out she handed me a new glassful. It looked about the same, but the red juice was diluted by something brown.

Probably real prune juice. Great. Michele had some paper towels. She started wiping juice off the porch.

She noticed I was staring at the glass. "I mixed it with apple juice."

I took a small sip. Actually, it tasted real good. I downed it, my Adam's apple bobbing like a buoy in rough waves. I didn't realize how thirsty I was.

"Want another?"

I handed her the glass. "Sure."

She went back inside, came back out with a new glassful. As she sat down she said, "You should try to finish the bottles I opened tonight."

"No problem. How much's that?"

"Half-gallon of each."

I almost choked. "Give me a fucking break."

She ignored my objection. She was serious. Then she said, "Do you have to swear so much?"

I couldn't believe it—I was stuck camping out with a Girl Scout. I lit a cigarette. She sighed.

All night I drank cranberry juice mixed with apple juice. Michele kept walking back and forth, getting me drinks. I kept walking back and forth, going to the bathroom. I worked through all my harmonicas, moving slowly through the lower-tuned harps, then slowly working through the higher-tuned harps. It was nice to be away from the band, but I would've chosen a simpler way to take time off. I took a break and had a cigarette. Hell, probably be back at the Armadillo's Armpit next week. Back to the grind.

Michele said, "I wish I'd played an instrument."

"Why didn't you?"

"In fifth grade the music teacher said I was tone deaf."

"That's bullshit. Here, sing after me: Laaaa ..."

She sang back: "Laaaa ..."

She sounded like a duck with a belly ache. Her fifth-grade teacher had a point. But I didn't let on. "See, you're not tone deaf."

She didn't believe me. Oh well.

I'd already had ten glasses of cranberry and apple juice. And I thought I was going to die: Michele had gotten up after her singing lesson and came back out, handing me yet another glass, full.

"How much is left?"

"Not much."

"Well, bring it all out. Mix it up."

And she did. There was about a quarter gallon left. I tilted my head back, chugged it all down.

She groaned. "How can you drink so fast?"

"Easy. I imagined it was beer."

She shook her head—when would I grow up? She got up and stretched. "Well, I guess I'm going to go to bed."

"I'll stay up. I need to use the bathroom for six hours."

"It's good for you."

"Hell, I'm not worried about me. I'm worried about the rickety toilet."

"It'll be fine."

Always matter of fact, like a bored phone opera-tor. She wasn't big on jokes. Or maybe I wasn't funny. Hadn't thought of that. Humm. I told her good night.

"Good night." She went off to bed. Then she came back out on the porch, holding my spent cig-arette butt, the one I'd squashed out in her room.

"If you're going to smoke, don't smoke in my room."

I tried to defend myself. All I could muster was a gargling of vowels.

With my bladder swollen double size, I woke in the night, stumbled to the bathroom, fumbled for the light, and relieved myself—simple pleasures are the most profound. Back in bed I couldn't sleep. I lay there. My eyes got used to the darkness. I tried lying on my back. I tried lying on my stom-ach. I couldn't stop thinking of Trip lying in a hos-pital bed, tangled in wires and flanked by screens showing his heart jitters, his head squashed soft as orange pulp. Couldn't stop thinking of Eddy, his shadow in flames as he tried to stand and run, and how he's lying in some hospital bed, charred like burned chicken—how could I think of him as burned chicken? I'm glad he's alive, anyway. I tried to sleep on my side. And Nicky, her eye swol-len, bruises dotting her skin like large measles, knife slices mapping over her. I wanted sleep. And it didn't come. Michele. She was methodical, no time for anything trivial, my God, no. No time for jokes, suntanning, being goofy and silly like kids pillow fighting at a slumber party. Oh, no. Time was Important; Life was Important. I tried sleep-ing on my side again. No sleep. Instead, an image

of Michele as a child—I saw her carrying a briefcase and dressed in a pin-striped suit, going door
to door selling Girl Scout cookies. As a child refusing to go out on Halloween because English and
math were more important. I saw her sitting in
front of a TV; she'd only watch PBS, channel 13.
Damn it! What's this shit? I wanted sleep. I turned
to my other side. She probably reads the *New York
Times*. I hate the *Times;* it has no comics. She probably reads *The Wall Street Journal*, too. If she went
to the theater, the play'd have to be about death
and dying or AIDS or religious and political perse-
cution. At least plain old injustice. Anything depressing would do. For fun, she probably taught
herself how to use the computer. Shit. I tried lying
on my back; I could see the cement ripples in the
ceiling. To her it was important to pay the phone
bill on time, to have proper car insurance, not to
enter exits, to put plenty of nickels in the parking
meter, to donate to Save the Children, to claim interest on income tax. Me? Hell, always time to take
it easy. We got the whole day. Let's kick back, crack
a beer, blow a joint, suntan, and fall asleep, then
wake and cruise on down to the Big Apple for some
late-night comedy and music, hit some all-night
diners, and fuel up with some chow—hamburgers
—and do up some toot, and throw everything on
the credit cards and worry about it next month,
mañana, as Eddy'd say—shit! I needed sleep. I
started breathing deep, counting my breaths. I lost
count after three. Damn it. I wanted sleep. Please?
I lay on my back. Why'd these thoughts come to
me? I didn't even know her. But I wanted to go out
and buy water pistols and play cowboys and Indians. I doubted she had much fun as a child. Shit.
I wanted sleep . . .

Chapter Twenty-three

|||| |||| |||| |||| ||||

I WOKE UP to the sound of groaning, grunting, and panting. It sounded like heavy sex; naturally, I wanted to see as much as I could. Blunder-headed, I stumbled out of bed and over to the window, looked out. No sex, only Michele. I thought about going to bed, then decided to watch.

She was practicing karate, dressed in whites. Wrapped around her head was a bandana, and wrapped around her waist was a brown belt. Walking away from me, in bare feet, she did a series of hand punches in the air. Turning around, walking toward me, she repeated the punches, grunting and groaning in Japanese—something Oriental, anyway. Then she started kicking: left, right, left, right. Then she hit the ground and went through a set of push-ups; I lost count around 50. Then she did a set of deep knee bends, about 50. Then sit-ups. Then she repeated the whole routine.

The sun was behind her, its hot flaring diffused through pine trees. The ankle-high grass was wet. The dew shone like fluid rounded flecks from a mirror. As she walked she left trails of dark green slicing through grass silvered by dew. Her thick, dark hair was held flat against her head with a pink bandana. Her high cheekbones were flushed like red dark orchids. Her clear blue eyes were like the shallow ocean waters off the Mosquito Coast, the wild, unspoiled Caribbean. She was the goddess of earth and land and the full moon rising, a virgin—it was hopeless for me to be objective when a beautiful woman was knocking about, and why should I bother?

I decided cranberry and apple juice was as good as bean sprouts: I was feeling my health, mostly in the groin area, not that my health ever left me there. I wanted Michele next to me. Wanted the rising sun to wash over her skin as I spread baby oil over her legs, arms, back, stomach, and breasts; wanted the sun washing over her as I kissed her neck—my tongue parting her lips, lapping her skin, leaving moist kisses to cool in the morning air—and kissed her breast, slowly past her stomach, parting her legs, kissing her, licking a sweet wetness like morning dew...

I needed a cold shower, bad.

Michele finished and walked toward me. She was drenched in sweat. I walked out onto the porch, lit a cigarette.

"When you going teach me all that?"

"Soon as you quit smoking."

All my dreams gone—never, never try to molest a Girl Scout.

"Anybody ever tell you you're beautiful?"

She frowned, irritated like fleas kept pinching her. "Save the movie lines for teeny-bopper groupies."

She walked past me, into her cabin.

I spent the morning walking around the old artists' colony. How any artist got any work done here I'd never know—there were horse stables, soccer fields, tennis courts, a pool, a river for swimming and canoeing, a barn theater. If I came here, I'd suntan, fish, swim, ride horses, and spend my days talking to women. I guessed it had been ten years or more since anybody had used this place. Grass and weeds and rot and decay had taken over—the place was like a burned-out fire, the ashes slowly dissolving into earth.

Across from the cabin was a field, where Michele practiced karate. I cut across it and came onto the tennis courts. They were in sad shape. Along the base lines grass poked out in clumps like hair from old men's ears. The nets, still up, were torn and looked like shreds from useless sneakers. The all-weather surface was buckling, cracking. And compared to the rest of the place, the tennis courts were in excellent shape.

Behind the courts was a small pool filled with algae-thick water. The water looked like cream of zucchini soup. There were only a couple of feet of water. I noticed a pair of frog eyes, floating, the frog, I guessed, staring at me—home sweet home for a frog.

Behind the pool was a white colonial house with black shutters, somber as a funeral home. It must have been the main office. I walked onto the front porch, tried the door. Locked. Oh well. I sat down and had a cigarette. Across the way I could see Michele sitting on our cabin porch, leaning against the post, writing in a notepad. I'd hoped my tour would've lasted hours, days, providing weeks of endless intrigue and mystery. It took a half-hour. Here I was, wanted by the police, the state police, the FBI—or part of it, anyway—and there was a $25,000 reward for me. I was a wanted man. And how did I feel? Bored. Safe. Unthreatened. Well, I guess being bored is better than being hunted. I stubbed out my cigarette. Shit. I had the rest of the day to do nothing.

I got up and followed a trail behind our cabin; it sloped down a steep bank to the river. The river was wide, twenty yards or more. It was brown colored, like a dirt road after heavy rains. It didn't make me thirsty. It looked like zoo water. All it needed was old peanut shells floating around and it'd look like the moat surrounding a monkey enclave. A dirt road followed the riverbank. It was overgrown with weeds. Skinny poplar trees sprigged up on the sides and tangled above the road, forming a green shadowed tunnel. Down fifty yards or so I could see a pile of old, aluminum canoes. Maybe I'd take a paddle about. But then I'd risk falling into the water.

I walked up and sat with Michele on the porch. She was still writing away in her notepad.

"What are you doing?"

"Making a list of everything we have to do."

"What could we possibly have to do?" I asked.

"Plenty, if we want to be safe."

"Oh." I stretched out on the porch. "You want to fill me in?"

"Tonight. After dinner."

The sun was hot. I felt like basking in it, lying around like an old cat. "No hurry, I guess."

"There's nothing we can do anyway. But wait."

"For what?" I closed my eyes.

"Until I hear from Hank Stewer."

"Who's that?"

"The man I work for."

I shifted my position on the porch, trying to settle into a good sleep. "It's kind of boring just hanging out."

"When people want you dead, being bored is a luxury."

"Humm, true." I'm not sure if she said anything else. I fell asleep.

Chapter Twenty-four

IIII IIII IIII IIII IIII

EARLY EVENING WE sat on the porch eating Granny
Smith apples. When I finished, I tossed my core
into some bushes and lit a cigarette. When Michele
finished, she threaded the pocket-sized, reel-to-reel
recorder; it was Swiss made, a Nagra, the Rolls
Royce of recording equipment. Trip used to use the
larger model for making bootleg tapes of concerts.
As she fiddled with the recorder I looked out across
the field. Darkness spread over the sky like a
sheathing of a dull, black plastic garbage bag.
Stars pricked the black. The new moon hung in the
sky, white like a clipped thumbnail. Tree frogs and
crickets popped off in their rhythmical ricochet
song. Michele clicked the tape recorder onto
"play."

The tape modulated from dry, flat, unrecorded
sound, to the faint sounds of the seashore—waves,
wind, sea gulls. The recording was made with a
shotgun microphone and picked up the hissing of
dead air. From behind the microphone I could
hear voices. Someone said, "Here it comes again."
I could hear the van, the whirring of rubber tires
over asphalt. There were muted shrieks from sea
gulls, and the hissing of dead air and wind. The
van stopped, turned around. I could hear the back
doors of my van swing open. Someone said; "What
the hell they doing?" I knew. Eddy was taking a
leak in the mailbox.

"Turn it off."

"No. You have to listen to this, at least." Michele
clicked the tape player into "fast forward," stopped

it, and switched it to "play." Gunfire came through the speaker, sounding like caps popping off.

"Turn it off!"

"Listen!" She grabbed my head and held the tape recorder closer, like a mechanical sea conch. Then I heard what she wanted. Someone said, "Now! Do it fucking now!" And the bomb's explosion squelched through the tiny playback speaker. I yanked my head back from her grip. She turned it off. I stubbed out my cigarette and held my head in my hands, rubbed my temples; a soft pounding was coming.

She said, "You were set up."

"I know that."

"Well, you might as well know it for a fact."

I lit another cigarette. As I exhaled, the smoke looked like the winter shadows of cold breath. "So what's going on."

"Okay. I was working undercover, gathering information on Scruggers." She started rewinding the tape.

"For the FBI?"

"That's right. See, after Scruggers got the bomb threats, he assembled a special security force. He hired explosives experts to check his car, house, mail, whatever, for bombs. It seems they were making a few, too. He also hired a photographer who could take pictures day and night. And I got in as an audio specialist. I was supposed to make recordings of suspicious vehicles, people who kept hanging around, anything."

"What were you after?"

"Well, Scruggers might've been getting kickbacks for letting drugs route through Riverton. I was trying to gather evidence."

Michele pulled out another notepad and flipped

through it. On a blank page she marked a footage count from the tape, made a brief note about content.

"How'd you get in?"

She folded the notepad closed. "I'm sorry?"

"How'd you get in."

"Hank Stewer. He was contacted by the FBI. He pulled strings and I got hired. It was a perfect cover. Gave me a natural reason for walking around with a high-powered tape recorder."

"Is he the one who owns the building we were in the other night?"

"That's right. It's the Institute for Undercover Training. We train policemen, detectives, FBI, CIA. Our specialty's training for deep cover."

"Jesus, sounds like my kind of place." I tried to imagine myself having cocktails with someone from the CIA; I'd have better luck smoking dope with a moose. The tape rewound completely and flickered round and round like a card in a bicycle's spoke.

I stubbed out my cigarette and lit another. Fucking things. I'd have to quit.

"I can't understand why Scruggers would set me up."

Michele shook her head. "I don't know. It's strange."

"I heard on the streets he was working with a guy, Raymond Broderick?"

"Maybe. I don't know." Michele clicked off the tape recorder and carefully wrapped the tailpiece of the tape around the spool.

"They really think I'm so stupid I'd send a bomb threat in the mail, in my own handwriting?"

"You were set up. My guess is after Scruggers went public with the confirmation you'd sent the

bomb threat, somehow, you'd 'accidentally' blow
yourself up. I'm not sure."

I stood up, just for something to do. "So what
can we do?"

"Nothing. Until I hear from Hank, anyway."

"Why don't we just turn the tape in?"

"It's nothing."

"What do you mean, nothing. We got someone
saying, 'Blow him now.'"

"No. All we have is someone saying, 'now.' It
could've meant anything."

"Shit." I sat back down, rubbed my forehead.
"The tapes aren't enough for the cops?"

"They're nothing." She placed the tape in a thin
box. After closing the box, she sealed it with electrical tape, then marked the box.

"How come it was enough for you?"

She looked away from me. "I had a feeling."

"Your FBI pal know about these feelings?"

"No." She wouldn't look at me.

"So. On feelings, you throw cops into car trunks
to save a drunk, right?"

"They were going to kill you."

"Another feeling?"

"No."

"So?"

"I have other tapes."

I could see myself walking out from my barn,
maybe with Nicky. We climb into the van. I start it
up. And ka-boom, we explode. Incinerated. It was
a showy bomb. I would've made the front cover of
the *New York Post:* Encrazed Bomber Blows Self
Up! I'd be dead. Trip would be dead soon. Only
official evidence would remain. It was a lot of trouble, very complicated setup; Trip and I had to go

down as cocaine pirates. Scruggers now looked like a lucky escapee from a maniac bomber. But, after I'd gotten away, after the fire engines, ambulance, and police had come and gone, after everything settled, Michele kept working. She recorded Scruggers talking on the phone; she played the tape, spinning "fast forward" through the dead zones.

"So that's how you got your feeling?"

"That's how." She started rewinding the tape.

"So why don't we just turn in that tape?"

"It's nothing."

"Again? Come on."

"Look. To you, to me, it sounds like Scruggers is planning to have you killed. To anybody else, it's someone, maybe not even Scruggers, saying, 'How was I supposed to know he'd show.' Whatever. It's nothing."

I was losing my sense of humor about life; I'd rather wake up and find I'd turned into a cockroach. "Well, I guess we got to do a little muckraking on Scruggers."

Michele rolled her eyes—I might as well pedal a bicycle to the moon. "Sure."

"Well, what else?"

"How?"

I thought about it. Wanted by the local police, state police; rewards were offered for information, so anybody—like a hotel clerk—who recognized me was dangerous. Also, I'm sure some private hit men were poking around. I said, confidently: "I don't know. Yet."

Michele sealed the second tape box with electrical tape and placed the box, like the other one, in a sandwich-sized Ziploc bag.

"Who was Scruggers talking to, anyway?"

"I'm not sure." She sealed the Ziploc bag, making sure there was no air inside; the bag wrapped flaccid around the tape box like the dried skin of a white grape. She sheathed a second Ziploc bag around the box.

"So you never heard him mention a guy named Broderick?"

Michele thought about it. "No. I don't think so. You mentioned him before. Who's he?"

"Some guy. I don't know. A friend told me he and Scruggers were buddy-buddy."

"Your friend seems to know a lot."

"Word travels fast."

She finished wrapping the second tape box and placed it into a nylon camera bag. Then, she wrapped the Nagra tape recorder in its leather case. She put the tape recorder in the camera bag, too. It was a professional camera bag, the size of a carry-on luggage piece, with enough room for two or three cameras and multiple lenses.

Always a thinking man, I said, "Why don't we get more tapes of Scruggers blabbing away?"

Michele rolled her eyes again. It was a sensible idea, like betting her life savings on a three-legged horse. "Fine. How would you like to do it?"

As usual, my brilliant ideas lacked substance. "I don't know. Yet."

Michele zipped up the camera bag, carefully, like she was zipping up her too-tight dress, not wanting to pinch her skin. She stared out across the field.

Chapter Twenty-five

IIII IIII IIII IIII IIII

IN THE MORNING I got a haircut. We set up in the field. I went outside straight from the shower, my hair still wet. I brought one of the red kitchen chairs. After I sat down, Michele wrapped a towel under my chin. She had a barber's kit—a monogrammed leather case that unfolded, revealing scissors, metal and plastic combs, brushes, clips. Michele combed my hair with a wide-toothed comb and started snipping.

Usually I let my hair wisp around sort of long. I'll wash it and let it dry free as a tumbleweed. Michele snipped and snipped. We didn't talk. She kept pushing my head gently around, snipping and snipping. I couldn't see and she wouldn't let me. When she finished, she made a few exact snips, then gave me a hand mirror. I almost choked: it looked like I was going to apply for a job at IBM.

"What the hell is this?"

"What?"

"Why'd you do this?" I felt naked with no hair over my ears.

"What? I told you." She started putting away her things.

"I look like a Wall Street zombie."

"Fine. Best way to be underground is to have no one know who you are." She finished packing away her barber's kit.

"I don't even know who I am." I kept adjusting the mirror from angle to angle. No way to get around it. I had a butch.

"Look, don't be silly. What's more important? Your haircut, or staying alive."

That almost shut me up. "My haircut."

"Oh God," she groaned like I'd just walked over her new carpet with muddy boots.

In the afternoon we set up in the old barn theater, going through costume after costume. No real theatrics, just simple changes of clothes. The idea was to blend in with the background, unnoticed, to be part of the scenery. Michele was big on hats and sunglasses, to "break profile," she said. Simple clothes make dramatic differences. I dressed as a preppy jock: football jersey, jeans, and penny loafers. I dressed as a house painter: painter pants, work boots, and a ragged tee-shirt splattered with paint. Me as a Wall Street zombie—pin-striped suit, white oxford shirt, yellow tie, cordovan wingtips. Most of the costumes were straight, but there were some odd ones, like a pair of Hare Krishnas, one of my favorites. And each costume had a double. The painter could be transformed to modern artist: I'd switch into a french beret and granny glasses and Museum of Modern Art tee shirt. The Wall Street zombie gig came with a briefcase; inside was a hat, glasses, and umbrella. The preppy stint came with a daypack; I could pull out a pair of tennis sweats and headband, walk out of a bathroom as a tennis jock. For fun, Michele dressed us up as a pair of punk-rockers. My hair had a green streak, and I had a fake safety pin sticking through my nose.

"Where'd you learn all this shit?"

"Well, undergraduate I was an acting major. And I got my MFA in directing at NYU."

"You're amazing." I kept looking at myself in the mirror. I was kind of taken by how good I looked as a punk-rocker.

"It's nothing," Michele said. She started taking off her rainbow makeup job. She looked funny as a punk-rocker. She greased her hair so it stood straight in spikes; her head looked like the arched back of an angry, dayglow porcupine.

"Why'd you quit acting?"

"I didn't have enough talent." She was using a cotton swab to smudge the makeup off her face. It looked like she was finger-painting her cheeks.

I was still turning from angle to angle in the mirror. I felt like walking around all day in this costume. "How the hell did you land this gig?"

She stopped taking off her makeup. "I don't know. A lot of things. A friend of a friend of a friend kind of thing got me introduced to Hank Stewer. He offered me $30,000 a year. It was that, or waitress and direct off-off-off-off Broadway. And also, I wanted to do something where I could really help people, do something that made a difference. Something. I mean, what does acting really do for anybody? Directing, plays—what's it do?"

I sat next to her. "Ah, the meaning of art. I know that feeling. I once had this dream. I was in Ethiopia with all the starving children. And I sat down to play my harmonica. And instead of music, out came these giant asparagus, asparagus the size of palm trees. Out of my harmonica. So, by playing music I could feed the starving. The bloated-belly kids went wild eating asparagus the size of palm trees."

She stared at me blankly. "Get out of here."

"It's true. You think I could make up something like that?"

"What happened?"

"It turned into a nightmare."

"Why?"

"Well, there was this pay phone all of a sudden, see. And my girlfriend called. She wanted to come over. I told her she could only come over if she brought a hundred gallons of homemade hollandaise sauce."

"Get out of here. Now I know you're lying. I try to be serious and all you do is crack jokes."

"It's true. We got into a huge fight. It was a nightmare."

She swatted away my story like she was shooing away a fat fly.

"You don't believe me?"

"No."

"Well, I'll show you." And I swatted my hand down flat on her greasy head and squashed her spiky hairdo. I rubbed it around. Her hair looked like oil-covered sea marsh. She ducked from under my mashing hand.

"Stop." She kept ducking. But my hand stayed with her head.

"Time for a super-duper, punk-rock nuggy!"

She ducked and scrambled out from my hand, parked herself in a karate stance. I stopped.

"Hey," I said, changing the subject. "Let's go suntanning."

She scrunched her face into a question mark.

It took a little doing, but I managed to convince Michele that relaxing for an hour was good for her, and what the hell else was she going to do, read the dictionary? We spread a sheet over the grass in the field. I was lounging in my new Hawaiian boxer shorts. The shorts had Froot Loop birds flying around in a jungle with pineapples; they fit me like a pillowcase. Michele had on running shorts with a bikini top. I was just lounging. She was reading *Crime and Punishment*.

"How can you read that junk?" I asked.

"Junk? This is a masterpiece."

"It's just a dumb cop and robber story. Like Starsky and Hutch."

"How do you know?"

"I can tell by the cover."

She groaned.

"You know, that's what people say about me."

"What? You're a dumb cop and robber story?"

"Funny, real funny. People say, "Ahh, he's not a real musician, he's just a dumb harmonica player." I wish I had a nickel for every time someone said that. Actually, I'd prefer a ten-dollar bill."

"Would you mind being quiet. I'm trying to read."

"Fine . . ." I zenned out to the heat of the sun.

Chapter Twenty-six

IIII IIII IIII IIII IIII

I FELT LIKE a little boy. Michele had picked out my clothes, made me wear them. I bitched and complained. And moaned and groaned and provided an encyclopedia of reasons why the outfit was all wrong. I had on a pink, Ralph Lauren tennis shirt with white linen pants and Topsider shoes. I felt like I had a lifetime subscription to *Yachting Digest*. I kept complaining. I wanted to wear my slobbering pig shirt.

"Look," Michele turned her Izod shirt collar up.

"They're looking for a maniac, drunken, drug-doing harmonica player who beats up old ladies. Now look at yourself in the mirror. What do you see?"

I looked in the mirror. I started shivering. For the first time in my life I prayed, "God, please let this woman be wrong." As I expected, I got no answer; maybe I was put on hold, but I heard no divine elevator music.

"All right. I guess you're right."

"I don't even want your brother to know who you are."

I pointed to myself. "My brother wouldn't let someone like this in his room. He'd rather mop floors at a nuclear power plant."

We went outside and got into the Volvo, which, besides Saabs and BMWs, is the ultimate yuppy mobile. I started feeling nauseous.

"Now look," Michele started the car. "Remember. We're up here on vacation, camping out at my uncle's place, the abandoned artists' camp."

"Michele, I'm having a problem with this. I feel it's out of context for my character to risk getting his pants dirty."

Michele shook her head. "Shut up. Just don't talk. And no one will ask you advanced questions." Michele put the car into first gear and started off.

It felt good to get out of camp. When we pulled onto the main road, I suggested we take a drive. Michele said fine.

Route 7 cuts through the Housatonic valley. We headed south. Sometimes jagged, small cliffs crushed up tight on the sides of the road with waterfalls and scruggs of pines. Other times, we drove through forests with oaks, beeches, maples, and birches. Sometimes we'd crest over a hill, and the view would unfold for miles, the Housatonic River winding through the valley like a trail left by a fat, lazy snake swaying through hot, wet sand. We didn't speak. I had my seat pitched back halfway between lying down and sitting up. It was dusk.

I tried to dissolve into the blurring images—and we came out of a cluster of trees. We could see the foothills of the Berkshires. A mist was rising, turning the trees into blurred, muted stains of green. The sky was pink with the setting sun, a few clouds glowing from the underlighting. The river seemed black and reflected a bluff of willows spreading out and over the water, the willows rooted on a mushy jetty. I tried not to think. I tried to let the setting sun, black river, mist, and gentle warm air and soft breeze be my moods, my serenity.

Michele said, "We should turn back. Okay?"

"I guess."

I could've driven for hours. Movement felt good. Michele swung off the road onto a dirt patch fishermen used to park their cars and turned us around. We headed back. She was right about the yuppy gig. As we drove through Kent, we saw Saabs, BMWs, Volvos; the tops of the cars had canoes, kayaks, fishing and camping equipment strapped to ski racks. We saw couples with daypacks going in and out of restaurants. We could get out and walk around and nobody would even notice. I'd be able to say, "How's it going?" to everybody. I was glad we drove through Kent.

We stopped at a country store at the junction of Route 7 and Route 4. Michele went inside. I got out of the car, sat on the hood, had a cigarette. Michele walked up three steps, across the porch and through the screen door, the screen door knocking itself into place after she disappeared. The porch was covered with black metal racks filled with newspapers. A couple of pick-up trucks were parked in the dirt and gravel lot. Over by a green dumpster a chicken was scratching and poking about. I stubbed out my cigarette and tossed the butt into the oil-drum garbage can. It seemed out of nowhere, a backpacking couple appeared. They clomped up the three stairs to the porch, threw off their orange and red packs. The guy went inside. The woman sat on the porch. Her hair was clumped into thick, black strands of sweat; it looked like a bunch of rotten bananas. She pulled out a granola bar, started munching. It was almost dark.

"Where you camping tonight?"

She jerked her thumb to the left and up the road, unable to stop gnawing on her granola bar. I looked up the road. In neon the sign blurbed MOTEL.

"You been on the Appalachian Trail?"

She spoke with a mouthful of chipped granola. "Been out for three days."

She looked pretty battered for three days; she said it like she'd just finished a National Geographic expedition. Not the outdoor type. Probably couldn't figure out how to use the hairdryer in the woods. Michele came back out.

"You get some cigarettes?" I felt like I was swearing in church, asking about cigarettes in front of a granola eater.

"No. Get them yourself."

Michele started helping herself to every newspaper on the racks. I hopped off the car and went inside, roamed around. The floors were wooden, not stained or painted, just natural and worn. I

grabbed a bag of Barb-BQ potato chips and a Coke
and walked up to the L-shaped checkout counter,
looked over the selection of cigarettes.

"Whoa," I said. "You got Old Gold filters?"

"Yes sir." The old man pulled them off the rack.
He had a wart on the side of his cheek, and it
looked like a miniature cow chip.

"Make it three packs."

He handed them to me and I paid.

Outside, Michele was throwing a bundle of
papers into the back seat.

"Hey, lady!" I barked. "You pay for them
papers?"

She gave me a look, telling me I was immature
and hoped I'd grow up before dinner. The two
backpackers were clomping up the road, up to the
motel.

At camp Michele went to work on the newspapers. She sat in the kitchen with the scissors and
went through all the papers, one by one. She had
the *New York Times*, the *Wall Street Journal*, the
Boston Globe, *Waterbury Republican*, *Bridgeport
Post*, *Hartford Courant*, *New Haven Register*, *Riverton Dispatch*, *Litchfield Times*, *Gaylord Gazette*,
Newtown Bee—towns I never heard of had papers.
I grabbed my saddle of harmonicas and went out
onto the porch. I'd changed: I wore blue jeans,
sneakers, and my slobbering pig shirt—what a relief.

It was dark. A mist, a muting silver, was rising
over the fields; the trees were only dark blotches
rising above the fields. A few crickets and tree
frogs carried on. It was cool, good sleeping
weather. Before I started playing, I remembered I
was hungry.

"Yo," I yelled to Michele. "Let's go out for dinner. On me."

"No."

"Why not? No one knows who we are."

"It's not good to flaunt it."

"What?"

"This afternoon you were running off at the mouth to everybody."

"You're crazy. I was not."

"I could see you through the window. You even tried to pick up that backpacker."

"What? The one with the overripe banana hairdo? You're crazy."

"Forget dinner. We're not on holiday." For an instant, she sounded British, a bloke.

"No shit. You're making sure of that."

"Anyway, I bought dinner."

We had salad, wheat bread, and farmer's cheese. We had a choice of seltzer or apple cider. I felt like I was trapped in Dannon Yogurt land. As I buttered my fourth piece of bread I asked, "This place is safe, right?"

"Sure, to a point. It's spring. And there's a lot of tourism around here. So the locals aren't surprised by strange people coming and going. But we shouldn't try to make any lasting impressions."

"Like buying a porchful of papers?"

"I covered myself, wise guy. I told him I was a sales rep for the Connecticut section of the *New York Times*. The only way I could write off my vacation was by doing some work."

"Oh." Quite the Yuppy thing to say, writing vacations off on taxes. I remembered I made a big deal about Old Gold filters—he'd remember me as the guy who had orgasms over Old Golds. I remembered the old lady at the motel who stared me down, then called the police. I remembered the backpacker. Shit. Anyone might notice me.

"Are you sure we're safe?" I hoped the paranoia didn't seep through my voice.

"Mostly, yes. Look, most people don't know how to go underground. They show up at their favorite uncle's for dinner. They bum money from dad at work. They take girlfriends out for drinks at local bars. Stupid things. As long as we make a clean break, we'll be okay. Theoretically."

"What do you mean?"

"Well, I've never been undercover for real. All I've done is train people. Probably thousands."

"I feel safe with you."

"We haven't done anything yet."

I buttered my fifth piece of bread. "What about the police?"

"Well, they'll do a little. Not much. The FBI will circulate pictures and blurbs. The local police in your town will keep a watch out. Your girlfriend and brother will be watched, and the guys in your band. But the local cops around here could care less. They don't have time to look for every underground criminal. Go into any post office and you'll see how many criminals are wanted nationwide. We're just two in a group of thousands."

"Humm. So why'd you get all those papers?"

"Couple of reasons. To find out if we're still a big story. And we're not; we're fading to the back pages, which is good news. But more important..."

She flopped a copy of the *Litchfield Times* in front of me, folded to the classified section, a Want Ad circled in red:

> CLEANING LADY. Ts, Thurs, nights.
> 1–7 am. Call MWF, 2:30–3:30 only.

"Wednesday, I can contact Hank Stewer."

I said, "Tomorrow's Wednesday."

"Boy, you're a walking calendar." It was the first joke she'd actually cracked. There was hope. I wanted to say, "Yeah, a calendar with a bum date," but I let her have it.

"This mean we'll be home by Friday?"

"I wouldn't count on it."

Chapter Twenty-seven

IIII IIII IIII IIII IIII

WEDNESDAY, 2:30, we were back at the country store. The same chicken was poking around. It was white with orange splotches. I was leafing through the *Cornwall Crier*, a small local paper. People around here actually bought and sold cows, pigs, sheep, and goats. There were more used tractors and hay mulchers than used cars. I thought all the farms were for show, bought and restored by rich, retiring, city folk. But there were a lot of working farms, too. Michele came out from the phone booth.

"Well?" I looked up from the paper—a poacher had shot someone's cow—as Michele got in the car. She sat in the seat and leaned back against the head rest.

"He said I should've let them take you."

"Great ..." I put the paper down. Suddenly my stomach felt empty and hollow like I'd been fasting.

She shook her head. "He said I may be right, but I don't have enough on Scruggers."

"The tapes aren't good enough?"

"No. They're nothing. I told you."

"So what're we supposed to do?"

"Keep our cover. Wait until we hear from him."

"How long's that?"

"Week, maybe two. The FBI's pulled out."

"Shit."

Michele got out and went inside. I was right behind her. I didn't care what she had in mind for lunch, I was getting my own. Ordered a ham and Swiss on rye with mayo and mustard, lettuce and tomato. Picked up an order of potato salad. Grabbed a six-pack of Coors in long-neck bottles from the cooler. Picked up some sour cream and chive potato chips. As I paid for everything, I could see Michele on the porch picking up newspapers. When I went outside, Michele was already in the car, the engine running. I climbed in and she slipped into reverse and started rolling backward before I even closed the door.

We didn't talk.

Back at camp I snooped around the theater barn. I found an old pool chair with plastic tubes strapped around a metal frame, the frame rusting like a tin can soaking in salt water.

I set up by the pool. I brought my lunch, beer, harmonicas, cocaine, cigarettes, and newspapers.

First I had a beer. It was the first drink I'd had in a few days—on an empty stomach—and it went right to my head. My brain went mushy, like thin grits. I looked down into the pool. The water still looked like zucchini soup. I noticed the frog was still there, its eyes floating over the green slime. I got the notion I'd go on a frog crusade, save the frog from the slime pool, might even turn the idea into a political bumper sticker. Across the pool and through the tennis courts I could see Michele walking out into the field in her karate suit. She started stretching.

I turned to my sandwich. It was three fingers fat. I opened another beer and chomped into the ham and Swiss, ripped open the potato chips and started munching. Swigged some beer. Now Michele was going through a set of kicking exercises. It took a little imagination, but I could do it: I dreamed I was poolside at a Club Med, the sun washing over me, watching women dance nude, having only to click my fingers to get piña coladas in coconuts or rum punches in pineapples, click my fingers for bronzed women to spread oil all over me, click my fingers—the frog ruined it. He started hopping, trying to get out, his fat, slimy belly flopping against the tile wall, a repeated sloshing as the frog kept hopping and falling back into sludge. He was stuck.

I finished my sandwich and popped open another beer. My stomach felt bloated and soft with fat. My lungs ached from smoke. My head felt squishy, soft from the light drunk—shit, I should've eaten bean sprouts. Anyway, I went to work. One thing I knew for sure, whatever Michele was going to do, I wasn't going to wait to hear from some guy who felt I was better off dead. I went through the classifieds of every paper, scanning the Help Wanted ads, finally found what I was looking for:

WORK AT THE BEACH! BE YOUR OWN BOSS!
WORK YOUR OWN HOURS! UNLIMITED INCOME!
Run a Hot and Cold Tasty Treats concession truck.
Call now! 576–1313. Ask for Len.

The ad was so good; it sounded like I should quit buying lottery tickets and go to work for them. I ripped out the ad and put it in my saddle of harmonicas.

Soon as Michele was done, I'd pitch the idea. Now I was going to do some suntanning. I stripped down to my boxer shorts. The late May sun wasn't strong—when clouds blotted it out, it was cool, goose bump degrees—but, it was good enough. I closed my eyes. And drifted into the whiteout of afternoon sleep....

I woke when Michele sat on the end of my pool chair. How long had I slept? Ten minutes? An hour? I didn't know.

"If I were to look at you, I'd say you're in pretty good shape." She was mopping sweat off her face and neck with a towel.

Was I dreaming or was she paying me a compliment? "When you going to teach me karate?"

"Soon as you quit smoking."

No dreams, all true. I shook my head and rubbed my eyes, trying to bring the world and my thoughts into focus.

"Look," I said. "I got an idea."

* * *

It only took a few minutes. When I finished, Michele sat and stared across the field, not very enthusiastic.

"Well, what do you think?"

"I don't like it."

"Why not?"

"I don't know. I just don't."

"Come on. I can't sit around this camp and twiddle my toes."

"I don't want to do anything until I hear from Hank."

"Fuck that. A week, maybe two. I want to be with my brother as he dies." The muddle had returned: now that I couldn't be with Trip, I had to see him—he was going to die. But I knew as soon as I was with him, I wouldn't be able to handle his dying. Shit.

"Jocko, what can I do?"

"I'm not waiting for this dip to send us a cleaning lady ad."

"He's not a dip."

"I don't care what he is. If you're not going to help, then I'll do it myself."

"Oh right. How?"

"Anyway I can."

"Good luck."

"Your boss doesn't have to know if you help me."

"I told you: I just don't like it. All right?"

"Why?"

"There's too many loop holes."

"Then help me with them."

"Jocko, please."

"And how do I know what your big boss man's going to do with me, huh? He told you you should've let them kill me. Right? He's not looking after my ass."

"He didn't say I should have let them kill you. He said I didn't have enough—I mean..."

"I bet he pulls you up and leaves me dumped."

Late afternoon, out by the pool, feeling good, late afternoon. Had a plan to burn Scruggers's ass. Michele or not. I knew it'd work. The wonder drug, cocaine, made me feel it so. I had worked through my harmonicas. Had dipped into the cocaine big time. Had so much cocaine I didn't bother to cut picayune lines. Just slip my pinky in the bag and glide my pinky under my nose. Oh yeah. Cocaine running through my blood like the fountain of youth. Like champagne. Happy. I'd settled down with my E-flat harmonica. Wailing through a country shuffle. Playing so fast I could barely catch my breath. My throat raw from playing two hours. The hinge of my jaw aching. My temples throbbing, not used to the pain—had taken too much time off from harp playing. I missed the band. Missed feeling the drums hammering and the bass swinging and the guitar chopping and the feel of a room full of dancers in rhythm with my song and the heat and sweat and ache from playing all night.

I stopped...

I wanted to hear people whooping and hollering and stomping their feet and screaming, "More! More! More!"—only trees and grass and the setting sun. I was coming down from the cocaine. Thing about me and coke, start doing it and can't quit.

Feel great when I'm high, like shit when I'm down. And all I think about is keeping high-high-high! Time to put my pinky in the bag. Time to arrange my white-tipped pinky under my nose—Michele was sitting at the end of my lawn chair, the bag of coke in her hand.

Chapter Twenty-eight

‖‖ ‖‖ ‖‖ ‖‖ ‖‖

"HOWDY!" I BELLOWED in a cowfolk mood.

"Having fun?" Michele held the coke for me to see.

"Just about to do some up. Care for any?"

"No."

"Good stuff." I reached for the bag.

She pulled it away. "You've had enough."

"Now, come on. Party time. We're going to burn Scruggers's ass."

"Not if you're stoned. And I don't remember saying I was doing anything." She looked at the ground, thinking.

"Come on." I reached for the bag again. She wouldn't let me have it.

She looked at me. "So. Who's going to do it?"

"Do what?"

"Pour this stuff in the pool."

"Nobody!" My mind went crazy with the idea of there being no cocaine and having to come down and go through the dregs of cocaine blues—like standing in a sleet storm. Crazy with the thought of 20 grams—at least—or $2,000 of coke dissolving in green slime. I tried to grab the bag. She blocked my hand with some karate shit.

"I guess it's me." She got up and started for the pool.

I lunged at her. She sidestepped and hammered her fist into the broad of my shoulders; it felt like I'd been hit with a two-by-four. I fell flat on the ground, out of breath. But I heaved myself up with both arms, and she kicked me in the stomach, under the ribs; it felt like a running back had gutted me with his helmeted, ducked head. I choked on air. My head swirled into blackout. Then my vision swirled back into focus; I felt like someone was swishing me in his cocktail glass. I saw Michele pouring cocaine into the green slime of the pool, the coke pouring out like a stream of damp sugar. She let go of the empty plastic bag, and it fluttered like a falling leaf, right, then left, right, left, finally spreading flat on the algae-thick water. Michele walked away.

I scrambled down the steps to the shallow end, scared shitless I wouldn't be able to toot up. I slipped on the tile bottom, slapped down hard on my hands and knees, but kept going. I scurried into the slime. Algae coated my arms, chest, legs, and stomach. I slipped again and algae gushed into my open mouth, glued to my hair. I arched my head back, choking, gagging with slime spraying out of my mouth as I coughed and coughed. The cocaine had dissolved. In my desperate grab for the plastic bag—enough inside to dust my nose, stall the dregs—I swatted the bag. It bloated with green water. And the cocaine was all gone. All gone.

* * *

In the morning, after sobering, after a pot of coffee, after three hot showers, the only trace of cocaine was a pounding sinus headache. The harsh sunlight hurt my eyes and made the pounding worse. But I walked out and sat next to Michele on the porch. My stomach and back still hurt from her kicking and hitting me. Michele wouldn't look at me. I couldn't think of anything to say.

I tried: "I'm sorry."

She didn't say anything. She had her arms crossed over her stomach. She was hunched into herself, looking away, across the field.

"Just say something."

Still she didn't look at me. "I save your dumb life and all you do is suntan and get stoned."

"I'm sorry."

"If you didn't get drunk, the police may never have found you."

"I'm sorry, all right?"

"Don't you understand? It's you and me. Against the police. The state police. The FBI. And every hoot-nanny creep with a shotgun who wants to make $25,000. Everybody!"

"I thought you worked for the FBI."

"I did. Did. And they don't want anything to do with us now. We're an embarrassment."

"All right. All right."

"We don't stand a chance. And we have a worse chance when you're stoned, waddling around like a drunk duck."

She almost cried. But she choked off her tears. She bit her hand and crunched her eyes shut to keep the tears from flowing. She turned her head from me, putting her shirt sleeve over her eyes, wiping them dry.

"I'll stay sober. I promise."

She drew a deep breath and sighed, shaking her head. "I can't believe I'm saying this. But I guess I'll help you with that stupid idea."

"You don't have to."

"If you do it yourself, you'll get killed."

"Really, we can just hang out and wait."

"You're right. If I don't prove they were going to kill you, Hank'll leave you out. You'll either go to jail, or he'll leave you for the underground. It was my hunch. I know I'm right. And I have to prove it."

Chapter Twenty-nine

IN THE MORNING we drove to the south side of Bridgeport. It took a while to find the place, but we finally did. A parking lot was guarded by a ten-foot wire fence, topped with curls of barbed wire. The lot was filled with red and white Tasty Treat trucks. We walked up the wooden steps of the white construction trailer and knocked on the door.

A small, old man opened the door. He stared at me with gray-blue eyes. He was over sixty, his hair thick and gray. His cheeks were pink from a fresh, tight shave—pink like they'd been slapped with hard, cold winds day after day. He just stared at me. Then he peeked around, looked at Michele, then at me.

"Morning. Len?" I stuck out my hand to shake.

He stared at me like I was lying about sleeping with his high school granddaughter.

"Yeap," he finally said. "I'm Len. Looking for work?"

"Yes sir."

"Well, come on in. Might as well fill out an application anyways."

He let us in, closing the door behind us. I felt like I was in a Salvation Army living room: an old orange and flowered sofa; a fake, stone coffee table; a card table by the kitchenette; a green Lazy-Boy recliner, the stuffing held in with electrical tape; a carpet spotted with old cat pee.

"I'm the manager." He was over by a rusting file cabinet, pulling out applications. "Lots of kids want these jobs. And I'm picky." For him, anyone under fifty-five was a kid. He shut the file drawer, came over and handed us our applications.

"Sit yourself at the table. Take your time. I've all day."

We sat at the card table. He sat on the couch and went back to reading the *New York Post*, drinking instant coffee. When I finished my application I had a new name, Bill Hollin. Michele fixed me up with a set of fake ID's—driver's license, social security, credit cards. On the application I listed I'd worked in seven restaurants. I actually did work as a cook once; I was fired after screwing up seventeen orders of Nachos. Michele listed she'd worked as a waitress. The restaurants were in Nashville; Michele had gone to Vanderbilt as an undergraduate, and I'd spent a summer there doing studio work. When we finished, Len looked over our applications. I was flipping through a *Popular Mechanics*.

"So, Bill, why'd you want this job?"

I kept flipping through the magazine. I'd forgotten I was Bill. Michele jabbed me in the side.

"Bill, the man's asking you a question."

"Oh, I'm sorry. Sir?"

I guess we were hired, but Len never said so. He brought us out and showed us around one of the trucks. He showed us how to turn the key—to the right, not the left. He showed us the steering wheel, the stick shift. He showed us the turn signal, the gas pedal, brake, and clutch. I was only interested in two things—the bumpers and the roof. The bumpers were made of half-inch steel. Good. The roof had a loudspeaker funnel on it for Muzak. But not for Muzak—the speaker was for the Tasty Treats theme song. Len flipped it on and warned us not to overplay it because nobody liked it, not even him. After two and a half hours of how-to instruction, we were able to go, but only after promising, over and over, to be back no later than eight-thirty Monday morning.

Early Sunday morning we were on the road, heading for Portsmouth, New Hampshire. We took Route 4 to Hartford, got onto Route 84 and then followed the toll roads through the old, industrial Northeast. It's a landscape of asphalt and office buildings and crumbling brick warehouses: gray buildings with gray and yellow smog. The only splashes, only relief, of color came from the poor sections where immigrants—Cambodian, Mexican, Haitian—hung their wash out to dry: 25 cents saved on a dryer is 25 cents earned. And color splashes came from advertisements and bright-colored cement silos. In the older parts of towns, the buildings were crunched together like a pile of

tin cans and cardboard, left to rust and dissolve in
acid rain; in the new parts, buildings shone like
new cars. I wondered what people grew up dreaming about in these towns, what kinds of lives did
they imagine?

After four hours we were in Portsmouth. Highways came in from Maine, northern New Hampshire, and Vermont; highways headed to Boston
and Rhode Island. The skyline was cluttered with
green and white highway signs hanging down
from steel frames or sticking up on metal posts. We
ended up on a six-lane bridge that arched over a
river to Maine. With so many directions, how
could we not get lost? Finally we found the signs
for the bus station and followed the arrows.

The bus station was made out of little cinderblocks and looked like a big cinderblock. We got
our parking ticket from the automatic entrance
gate and left the Volvo in long-term parking, very
long-term. Inside the bus station, Michele rented a
car. She got a simple, nondescript, beige Chevette.
She had to take a shuttle bus to the rent-a-car
parking lot. As she did that, I'd call Scruggers. We
found a cluster of phone booths, and I stepped into
an empty one.

"I'll make the phone call in fifteen minutes. That
should give you enough time."

"Okay." Michele turned and left. Then she doubled back, unstrapped her wrist watch and handed
it to me.

"Good luck."

"Good luck to you too." I blew her a kiss. She
turned and left.

I made a fake phone call, lit a cigarette. I sat
down and pressed my foot against the door so no
upset traveler would shove in to use the phone. I

sat there and fake-talked and smoked and stared at
exhausted travelers—people with uncombed hair,
unshaven faces, with bags under their eyes and
unbrushed teeth. I talked about basketball, which
I know nothing about. I counted how many pieces
of chewed gum were stuck in the phone booth—
twenty-seven. I talked about baseball, which bores
me, so I didn't talk long. Then I talked about this
new woman I'd met, under unusual circum-
stances; she was different from any other woman
I'd known. I was talking to Will, my long-lost
friend from Omaha. As I looked at Michele's watch
constantly, I noticed time sure went slow. After my
third cigarette, I put in my call to Scruggers, using
a fake long-distance calling card, the area code in
Montana. After a few rings, a woman answered the
phone, I guess his wife.

"I want to talk to Jack."

"May I ask who's calling, please?"

"You surely please may. Jocko Miles. The drunk
who tried to blow him up. If he's not on right
away, I'm going to try to blow him up again!"

"Oh, yes, please, just a minute." Flutters of
panic, like birds scurrying off telephone wires,
were in her voice. She rested the phone. It hissed
with dead air. After forty-five seconds he still
hadn't answered. He was stalling, trying to get a
trace. Fine with me—we wanted to act a little
dumb, wanted him to think we were north.

He answered. "Yes?"

"Jack, old buddy."

"Jocko, you're crazy."

"Could be."

"What the hell you want?"

"We want to make a little deal."

"What could you possibly have to deal with?"

"Tapes. Recordings. Nice, high-fi quality."

I let it sink in. He didn't say anything. So I went on: "Quite a few, actually. Of you and Mr. Broderick chit-chatting. Let's see, ... we have tape of you talking about my 'accidental' death, and—"

"Bullshit, Jocko."

"It's true, Jack old boy. What do you think she was doing? Using that fancy ass recorder to tape mating birds? We've got hours."

"She was only here a few days." He was going through his mind, running through the days, trying to remember how many times he'd talked.

"Well, what can I say? You got a big mouth."

"I'll play your bluff. What kind of deal did you have in mind?"

"Simple. Grab two lowlifes off the street, man and woman. Stage a shoot out, blow them to pieces. Burn them. No finger prints, nothing. You get two dead bodies you can pass off as us. We give you the tapes and skip to Canada as new people, using the IDs of the goons you mutilate."

He didn't say anything. It was working. Michele and I had no plans for that kind of deal. It was her idea. Killing two people had overtones of blackmail, entrapment, murder. Michele figured if we gave Scruggers plenty of ways to snag us—legal, illegal—he'd play further along, planning he'd always be able to grab us when he wanted.

He broke the silence. "You're crazy."

"You didn't have any problems staging a blowout for my brother."

"I want to hear the tapes."

"All right. Tomorrow, between twelve and one. Go to Riverton's Cove Point Beach. By the seawall on the south side, there's a double phone booth.

Pull up and wait for us to call. You and Broderick.
If you mess up, the tapes go to the FBI."

I hung up.

I stepped out of the phone booth. I was shaking
like I'd overdosed on coffee and NoDoz and Coca
Cola and Reeses Pieces. When I went through the
doors and outside, Michele was waiting for me in
the fire lane, the car running. She slid the car into
gear and pulled up to me. I stubbed out one cigarette and lit another.

"Well?" She checked oncoming traffic, then
pulled out into the lane.

"Nothing definite. But I think he'll show."

Chapter Thirty

IIII IIII IIII IIII IIII

MONDAY, MICHELE WOKE me early.

I dressed as a football jock. I had a yellow football jersey, cut off midway at the stomach, with
blue numbers, "29." I had a pair of gray sweat-
pants, cut off into shorts, and a pair of tennis
shoes, no socks. Michele was supposed to look like
my girlfriend—running shoes, tank-top, pink bandana, sneakers, and pink puff balls dangling from
her ankle socks.

A little past eight I was getting out at a mom
and pop deli just down from Hot and Cold Tasty
Treats' headquarters. We didn't want Len to see
the new car—we'd dumped the Volvo because he'd
seen it—so Michele was going to wait for me at
another corner. I walked to the lot. It seemed I was

the first one there. All the trucks were in. When I
knocked on the door, Len opened it.

"Good morning, sir."

He looked at his watch. I was early. "Morning."

He went inside and came out with an oversized
clipboard, big enough for legal pads.

"Where's the wife, Bill?"

"Girlfriend. She has to leave the Volvo for a
friend. I'll pick her up on the way."

"Whatever." He handed me the clipboard.
"This's for you. Keep track of what you sell."

We walked over to the gates. Len unlocked the
padlock and rolled back the gates. It put him a
little out of breath. He pulled out a pack of Ches-
terfield unfilters and lit one with a Bic lighter.

"Smoke?"

"Sure." I pulled one out. He lit it for me.

"What you doing smoking if you play football?"

"Don't play any more. Used to." It tasted good to
smoke a strong cigarette.

"Oh."

He took me over to the truck we were going to
use, gave me another tour. It was stocked with 100
hot dogs, 100 hamburgers, six cases of soda, rolls,
buns, popsicles, ice cream, frozen fries, and onion
rings. He showed me how to get the loudspeaker
cranking. A flick of the switch and the Hot and
Cold Tasty Treats theme song came on; it was an
amusement park romp. He flicked it off.

"I hate that song."

I had a big ash on my cigarette. I looked around
for a place to flick it. He noticed.

"Just flick it on the floor." He flicked his ash on
the floor then dropped his butt and squashed it out
with his work boot. "But make sure you sweep

clean at the end of the day." He jerked his thumb at a broom stashed behind the stove.

He showed me how to track what I sold, using the clipboard. He explained everything twice, positive I couldn't follow the first time. Then, positive I couldn't figure it, he started the truck. He got out the driver's side where the walk-through door was. I climbed into the driver's seat.

"Make sure you're back by six."

"Yes, sir."

I eased the truck into gear. The transmission grinded. Then I pulled out of the parking lot. In my rearview mirror I could see Len closing the gates, then slowly walking back to his office, walking into another day of reading the paper cover to cover and hoping someone applies for a job so he'll have something to do. I hope when I'm old I don't have to fight boredom and loneliness with a boring, meaningless job. Getting old. Maybe Trip was right—dying young's not so bad. Shit. I rattled my head, tried to clear it.

The gears were set on such a low ratio, the truck drove like a car with its parking brake on. When I passed the empty parking lot of the bank, Michele pulled out behind me and followed. We got onto the highway, headed south, then pulled into a commuter's parking lot to fix the recording equipment. Michele parked next to me and got out and came over to the truck.

It was an easy job. Two wires, red and black, led from the music box up to the loudspeaker on the roof. Michele handled the inside wiring. When she finished, I climbed on top of the truck's roof with the microphone. The microphone was about two-feet long, as fat as a good cigar. It was a highly sensitive shotgun microphone, designed for eavesdropping; it could pick up whispers from a 100 yards.

The Tasty Treats speaker housing was simple: a cone-shaped funnel, a few years ahead of the first bullhorns. I plugged the microphone into the hook-up jack Michele was wiggling in the speaker housing. The speaker looked like an old microphone from the golden days of radio. With electrical tape I secured the shotgun microphone to the underside of the speaker, then covered both with a black sock. I hopped down and went back into the truck. On the ceiling was a round plate, and the plating fastened with one large bolt, through the roof, to the bottom of the speaker housing. I loosened the bolt so we could adjust the angle of the microphone by turning the fastening plate.

We were ready. I started up the truck. Michele got back in the rented car and followed. On the way to Cove Point, we parked the rented car behind an empty apartment house. Years ago it was called the Arctic Bird, a whorehouse, a stucco building with arched windows and blue trim. After upright citizens shut it down as a house of pleasure, it was converted into cheap apartments. Now the building was abandoned, awaiting its death—it was going to be torn down, making room for condos. I preferred a whorehouse to a condominium any day. All the windows were broken, and the inside was weathering. Trip and I used to have a gig here; he'd play acoustic guitar, I'd play harmonica and sing. We got our choice of women, and they all wanted me—I was only fifteen, an easy trick. I didn't tell Michele any of this. We hid the rented car in back, behind a dumpster.

Michele locked the car and walked into the truck.
  "Ready?"
  "I guess," she said.

Cove Point is not exactly what I consider a
beach. It's called sand, but it's really gravel and
sand, perfect for driveways. To take a swim, you
had to walk over a field of algae-slick rocks—they
threw you off balance and cut your feet. And of
course crabs went for the feet, too. Once, when I
was a kid, I roughed it all and went for a dip. After
clearing the rock and crab zone, I dove under and
came up wrapped in a slime wad, figured it was
seaweed. When I finally untangled myself, I found
I was wrapped in a roll of toilet paper. I don't
swim at Cove Point much anymore.
  We parked about fifteen yards past the phones,
along the seawall. It was a good beach day. The
sun was glaring white, bleaching the ocean as it
rose. It was going to be hot. A slight breeze came
from off shore. Scruggers was supposed to be here
around lunch, prime time. After the late snows in
April, most people would be suntan crazy. During
lunch, everybody would try to catch some rays
while scarfing down tunafish. If it had been raining out, our Tasty Treats cover would have been as
useless as a wetsuit in the desert.
  Michele had wired herself into the Nagra tape
recorder with pair of Walkman headphones. She
was supposed to act cool, uncaring and rocking.
Now there was nothing to do but wait, maybe sell
a few popsicles.
  Around 11:30 the beach crowd started thicken-
ing. A lot of women—secretaries, bank tellers, rising executives—had hightailed it out of work,
changed into makeshift tanning suits, and were

lying out, trying to get a bronze base for a summer
of tanning. People who had their days off came
with chairs, books, coolers, suntan lotions, snacks.
One group was having a beach party and brought
their own potted palm tree, had a blender powered
by a car battery whipping up piña coladas. The
beach was checkered and cubed with radios,
ghetto blasters, and whenever the wind blew hard,
the sound of thirty-nine radio stations swept over
me. And people were actually ordering Tasty
Treats, lots—the public concession stand was
closed. I had no competition. And I was going nuts.
People were three deep, mostly wanting sodas—
all diet—and popsicles and ice cream. To make
things easy, I charged a buck for everything. Michele wasn't helping, wasn't supposed to.

When she tapped me on the shoulder, I looked
back through the grime-blurred windows of the
truck. A white, stretch Cadillac limo pulled up in
front of the phone booths. Michele reached behind
the cabinet and turned on the recorder.

I didn't have time to think about Scruggers.
There were more important matters than someone
wanting to kill me—the lunch crowd had descended. I had seven hot dogs and five hamburgers
and french fries and onion rings all being nuked in
the microwave. I glanced over to Michele. She
nodded. It was them.

Meanwhile, back at the lunch crowd, I explained
why everything was a buck. Why I had no diet
soda left. Why grape popsicles are so popular. Why
microwaved hot dogs taste so funny, never like
ballpark dogs. And, no, I didn't know microwaved
hamburgers tasted like warm horseshit. I never ate
warm horseshit—why'd you eat horseshit, buddy?
And I know my girlfriend has huge knockers, punk.

But why don't you tell her yourself? She'll knocker your teeth through your ears. And, of course, sodas cost a buck everywhere; who cares if the price of gas is going down? When it comes to being waited on, people can be the biggest assholes. I made a mental note: Never open a restaurant. Somehow I made it. The microwave dinged for the last time, and the lunch rush was over.

Michele patted me on the back. I looked over to the white Cadillac. The driver was getting out of the front. Michele pulled the headphones off and draped them around her neck.

"He's coming over to buy sodas."

"All right. Well, I'll just serve him."

"Just serve him like normal."

"I got it. I know."

"Good." She started putting the headphones back on.

"What's it sound like?"

"Good. Bad. Good news is they rolled down the window to make sure they could hear the phone ring."

"That's it for the good?"

"That's it." She put the headphones on.

Chapter Thirty-one

IIII IIII IIII IIII IIII

THE DRIVER HAD black hair, coffee black eyes, and an olive, always tanned complexion. He wore white linen pants. His flower print Hawaiian shirt had nude windsurfers—all men—whipping about, chasing other nude windsurfers; all the wind-

surfers had prominent hard-ons. His feet poked out
of black Chinese sandals. His white, linen jacket
looked clean as the un-cola.

He was gay and loved it. First thing he did was
stare me down, undressing me in his mind, una-
shamed he wanted my ass. I ignored him. I don't
mind gay men, nothing against them. But I don't
want them coming onto me. Mostly I didn't want
this bimbo staring me down. He might remember
what I looked like.

"What can I get for you?"

"Some colas, please." His English was colored
with a Brazilian accent. He spoke with an effemi-
nate lisp.

"What kind?"

"Low calorie, please."

"All out of diet, bub." I talked like I had Cheerios
and Budweiser for breakfast.

I pulled out my Old Gold Filters and stared into
the pack, counting how many I had left. Six. I
pulled one out, lit up.

"Well, what kind of colas do you have?" He was
getting snippy.

"Let's see." I fiddled through the icebox. "Coke,
orange, root beer, Dr. Pepper, 7-Up."

"Well, I guess, humm. Two Coca-Colas, and one
orange, please. I'm fond of orange soda."

"Glad to hear it, pal." I handed him the sodas.

"How much, please?"

"Let's see. Buck each. Three bucks clean."

The dollar sodas blew his composure. "One dollar for a soft drink?!"

I shrugged, suggesting life's tough all over, and
before you know it even ducks will be extinct. He
peeled three dollars off the bottom of a folded

square of bills. A small, gold dildo was his money
clip. When he put the money in my hand, he gave
me the French tickle. He knew I was straight, but
he was into teasing straight men, watching them
panic as he put the moves on them. I ignored him,
kept smoking.

"Thanks," I said.

"Of course, you're welcome."

He reached across his chest with his left hand for
napkins and straws. His linen jacket molded
against the shape of a gun and holster. After getting his napkins and straws, he winked at me, then
twitched his ass at me as he walked back to the
car. Michele kept cleaning and started talking to
me, acting like she wasn't.

"They're onto something."

"What?"

"Scruggers is trying to figure out why our music
speaker is pointed at him and not the beach."

"We can't leave until they go."

"I know."

"Kill the tape and play the Tasty Treats theme.
Then kill the Muzak and roll the tape. We'll act like
it's last call."

Through the blurred windows, I could see the
driver climbing into the car. Michele was about to
throw on the Tasty Treats romp. She didn't.

Out of the corner of her mouth she said: "They're
pumping the driver for what we look like."

"Shit. Okay, go on. Kill the tape."

Michele clicked the tape player and flicked on
the Tasty Treats theme. The cheap recording—an
organ waltz—romped over the beach. I looked
through the window. The driver got out of the car,
clutching his left side like he had heart burn. I
went and started up the truck. Then I grabbed a

soda and shook it up. Michele had cut the Tasty Treats theme and had the tape rolling again. A metal slatted door rolled over the serving window like a garage door. I undid the latch on the ceiling. Then the driver was at the window.

"How's it going?" I said. "Last call, what can I get for you?"

"My employer would like to speak with you."

"I'd love to chat but can't leave the truck. Tell him to come on over."

"I'm afraid you misunderstand." A smile spread from ear to ear, and his teeth gleamed like a fresh cleaned, porcelain toilet.

He made his point clearly. He pulled out his gun, pointed it at my vitals. I sidestepped and opened the soda and sprayed soda all over his face. Then I slammed the metal slat door down onto his hand. His wrist snapped like brittle, dry spaghetti. He screamed like a child having nightmares. I slid open the metal slat door and rammed the butt of my palm into the top of his chest. He toppled over the seawall into the sand, clutching his smashed wrist. I scrambled into the driver's seat and crunched the truck into gear. Michele, her back to me, still listening to the taping, missed it all. She didn't know anything had gone wrong until the truck bucked into gear, slapping her against the back wall.

"What are you doing?!" she yelled.

"Just stay low."

I crunched the truck into second gear. In the rearview mirror I could see the driver shuffling back to the Cadillac. Both Scruggers and Broderick had stepped out, and both had one foot on the pavement, one foot in the car. The driver opened his door, then all three were swallowed behind closing doors and tinted windows.

A one-way road followed the seawall for an eighth of a mile to a stop sign. I knew I couldn't out-run the Cadillac. So I stopped and angled the truck sharply to the left for a turn and waited for the Cadillac. Like I hoped, it pulled in straight behind me, angling for a left turn. Time to use the bumpers. I slammed into reverse and popped the clutch, pinned the gas pedal to the floor. The truck lurched back into the Cadillac. I saw, in the rear-view mirror, the half-inch steel bumpers crushing the headlight into the wheel. The Cadillac mushed like an aluminum can. After just standing up, Michele went flying back onto the floor.

I slipped the truck into first, pulled ahead, then yanked back into reverse, slamming again into the Cadillac. I crunched the front-end back behind the left wheel; now the Cadillac could only swirl left in circles.

But the driver could still run anywhere he liked. And he got out of the car waving another gun wildly in his left hand. I slammed the truck into first gear and took off. In the jangling rearview mirror, I could see the driver starting to shoot wildly. I heard gunshots cracking through the air. Then I saw him, again. Tall, lean, in black sunglasses, a soft lemon yellow jacket, walking quickly to the driver, gently reaching and pulling the driver's shooting arm down—Broderick. I ripped the truck through all its gears, the transmission grinding with each shift. The image of Broderick bounced and jolted in the mirror, getting smaller, finally disappearing behind a turn.

Back at the Arctic Bird we hustled into a change of clothes. Both of us put on tennis warm-up suits and sunglasses and sun visors. I took the cash we made for the day. I took the driver's gun. Michele wrapped up the recording equipment, not asking questions, knowing we had to move and move fast. I climbed on top of the truck, ripped off the sock, unwrapped the tape from the microphone, grabbed the microphone, and hopped down. Michele was in the beige Chevette, the car already started. I ran around and got inside. I put the microphone in a Prince tennis bag with the recording equipment. Between my legs were two tennis racquets. Michele swung back in reverse.

"What happened?"

"He pulled this." I showed her the snubnose .38.

"What'd he want?"

"He wanted us to join them in the Cadillac."

Michele shifted the automatic into drive. "Great. Just great."

A police car, its siren wailing, screamed past us as we ambled along in our modest Chevette; we looked like a frustrated couple, searching for empty tennis courts.

Chapter Thirty-two

|||| |||| |||| |||| ||||

BACK AT CAMP we didn't talk. Michele showered. I showered. Then I sat on the porch, playing my harmonicas. My hands shook. I couldn't stop thinking of Broderick walking out, relaxed, his yellow blazer, black pants—white wicker shoes, too —and all he did was put his hand over the driver's hand, calmly pulled down the gun. I only saw his image bouncing in a mirror. He was fifty yards away, at least. Yet he reeked of composure. Michele came out and sat down. She had the tape recorder.

"We should listen to this."

"Guess so," I said.

The tape was threaded and ready to play. Michele clicked it on. Out of the speaker came the sound of hissing, dead air. And the sound of children playing on swings. Ocean waves and seagulls and cars—rubber tires whirring over dry asphalt. The voices of Scruggers and Broderick talking. Easy listening jazz, a piano trio. It seemed Scruggers's blood pressure had shot up to 240 over 170; it seemed Broderick was floating in an isolation tank, his pulse down to 50.

"That bitch was around my house," Scruggers said. It had been so long since I'd heard his harsh, Long Island accent. It grated my nerves.

"Jack, she probably has nothing." Broderick's voice was resonant, well-modulated, melodious— like a retired opera tenor.

"I wish I could remember what we talked about. Did I talk to you anyways?"

"I don't recall, Jack. Regardless, it doesn't matter. We find out what they have, retrieve it, and put them to rest."

"They're already supposed to be. Jesus."

"Next time, next. Be calm, Jack."

There was the sound of ice swirling in cocktail glasses. Michele had made notes to herself, indicating footage counts of important parts. She clicked the recorder to "fast forward" then switched it back to "play".

"When the hell they going to call?" Scruggers blurted.

"Jack, please, relax. It's probably a hoax. Would you care for some tobacco?"

I imagined Broderick having a selection of pipe tobacco, cigars, and international cigarettes.

"No thanks," Scruggers said. "Oh, man. Look at that woman's piece. Sweet, huh?"

"Francis's is nicer."

"Yeah, give me a fucking break. And tell him to stop pinching me anyways."

"But Jacky, doesn't it make you tingle?"

Someone giggled, I guessed Francis.

"It makes me want to throw up."

I decided Francis was the driver. Michele obviously didn't think the exchange was important; she scribbled over her original footage note, marking a new count.

"I believe," Broderick said, "you should suggest we cancel the Wednesday meeting, just until this mess is tidy."

"I did, I did already. And he went fucking nuts, I'm talking—crazy. On and on. It's all been set up; we have to move on schedule. And he's pissed we can't handle a couple of punks."

"You can't battle luck," Broderick said.

"Yeah, well, tell him."

"Personally, I'm not concerned. Squirts with a tape recorder. Maybe we should let them be."

"What? You bonkers? They got tapes."

"We don't know for sure. Besides, my lawyers have degrees from Columbia and Stanford. But, if it pleases you, we'll relax and see what they have to offer."

"When the hell these assholes going to call?"

"I'm not sure, Jack."

"Got any soda in this bar? Hell, if I can go back crocked."

"I'm afraid not, Jack. Sorry. But I'll have Francis get one for you, if you like. What kind would you care for?"

"Shit, I don't know. Anything diet, I guess."

"Francis, would you mind getting us some sodas. Two diets will be fine. Have one yourself, if you'd like."

"Sure," Francis said.

The door opened, then closed. There was no talking, only Broderick, I guess, whistling some classical melody. I couldn't imagine Scruggers whistling Brahms.

Scruggers snapped, "Hey, anything look funny about that truck?"

"Off hand, no."

"Look at the speaker."

"Yes. What of it?"

"It's pointed right at us."

"Yes. And what of it?"

"So how'd we know it's not them taping everything we fucking say?"

"Honestly, Jack. I believe you're becoming a twinge paranoid, really."

"Well, ask him anyways, when he gets back."

Silence. Then the front door opened and closed.

"Thank you, Francis. Would you please tell us who was serving you from the, humm, Tasty Treats truck?"

"This hung jock and a priss. Can I ask them over for a foursome?"

"Perhaps."

"I think we should fucking make them come over."

"Jack, honestly."

"Shit, it won't hurt."

"All right, fine. If it'll make you happy. Francis, please, invite them over."

"Surely."

And the door opened.

"Make damn sure they come," Scruggers said.

And the door closed.

"I do hope Francis doesn't play cowboy," Broderick said. "He's a bit thirsty for adventure."

Michele unwound the tape.

"Well," I said. "They're up to something." Sometimes my insights amaze me.

"No kidding."

"I got some ideas." I lit a cigarette.

"Like?"

"Well, they're pirating coke from the Colombians. Of course the Spanish neighbors aren't too happy; so, they pour on the heat. So, Broderick and Scruggers try to cover their asses; and they set up Trip and me as the cocaine pirates so we go down as the fall guys. I guess."

"Maybe." Michele put the tape in a quarter-inch reel box and started sealing it with electrical tape.

My thoughts drifted as Michele worked. I couldn't figure how Scruggers and Broderick ever met. It seemed impossible. Also, I didn't like the idea of the Colombian mafia; we could prove to the law we were innocent, but if the Colombians didn't like my face, that'd be it. If there were any Colombians involved. My cigarette tasted hot and foul. I stubbed it out.

"Maybe," I said, "we should find out who the other guy is."

"Sure. Why not." Michele rolled her eyes—when would I grow out of diapers? She sealed the taped box, then put the box in a side pocket of her camera bag.

Michele said, "I could call Hank and see what he says."

"Really. Tell him we got another tape."

"He'd kill me if he knew I was out making tapes when I'm supposed to just sit and wait."

"Then don't tell him. Maybe we should tail one of them on Wednesday."

"What?"

"Well, you know how to do it. Right?"

"I do. But it's not easy."

"We tail them. Find out who the other guy is. Get more tapes. Bingo."

"Of course. Simple." Michele shook her head in disbelief.

"Well, it's worth a try."

"And who we going to tail? Sheriff Scruggers?"

"All right, so we follow the other guy around."

"After today, we're not going anywhere." She wrapped the Nagra in its leather casing.

"What'd you mean?"

"It'll be in all the papers."

Chapter Thirty-three

‖‖‖ ‖‖‖ ‖‖‖ ‖‖‖ ‖‖‖

NEXT DAY DIDN'T bring good news; it brought news of Broderick. All the city papers ran stories about the county sheriff lunching with the underworld. Scruggers passed it off, explaining Broderick had information concerning my hideout. Broderick said it didn't matter how much money he had, he was always interested in more. Each article had blurbs on Broderick. I'm not sure they were accurate. Michele and I were described as con artists who'd ripped off Tasty Treats for over $600; our expert use of false identification implied we were professionals. The spat began when Scruggers asked Broderick's bodyguard to secure our vendor's license, wondering how we were able to charge one dollar per soda. Supposedly, Michele and I panicked when we thought our scam had been exposed.

Raymond Broderick was third generation, descended from Russian immigrants. His great-grandfather, friendly with the czar's family, had established a vodka exporting business. During the Russian Revolution, his great-grandfather escaped, leaving an estate and millions behind. After working his way to the United States, his great-grandfather built a second empire importing vodka. He changed the family name from Brodergravich to Broderick.

Broderick's grandfather carried on with the importing business. Diversification started with Broderick's father. He used his engineering degree and family money to start a manufacturing business, providing parts for the Connecticut military industry. Broderick's uncles started businesses in real estate, trucking, linen and laundry, shipping, construction—uncountable millions.

Raymond Broderick, a family oddball, used family money to open restaurants specializing in gourmet Russian food, patterned after the Russian Tea Room. He'd opened places in New York, Boston, Chicago, Los Angeles, New Orleans, Montreal, and Toronto. The IRS was investigating the family for laundering money through the cash-only restaurants.

Supposedly, there was no Mafia in Riverton, only the Brodericks. They controlled the loan-sharking, bookies, drugs, gambling, prostitution, black-market cigarettes, and alcohol. The unions for Riverton's docking industry had a fondness for Eastern Bloc Europeans. And Riverton had one of the largest concentrations of Eastern Europeans of any city in the country: Hungarians, Czechs, Polish, Rumanians, Bulgarians. It seemed that sooner or later everybody important—mayor, police chief, judges, prosecutors, newspaper publishers— was somehow related to the Brodericks, either by marriage, a distant cousin, or a close friend. It was the Brodericks who supplied Scruggers with most of his campaign funding.

Many times the Russian government had asked the United States to bring the family to trial, claiming the Brodericks ran an underground railroad for escaping iron curtain immigrants. The United States denied the request: there wasn't enough evidence. Also, the family had been accused of financing assassinations in communist, third-world countries. The Brodericks were violently anticommunist—the Réds had caused grandfather to lose millions—and went to church every Sunday together. They'd also been accused of sending hundreds of thousands in U.S. dollars to the Polish Catholic Church, contributing directly to the destabilization of the government.

I felt pretty small.

I used to figure, hell, we'd make a few tapes, turn them in to the FBI and they'd hurl the book. Now we were trying to peg someone who could hire international assassins. Michele assured me anyone with money could do it. But that didn't make me feel better: the Brodericks had money, lots. No wonder he was so calm. He was protected by millions, Columbia and Stanford lawyers, a personal army, and the government liked him, too. Shit.

I lit a cigarette. The porch was covered with shredded newspaper articles. All the background blurbs on Broderick had been underlined in red. All the background information on Scruggers was highlighted in yellow. All the information on us was underlined in green. I took the last sip of coffee from my cup. It was cold. Michele came out in her karate suit and sat down.

"Well?" I asked.

"It doesn't look good."

"What do you think?"

She rubbed her strained eyes. "I guess call Scruggers. Tell him we missed the call. And act like we don't know what happened. He's skittish. Hopefully, he'll start doubting himself."

"Maybe he'll fall for the con artist bit."

"Just so he doesn't trust himself."

It was hot and humid, and my cigarette smoke hung like a moist cloud of car exhaust, stagnant. Michele fanned away the smoke with her hand.

"Then what?" I asked.

"Then, tomorrow, I guess we tail Scruggers."

I chuckled. "Don't feel like tailing an international assassin, huh?"

"No." She stood up and stretched, bending her upper body so her nose almost touched her knees.

"Things are pretty grim, huh?"

"I'd say so." She stood up straight, stared blankly across the field.

"I guess we're lucky. They don't take us seriously."

"We've given them nothing to be serious about."

"Humm."

"And I'm sure they want to take care of us privately."

A nice, comforting thought. I stubbed out my cigarette. Whenever I stop drinking or doing drugs, I usually smoke like a fiend. Then, to cut down on my smoking, I start drinking and doing drugs. I lit another cigarette. It struck me—I hadn't worked out in a while. Suddenly, all my aches and creaks felt like cancer. I stubbed out my cigarette. I'd work out later.

"Where do we call Scruggers from?"

"New Hampshire. Let him get another trace."

"Today?"

"Soon as I'm finished." Michele went out into the field to practice her karate.

I went inside and pulled out my saddle of harmonicas, went back out on the porch. I juiced my C harp and cupped it in my mouth. But I didn't play. I watched Michele. I wanted all this to be over. I wanted to curl up to her, wrap around her, her soft skin and warmth meshing with mine; wrap close to her and sleep and wake in the morning with soft pink light coming through the windows, with a soft breeze whispering through leaves—the leaves still full and green and not wilted from summer heat—and have it be just a little too cold so we'd have to wrap closer together for warmth, and fall off to sleep again...

Around noon we packed for a road trip; a couple of Yuppies off motoring again. We took Route 22 through New York, then cut over to Massachusetts, picked up Route 7. In Pittsfield—an apt name— we changed cars. Now we had a nice, pale blue

Chevette. I felt like I was in a company car for *Encyclopaedia Britannica* salesmen. In Bennington, Vermont, we picked up Route 9 and cut across Vermont into New Hampshire, following Route 9 through Keene and into Henniker.

Henniker is a small college town in the White Mountains. When I was in Trip's blues band, we used to come here often. We'd play in fraternity parties for free beer and high exposure to the women. And of course Trip unloaded drugs, all kinds. We had a regular circuit. I know the colleges in the Northeast like a roach knows its favorite kitchen. It was my idea to come here; it always seems I'm driving around in my past.

The center of town had a grocery store, a knick-knack store for decorating college rooms, and a pharmacy with a 1950s soda bar. The stores shared the same communal porch, the porch the size of a basketball court sliced length-wise in half. The stores were flanked by a stone bridge that arched over the Black River. We pulled into an Exxon station around six. Michele gassed the car. I got out and walked over to the phone booth. I used the same long-distance calling card from Montana— poor folks. I expected Scruggers to be gone; all I wanted was to leave a message. But Scruggers answered himself.

"Home early, huh Jack?"

"Jocko? I'm going to burn your ass, you little shit."

"Sure. Wouldn't you like to hear the tapes? Look —sorry we couldn't place our phone call. Same place, same time, Thursday."

"What're you saying anyways?" His voice was strained with confusion.

I acted like I was being massaged, bedside. "You get any phone calls at the beach?"

"You telling me you weren't running a Tasty Treats truck yesterday or what?"

"What the *hell* you talking about?"

"Forget it. Why the fuck didn't you call?"

"We kind of got waylaid in a little lakeside romance. Didn't really oversleep, yet most of the day we were in bed."

He sneered. "New Hampshire's a nice state."

"Sure is. But we can be in a lot of places in one day. Thursday or Friday."

"What is this, anyways? Thursday or Friday. I got other shit to do, you know."

"You want the tapes?"

"Why can't you just fucking tell me what day?"

"Thursday or Friday."

I hung up.

Then I lit a cigarette—shit, still hadn't worked out. Anyway. Michele and I wanted two things to happen. First, Scruggers doubts we ran Tasty Treats; second, he thinks we're more concerned with romance than saving our lives. They didn't think we were a serious threat. If they thought we were whooping around, getting it on, they'd figure we were no threat. Hopefully. Also, we wanted them thinking we were silly enough to make careless phone calls. I wanted them to be unconcerned, let their guard down. After Michele finished, she pulled over to the phone booth. I stepped out as she rolled down the window.

"Well," I said. "I'm not sure he believed me. But I know I threw him for a loop."

"You tell him we'd call?"

"Thursday or Friday. He knows we're in New Hampshire."

"He's keeping that private."

"That doesn't settle my stomach."

"Mine either." She tapped her fingers on the dashboard, thinking.

"Hey, let's go for a walk. Stretch our legs before the drive."

"I guess it's okay."

"Meet me over at the grocery store."

"Fine."

She shifted into reverse, swirled back, then idled through the intersection. I walked over and clomped up the porch and went inside, bought a pack of Marlboros—no Old Golds—and a Tall Boy Budweiser. After paying, I went outside. Michele was leaning against the hood of the car, looking out toward the river. I opened my cigarettes and lit one. My pack of matches announced I had a bright future in hotel management, computers, or air-conditioning repair; well, always something to keep in mind if everything else crapped out. I popped open my beer.

"I'm sorry. Did you want anything?"

"No, that's all right." She didn't mind my drinking. But I didn't plan to get drunk.

I said, "Come on."

We started walking.

"So, what'd you say to Scruggers?

"I told him we got held up in a lakeside romance."

She laughed. "You wish."

"And you should be so lucky."

"Uh-huh. My foot."

"Feet, hey? You into feet? Bet you didn't know I can massage your feet and send you into multiple orgasms."

"You're right. I didn't know."

"Magic touch. Anyway, if they think we're romping and making whoopie, they'll definitely think we're harmless."

She tilted her chin down and rolled her eyes up, meeting mine with soft affection. "You could've thought of something else to say."

"Yeah, but I didn't."

We walked down the road, following the river. After passing a row of old colonials, we took the right fork and followed a dirt road along the river bank. The river made slow, lazy S turns into the setting sun, the sun still high in the spring sky. The river looked black, and the water was low. The blackness of the water was broken into ripples as the river flowed over beds of rounded rocks, rocks smoothed by aeons of flowing water. Down farther, bigger rocks jutted out in hard angles. Swirls of bugs whispered in patches across the river. There was no wind. We stopped to hear the soft churring of water flowing over rocks and sat in a patch of tall grass where young birches—maybe twenty feet high, and scraggly—sprigged out, some arching over so their leaves brushed against the ground. We sat, silent, and stayed watching the sun set; the soft pink-orange turned the trees into black shadows. I let myself melt into this dream. But as soon as I turned away, I'd be facing the garbage dump of my life, an old industrial New England town crumbling into no color—it wasn't true, I hoped. I wrapped my arms around Michele and hugged her. She drew back, startled, confused by the suddenness, her eyes questioning. Then she welcomed my warmth. And I needed hers.

Chapter Thirty-four

IIII IIII IIII IIII IIII

KEENE, NEW HAMPSHIRE, is an odd town, like many New England towns. It's divided into two sections, though no one planned it. One part is old, with immaculately restored colonials clustering around the Town Green, library, Town Hall, and court house; there are brick sidewalks with gas lamps, too. The other part has colonials smeared with clearance-sale paint, and the front yards border four-lane roads and buckling sidewalks. And the dark is bleached by neon—McDonald's, Burger King, Friendly's, Mobil, Exxon, GM.

We stopped at a Radio Shack, and Michele bought an array of splitters, wires, alligator clips —she tried explaining, but electronics made as much sense as voodoo; it had something to do with wiring the car for tailing Scruggers. We went into a grocery store and bought six gallons of orange juice, then bought a case of motor oil at a hardware store. I didn't bother asking what she was doing. After, we went into a small pizza place for dinner.

We were the only customers. The whole staff, a waitress and cook, were in the back talking. Finally the waitress, armed with a dupe-pad, came out and took our order: pizza with green peppers, onions, and mushrooms. Michele had club soda; I ordered a Molson.

I didn't want to talk about Scruggers and Broderick and the whole mess. Michele and I had been forced together, having to save our lives. But if we were going to sit around and talk about the movies or the news or weather, we didn't have much to say. Or so it seemed. I lit a cigarette, making sure I blew the smoke away from Michele. The waitress brought the drinks, poured them, and left.

I broke the silence. "You think tailing Scruggers will be a problem?"

Michele broke out of her blank stare. "I'm sorry." She shook her head, trying to clear her mind. "I hope not."

"I guess we'll see, Wednesday."

"Tomorrow."

"Yeah..."

"I hope they don't meet at his house. We can't hang around there."

"I guess so."

"We need more tapes."

"I guess."

Silence...

There's nothing worse than being in a restaurant, having nothing to say, having to wait forever for food. I noticed the cook and waitress chatting away.

"It was a nice day." I said.

"It was."

Talking about the weather has as much fizz as flat soda. I flung out another conversation sparkler. "How long you been out of school?"

"Humm...two years. No, I guess three. God, it's been three years."

"You been working the same place?"

"Yes. The man I work for, Hank Stewer, retired early from the CIA. He's brilliant, really brilliant. He graduated from Harvard Law School, top of his class. After retiring, he started his private seminars for undercover work. We had regular work with the FBI, CIA, Pinkerton Security, police forces, foreign governments. It was nuts. I worked seven days a week—at the institute, on the road. I've trained so many people for so many roles— bums, art traders, stock brokers, whores, dockmen, fur tycoons, diamond merchants, drug dealers."

"So you like it?"

"Well," she rolled it over in her mind. "I guess. I really didn't have time to think about it. I worked so hard. I don't know. It's just, well, when I first started, I thought I'd be able to fight for justice. You know?"

She laughed shyly like she was showing embar- rassing baby pictures. "Justice, with a capital J. It seems silly now. I don't know. I'm sure what I do is good. I'm able to teach a lot of people important things. I just feel the burning desire to 'Save the World' is gone."

Brushing away her childishness, she huddled into herself like she was cold. She wasn't used to telling anybody anything about herself.

"Well, come on," I said. "Nobody can carry that forever."

"I guess. Sometimes I feel so useless."

I reached over and stroked her cheek with the back of my hand. The waitress brought our pizza. I stubbed out my cigarette and ordered another beer.

"You know," she said. "I think about your dumb asparagus dream."

"You do?" I used a steak knife to recut the pizza.

"Yes, I do." She held her plate for me. I placed a wedge of pizza on it, catching the dangling cheese with the knife and putting it back on her pizza.

I took a piece for myself. "Yeah, well. I'm not sure what the hell good 'Art' is, but if I didn't have my harmonicas I'd be a heroin addict for sure."

"Have you always done so many drugs?"

I shrugged. "Nah. Only since I was eleven. So what's that? Seventeen and a half years?"

"God," she said. "You know I've only been drunk once?"

I gagged on mozzarella cheese. "Get off it. People have been to the moon more times than that."

"It's true. At a slumber party. I was only fourteen. We mixed gin and scotch and pineapple juice. I got sick for two days."

"No wonder."

"Really. Only once. I had such a normal upbringing. I went to church every Sunday. Loved school —almost got straight A's. I joined the Brownies and Girl Scouts."

I shook the knife triumphantly. "I knew you were a Girl Scout."

"How?"

"I just did."

"Every year I sold more cookies than any other girl."

"And did you wear a pin-striped suit?"

That stumped her. "What?"

"Nothing, nothing. Trip and I used to order cases and never pay for them."

"It figures." She shook her head. "Yes. I was a Girl Scout. And I said the 'Pledge of Allegiance' to the flag with reverence. I prayed dutifully. My life was filled with reverence for words with capital letters: Justice, Marriage, God, Government, Freedom."

"Whoa, welcome to lollipop land."

"Well," Michele said. "It sure seems some of my capital letters are shrinking."

"Don't worry. Mine are shrunk. I was thrown out of the Boy Scouts for selling pornographic pictures. Trip used to get these triple-X magazines

from Denmark. We'd cut them up, and I'd sell the
pictures to the highest bidders. The ring went bust
when the den mother found a picture of two black
guys doing a nurse; the picture was in her son's
pants. He panicked and spilled the beans."

Michele stared at me blankly. "Are you ever serious?"

"Dead serious."

Chapter Thirty-five

|||| |||| |||| |||| ||||

WE MESSED UP.

We talked and talked. Then realized we had a
hell of a lot to do. Like drive four hours. And when
we got back—at two in the morning—Michele
spent an hour wiring the car. When she finished,
she could click off one headlight, right or left, or
keep both on; and we could click off one taillight,
right or left, or keep both on. If we tailed Scruggers at night, he'd never know the same car was
following him. While Michele wired the car, I
dumped orange juice in the weeds and filled the
empty gallon containers with motor oil.

"What's this oil for anyway?" I asked.

"Let's hope we don't have to use it."

"Well, what should I do with it?"

"Just put it in the car."

Fine with me. I threw a case of orange juice oil
in the trunk. We got to sleep after three. And a little after six, Michele woke me. I was coughing my
brains out my ears. The top of my lungs felt like

they were clogged with sulfur-coated, broken fish eggs. My lungs ached. I fell off to sleep, but Michele shook me awake again. Dazed, I took a quick shower. When I came out with the towel wrapped around me, Michele was standing in my room dressed, again, in a preppy outfit.

"We have to wear the same thing?"

She nodded yes. "We're going to stake out in a library across from the county sheriff's office. We'll look like a couple of industrious students from Yale."

I groaned and got dressed, not caring Michele was standing around. Actually, I hoped it gave her some ideas. She wasn't talkative. I hoped she was staring at my body with awe, but I think she was sleeping with her eyes open. Everything was intact—hair, makeup, clothes—yet she looked like she was going to fall over. Her eyes were swollen, puffy with dark circles underneath. She was white from exhaustion.

"Did you sleep all right?" I asked.

"Not really."

"Me neither. Maybe tomorrow we should knock off and go suntanning."

"We'll see."

Looking at her, I started to feel pretty pale, too.

We stopped at a Dunkin' Donuts. I went inside and got coffee and doughnuts for myself, tea and a bran muffin for Michele. The place was crammed with men, all house workers—painters, carpenters, plumbers, landscapers. It was a collage of workboots, blue jeans, paint-spattered and cement-streaked tee shirts. Plenty of thick mustaches and unshaven faces. Hard workers, making honest, simple livings—these days I longed for the simple life of a carpenter.

We ate in the car as we drove. And a little after seven we headed into Riverton with the first cluttering of commuter traffic. The closer we got to downtown, the more snarled traffic became. In the city, traffic was stop and go through a maze of lights.

The county sheriff's building was a brick structure with tinted windows, five stories high, in the middle of the city. Across the street was a public park. Among the old maples was a statue of someone important, or at least someone who had money. Pigeons covered the statue like fat bums in dirty overcoats. It looked like the pigeons were playing king of the statue. There'd be a flutter, then a settling with one pigeon on top of the statue's head. Then another flutter, another settling, another lone pigeon. They all looked alike. I couldn't tell who was winning or why the statue's head was worth anything.

Roads came in from all angles and horns blew constantly. The sun was up, but tall buildings kept the park in shade, the morning dew still wet and cool on the grass. Harsh slabs of light burned through open spaces between buildings, blinding drivers. Michele found a parking space alongside the park and slotted in. Across the way I could see a private parking lot for the county sheriff's office.

Michele looked over, too. "He's not in yet."

"We going to sit here all day?"

"No. The library."

"Where's that?"

"There." Still looking at the parking lot, she pointed to the right. The library looked like a mirror image of the sheriff's office: red brick, tinted windows, and directly across from Scruggers's. We'd be able to watch all day. As we got out and started loading the parking meter with quarters, Scruggers pulled into the parking lot, parked in a reserved space, got out, and hustled inside.

Michele dropped another quarter in the meter. "He's late."

"I hope they haven't already met."

"Tell me about it."

We crossed the street and went into a diner for a second breakfast. I had two poached eggs, whole wheat toast, home fried potatoes, coffee, and orange juice for $1.10: the morning special. Michele had another bran muffin, more tea, orange juice, none on special, so it cost more than mine. I finished my shot glass of orange juice and ordered another. Michele was leafing through the *Riverton Dispatch*.

I looked at the wall clock. Only five after ten. "It's going to be a long day."

Michele flipped to another page. "They always are. His car still there?"

"Yep."

I pointed to my empty coffee cup. The waitress grabbed the coffee pot and headed over and refilled my cup. I thought of having a cigarette. But just the idea made me want to cough out my lungs and hang them on a clothesline and beat them with a broom to whack free all the shit. I walked over to the check-out counter, following the waitress, and picked up a mint-flavored toothpick and sat back down. Toothpicks are lower in tar than cigarettes. Probably the mint flavoring caused cancer. So what's new? And what doesn't? The waitress dropped the check. I looked it over. My second glass of orange juice cost fifty cents, some deal—the blind hand is always pulling an ace out from the bottom of the deck.

"Well," I said. "You ready for the library?"

Michele folded the newspaper neatly, leaving it for someone else. "I guess."

It had been a while since I'd been to a library. I'd forgotten how little encouragement there is to have fun. Libraries are somber business—libraries and funeral homes. I did my best. Figuring I'd catch up on the world, I pulled out a stack of the *New York Times*. As usual, the world was a complete mess, everybody fighting or cheating or lying. It's what I hated about politics: everything always changed, and I couldn't keep up with the goings on; but nothing ever changed, things were always a mess and very depressing. We hadn't advanced any further than those stupid pigeons flapping over who got to sit on the statue's head. After a few editions—I'm not sure I made it through a whole week—I was tired of reading how messed the earth was. My father was right. What could people possibly say intelligently about this world? Pollution. Cancer. Religious wars. Political wars. Nuclear weapons. Shit. I sing the blues: Life's a bitch, then you die. Sometimes I have enough love, sometimes I don't. But if you don't have food or water or a roof over your head, who needs love? Low-down basic blues: ain't got enough to eat and drink, and love don't fill my belly. So many—too many—people moan the blues....Anyway, by accident, I came across a series of articles on the background of my poem, "Skateboard Blues."

They called themselves the Snowman and the Coalman, and were featured at a street artists gathering last summer at Washington Square,

New York City. They placed an old police car in the
waterless fountain and surrounded it with six
ghetto blasters which blared out a long, droning
rap song. First they did an act with their skate-
boards, twirling, jumping, flipping around; then
they did a long break dance—no pun intended—
with sledge hammers, mashing the police car into
a dented, crushed heap. With spray cans they covered the car with their graffiti. When the Snowman
and Coalman finished, applause lasted for twenty
minutes or more. The Snowman was white. The
Coalman was black. The mauled and painted cop
car was auctioned, selling for $22,000. For a while,
it was exhibited at the Museum of Modern Art.

Skateboarders, break dancers, rap talkers—they
were also mural artists, painting ten-story buildings in the South Bronx where they both lived. But
they were best known for their outlaw graffiti. Underground heroes. They'd taken to painting their
insignia on police cars and vans, on precinct
houses and court houses. They painted a picture of
a white man holding hands with a black man,
their hands clasped about their heads in trium-
phant victory. Behind the two was a sea of red and
orange flames, above them, a rainbow. Very elabo-
rate graffiti. On the front cover of a *New York Times
Magazine* was a picture of their graffiti on the side
of a police van. The policeman in the picture was
frowning. The message was simple: Brotherhood
between whites and blacks.

Even though they sold the same paintings on
slabs of plywood to private collectors, they denied
ever painting a police car or public property. They
said they were imitating a real artist, an outlaw
artist they respected. Police suspected the plywood
paintings kept them in sharp practice for graffiti.

The Snowman and Coalman attracted national attention. College professors claimed America had never seen such a strong push toward unity between poor whites and blacks. Art critics claimed the graffiti was the next evolution in modern painting. But police didn't care about anyone's claims: they'd never had such a fight. In the South Bronx, through the whole city, once-rival gangs of blacks and whites and Puerto Ricans were finding out about strength in numbers. Big numbers. Police were powerless against the oversized gangs. The police commissioner told those with fancy theories to go to hell.

One night, on a local news program, the shadows of two men who claimed to be the Snowman and Coalman were interviewed. They spoke out because their message had been misunderstood. They didn't want gangs uniting and using power for violence, looting, and destruction. They painted police cars and court houses to dramatize how ill-served the poor are by the arms of justice. They wanted blacks and whites to join together to help each other offset injustice. Hopefully. Their spirit of brotherhood was in tune with the aims of the Guardian Angels. Afterward, the news station was in an exhausting court battle to protect its sources.

But after a while, the sources didn't need protection. Earl Leamore and Braxton McDonald weren't only the plywood artists; they were also the graffiti artists. They were caught painting a police car. And, after six policemen arrived, the Coalman and Snowman were dead. An army of specialists was called into the courtroom. Half were positive the autopsy indicated violent struggle, supporting the officers' pleas of self-defense. Half were positive the autopsy indicated the Snowman and Coalman were held and savagely beaten with no signs of resistance. Now the trial was a full-blown media event. And everybody was worried: if the policemen were acquitted, massive riots, similar to the race riots of the late sixties and the 1980 Miami riots, would burn through New York.

I guessed we'd soon find out.

After three hours of going through newspapers and microfilm, my eyes were watering, sore, and probably blurred red. I went back to where Michele was sitting. She had a stack of books on the history of drama.

"Well?" I asked.

She looked up from her book. "He hasn't left, yet." She nodded toward the parking lot, his car still there. Michele was sitting in a two-seater couch. I sat next to her and rested my feet on a coffee table.

"Find anything?" she asked.

"Nah. Just reading about a song I wrote. Found out I didn't really know what I was writing about. Poetic license, you know."

"I didn't know you knew how to use a library. I'm impressed."

"Funny. I went to college, sort of."

"Really?"

"Yeah. Music school. I did hundreds of hours of research on the history of the blues."

"Learn anything?"

"Yeah. No matter how hard I try, no one'll ever take me seriously as a musician."

"Come on. That's not true."

"I'd have better luck if I played the coconuts and told people I was a drummer."

"Jocko . . ."

I looked at what she was reading. It was a doctoral thesis entitled, *Fecus Metaphors in Shakespeare's Historical Plays*.

"What the hell you reading?"

"Oh, this." She looked at the 200-page paper. "Someone's idea of an original contribution."

"Trying to prove Shakespeare had an anal complex?"

She frowned. Poop jokes were only for kids. "If someone wants to know, I'll say I'm doing research on drama history."

"Well," I closed my eyes, ready for a nap. "I've been doing research on current events."

Michele asked, teasing, "And what did you learn today, little boy?"

"Well, I learned I feel like Leadbelly."

"Who?"

"A blues singer. Used to sing, 'Well, I feel like walking, mama ... But I don't know which way to go ...' I sang the mournful, field hollering blues softly, resting my head on her shoulder.

Chapter Thirty-six

IIII IIII IIII IIII IIII

WHEN MICHELE WOKE me from my afternoon nap, Scruggers was walking into the parking lot. We scrambled out of the library. After being in an air-conditioned room all day, the late afternoon was hot, like a sauna. Heat and humidity and smog blended in a leadened smear.

We walked across three lanes of one-way traffic

and were getting into our car as Scruggers pulled out. On the other side of the park was another one-way road, going the opposite direction. Two left turns and we were about ten cars behind Scruggers. Michele closed in, keeping five or six cars behind.

After a few miles of city traffic, Scruggers pulled onto the highway. We followed him in the middle lane, keeping behind by ten cars. We speeded up for exits, making sure Scruggers didn't get off. It was later than I thought. The rental car's digital clock blurted 7:33. Digitals. I hate them. No one ever said, quarter after five; now it was 5:17. And no one ever said, about twenty of six; now it was 5:43. How did people become so obsessed with time?

As we drove, the setting sun, blotted out behind a thin film of clouds, splashed the sky with hot orange. The orange muted into pink as the sun sank. Red taillights cut through the haze of humidity and dust.

"We're in luck," Michele said.

"Why?"

"Look up there. Who's Scruggers?"

I looked ahead. In the half-light I could see Scruggers. "Well, he's right there." I pointed.

"True. But how will you know when it's dark?"

"I don't know."

"Look at his taillights."

His right taillight had been knocked out. A hot white, like a flashlight, glared on the right side.

"One of his taillights is missing."

"Boy, you learn fast."

She was right. In the mass of commuter traffic, Scruggers stuck out like a match in a movie theater. He was easy to follow. And after about eight miles, Scruggers signaled and got off at the South Norwalk exit. When Scruggers rounded a corner, out of sight, Michele clicked some switches on her homemade panel box.

"Now, lie down," she said.

"What?"

"Just lie down," Michele said. "Next time he sees us, we'll be a car with one headlight and only one person."

I lay down, resting my head on Michele's right leg. Tree branches laced across the road over us. We came to a stop sign and Michele waited. She clicked another switch.

"Okay. Sit up. Put this on."

I sat up and she handed me a baseball hat. She put one on, too. Now, the next time Scruggers looked in his rearview mirror, he'd see a car with two people, two lights, and two baseball hats. Softball players, he'd think. I hoped. Of course, if a car wasn't behind us, he wouldn't see our shadowed outlines.

After going through a four-way stop sign, we followed Scruggers along a tidal river with two cars between us. When Scruggers rounded a long curve, we pulled over and let a car pass. We took off our hats, then pulled back into traffic.

Finally, we came to a drawbridge. As we pulled up, we could see flashing red lights. Something was coming down river, and the bridge was about to be raised. Scruggers, good cop he is, punched the gas to the floor and zipped through the red lights before the gates blocked his passage.

"Shit," I said.

Michele slapped the dashboard. "How'd he know we were behind him?"

"When the hell he make us?"

"I don't know."

"Damn it. I thought we had him." I looked out the window, across the river. And there was Scruggers's car pulling into a fenced-in boatyard, stopping, waiting for someone to open the gate for him.

"Yo, sweetie, we're in luck. He's right down there. Pulling in and parking."

Michele leaned over. "Where?"

Scruggers drove through the open gate. Then his car was swallowed by darkness. The boatyard was underneath a train bridge, the bridge the same color of a rusting tin can.

Michele slid back over to the driver's position. "I guess he didn't make us."

"No way, baby. You're the best tail in town."

She frowned—jokes about women's anatomy should be outgrown by the sixth grade.

We waited as a tugboat hauled a skinny barge up river. The flat barge was loaded with rocks the size of Volkswagens. When I grow up, I don't want to sell rocks for a living, but I guess someone has to. After twenty minutes, the drawbridge went down. Scruggers had zipped through so he wouldn't have to wait. He must have been caught by the drawbridge before. With traffic we crossed the bridge, then made a right turn.

Chapter Thirty-seven

IIII IIII IIII IIII IIII

SOUTH NORWALK USED to be a prosperous seaport. But the onion market and oyster and fishing business moved on, and this part of town was left to crumble. We were flanked by old brick warehouses; the lower windows were boarded, and the higher windows were black with soot and grime and neglect. Everything seemed to be rusting, crumbling, and forgotten. On the left was an eight-story warehouse, and to the right was the river.

We passed under the train bridge, passed by the boatyard Scruggers had pulled into. A small sign said the office was in back; it was the headquarters for a custom boat-building yard. Odd place for the sailboat industry, but I'm sure the rent was low. The grounds were surrounded by a ten-foot wire fence, the fence topped with snarls of razor wire. Off from the driveway was a guard house, a guard inside. We drove past like we knew where we were going.

The boatyard's fence followed the road for a hundred yards or more, then the fence sloped downhill toward the river. Where the fence turned right and sloped downhill, it was flanked by an empty brick warehouse. We came to a stop sign. The road split. An unused dirt and gravel road branched to the right; the paved road wound off to the left. We first followed the dirt and gravel road and came to a dead end with brick warehouses on the right and left, with a wire fence in the middle. Behind the fence was an open field with slabs of white rocks lying around like sun-bleached turtles.

We turned around and followed the paved road.

Still nothing. It didn't look good. No matter what we did, we'd still be two people walking around where nobody walked. And in the dark it was even funnier. We came to a traffic light. To the left was a run-down movie house that had been converted into a porno palace of sorts. To the right was a pizza parlor. Well, that was it: we were just having dinner and thought we'd take a stroll through the run-down warehouses and then catch a little triple-X action; I mean, even though I went to Yale, I still lust, and I'm an architecture major, so it was a perfect evening—don't you understand Mr. Police Officer? Sure.

I said, "Just park."

"But we have no reason to be here."

"I know."

Michele parked in front of Luigi's Pizza. "I don't like it."

"What else?"

"All right...then let's go." Michele grabbed her oversized pocket book. She got out. I got out, too, and locked my door.

Luigi's Pizza wasn't busy, but there was a crowd gathering at the porno palace. Lustful Linda was going to play to a full house. There was a picture of Lustful, in neon, her legs spread with black stars over her breasts and crotch. Her tongue stuck out like a thick slab of bologna.

"Perhaps we should see a film," I suggested.

"No thank you."

We turned down the side street. There was only one street light, and its cone of light wasn't wide. The absence of life reeked. No one came here at night. No one came here during the day. No one used the buildings. The warehouses were brick skeletons.

We passed under the chalk-white light of the street lamp. A peppering of bugs swirled under the light, batting lightly against our faces. Then we were in darkness again. The humidity was cooling, making the air damp and cold. And a fog was rolling in, muting sounds into dullness. The sky was covered with a thin, translucent film of clouds spread flat and even. The moon was a melted white smear.

As we passed the cross-street, I looked down the road to the entrance of the boatyard. Car lights blinded me, then turned left as the car stopped. It was a Cadillac limo.

"Michele."

"I saw it."

The headlights cut through the darkness of the boatyard, the car winding through the driveway. When the car stopped, the lights reflected hotly off the side of a metal trailer.

"Come on." I grabbed Michele by the arm, and we broke into a trot.

We followed the dirt and gravel road to its dead end. The ground-level windows of the warehouse were boarded. I decided on the last window. The plywood was nailed on from the inside. I climbed into the window well and faced the street, and with my heels kicked hard, over and over, until the boarding loosened and finally fell flat onto the inside floor. I helped Michele, and we climbed inside. As I replaced the board, Michele held a penlight to help me see.

Every window street-side was boarded. But the windows facing the river still had glass. The back wall was a checkering of black and light squares. Michele scanned the floor with the penlight: it was covered with broken glass, chips of brick and cinder block, rotting wood, rusting cans of food and soda and beer. There was even a charred pile of spent firewood, but I wouldn't want to build a fire and make soup—the place smelled like the dirty, long uncleaned bathroom in a forgotten truck stop. Along the back wall a staircase led to the second floor.

Michele clicked off the light. We waited for a minute or more, letting our eyes get used to the darkness. I took Michele's hand, and we walked over to the staircase. I jumped up and down on the first few stairs to see if they were stable. It was a metal staircase, and the stairs clanged like a broken church bell. When the noise stopped, fading into a dull echo, I could hear a dog barking in the boatyard.

After walking up the stairs, we set up in the far corner of the warehouse, closest to the river. None of the windows on the second floor was boarded, making it easier to see. Looking out a broken window, I could see down to the trailer, maybe thirty yards below and off to the right. A light glared out of what I guessed was the kitchen window. Curtains hung over what looked like a sink. Every now and then a shadow passed by.

"Think we'll get anything?" I asked.

"Pretty sure. We can only try."

A Doberman, calmed by a bowl of food, probably shark heads, was tied to the back door.

Michele threaded the tape, put on the headphones, and then scanned the trailer lengthwise, trying to find where they were seated. She stopped scanning, pointing the microphone just to the right of the kitchen at another window.

I whispered, "They all there?"

She pulled the earphone back. "I'm sorry?"

"They there?"

She shook her head no. "They're waiting for one last man."

She adjusted the tape player so she could listen without taping; when things got started, she'd flick it to record. Within ten minutes the Doberman was going bonkers, barking and lashing about, almost choking itself on the chain. Another car pulled in. For the first time, I realized we were looking at the back of the trailer. The last person had arrived. A few minutes later Michele was giving me the thumbs-up: the meeting was under way, and the tape was rolling. I had nothing to do but stare into the half-light, making sure nobody sneaked up on us. It was the first time I'd thought of a cigarette all day. I didn't have any. So I just waited.

Chapter Thirty-eight

IIII IIII IIII IIII IIII

AFTER ABOUT TWO HOURS the meeting broke up. Goodbyes weren't drawn out. The Doberman barked and thrashed violently against the limits of its chain as three cars started up and left. Even after Scruggers, Broderick, and the third man left, someone stayed in the trailer. A light was on.

Our eyes were used to the darkness. We walked across the second floor, down the stairs, and climbed back out the window we came in. As we walked to the car, no one drove by. As we got into the car the porno house was clearing out and another crowd was gathering to watch Lustful. Michele started the car, slipped into drive, saying nothing. The tape didn't make her happy. According to the digital, we drove in silence for twenty-one minutes.

Then Michele said, "Someone's following us."

"What?" I started to turn around to look.

"Don't turn around." Her eyes jittered back and forth between the road and the rearview mirror.

"You sure?"

"Almost positive."

My body tensed like I was straining to do a 500 pound leg squat—how'd they even know?

I tried looking out my sideview mirror. It was adjusted for Michele. I couldn't see anything. "How far back?"

"Six, seven cars."

We came to a four-way intersection with stop signs. Michele turned right. As soon as our car was blocked by a run-down deli, Michele punched the gas. I thought we were going to run for it. But Michele swung hard right into a side street, then left into a driveway.

"What're you doing?"

"Get in the back. Break profile with anything."

"What?"

"Please." She was calm, yet firm, demanding. "Just do it."

I climbed into the back. Michele clicked her switch box. Now the car was missing one taillight. She clicked another switch and killed the light above the license plate. In the back seat I pulled out the floor mats and crammed them into the window well of the passenger's side.

"Make a slot so you can watch. Just make sure

your head blends in." Michele backed out of the driveway into a side street.

I finished the adjustments. From a few cars back, we'd look like a car with one taillight, one person, and boxes or something in the window well. Michele turned back out onto the main road. As she pulled out, a second car went through the intersection and was now behind us. Then the car that was following us pulled onto the street; only one car separated us. Another car pulled behind the third and lit up two men, in shadows.

"It's the second car behind us," Michele said.

I looked at the shadowed men. The driver was huge—he was hunching to keep his head from sprouting out the roof of the car. The passenger was much, much smaller, his head just barely a notch over the dashboard. Michele had fooled them. They slowed down, turning their blinker for a right, then left turn. They pulled over and let the car behind them pass. Then they started down the road again, slowly, creeping, looking up and down all the side streets.

"I think we made it, Michele."

"I hope they're not looking now."

We passed under a street lamp, and our Chevette lit up like a pinball bonus bumper. And they saw us. Their car pulled out and passed the two other cars and hauled toward us, a steady sixty, ready to kiss our bumper.

"Michele, they got us."

"I know."

Michele crunched the gas to the floor. The digital speedometer flickered up to seventy. But they stayed with us, a clean three-car lengths behind.

"Jocko. Roll down the window on the driver's side. And get the oil ready."

"The what?" I rolled down the window.

"The bottles. With oil."

We were going eighty now, and the wind rushed through the open window. I yelled, "They're in the trunk."

"What?!"

"You said put them in the car."

"The back seat. The back seat."

"Just drive," I said.

Most cars have only a flimsy piece of plastic separating the back seat from the trunk. I yanked the seat cushions out of place. I was lucky. The plastic backing was fastened with only two bolts. I crammed my hands behind it and started yanking. I had to use all my weight. When the plastic tore free, I fell backward and sprawled out in the foot well. Shit.

I sat back up. "I'm in the trunk."

"Just hurry. And get those mats out of there so I can see."

I slashed the mats out the window. As we streaked under a street lamp, I could see the passenger leaning out his window, his left arm wrapped in the seatbelt, giving him something to hold onto. In his right arm he gripped a gun.

"Michele!" I screamed. "They're opening fire."

"I know. Get the oil."

"There a trunk latch?"

"Yes."

"Pop it open when I yell. And I'll throw the shit out."

"Don't use the oil until I say so."

"What?"

"Not until I say so."

"Got it."

"But throw anything else you can find at them."

I climbed into the trunk. Even with the muffling of the trunk I could hear the crack of gunfire. It was a rapid clicking, like a woodpecker working on a foggy day.

"Jocko. Hold on."

Michele started swerving the car back and forth. The firing stopped. In the dark I felt around for all the spare tire parts—tire, fastening plate, jack, four-pronged wheel-nut wrench. There was a set of generic tools wrapped in a vinyl sheath.

I screamed, "Pop the trunk!"

The trunk swished open, then bobbed up and down with the wind. First I threw the handful of tools. The car behind us slammed on its brakes, the odd clanking of screwdrivers and wrenches slapped against the car. No damage. They hit the gas and gained on us. I threw the four-pronged wheel-nut wrench out. It clanked against the road, bounced and smashed into the left headlight. The passenger ducked back into the car. Then leaned back out, ready to fire.

I took the jack and lofted a hook-shot and got lucky. The jack slapped down on the hood and slid back into the windshield. The windshield shattered and froze, looking like a forgotten spider web. The passenger ducked back into the car. But they kept coming. The passenger leaned out again. And the driver poked his head out, too.

"Michele. I've got nothing else."

"Get ready with the oil. Throw it. And try to cover the whole road."

When we arched into a long, lazy turn, I took the first four half-gallons and tossed them on the road. Then I did the same with the next four. And between the two patches of oil and broken glass I'd covered most of the road.

Their car screamed around the corner and hit the first oil patch. The back end fishtailed to the right so the car was broadside to oncoming traffic. Then it hit the second oil patch and swirled almost all the way around. I could see the taillights. Then the car slid out into the dry road. The driver had turned his wheel hard left at some point, trying to turn out of the skid, the wheels useless in the oil. But when the front wheels caught traction on dry asphalt, they snapped the car forward and left and out of control, broadside into an ancient oak. The car crushed like cellophane in a baby's hand.

When we were through the long turn, Michele punched the gas. The digital speedometer flickered up to 87. After a half-mile she stopped, almost slamming on the brakes. I hopped out of the trunk and slammed it shut, then got in on the passenger's side. Michele clicked on all our lights and handed me a baseball cap. Again, for some reason, she wanted to look like softball players in silhouette.

Chapter Thirty-nine

IIII IIII IIII IIII IIII

AT CAMP, the bare bulb in my room glared bald against the white ceiling. We sat on my bed with the recorder between us. I quivered with adrenaline overdrive, using a towel to mop sweat off me. Michele wasn't any better; she clicked the recorder to "play." And we listened to the taping. The first time through, Michele took notes. The second time, I took notes, marking the footage exactly. Everything was referred to offhandedly, and we had to listen three times before I could sketch out a rough idea.

There were four men: Broderick, Scruggers, a guard who barely said anything, and a Frenchman. Michele and I were the main topic of conversation. We were complications. But, in spite of us, the plan had to move. Hopefully, we'd be taken care of soon. They spoke about us like we were spots in a carpet that had to be tidied before guests arrived. The next time we called, Scruggers was to find out what we wanted, where we were. Then meet with us. Then take care of us. Scruggers was the only one who believed we were in the ice cream truck; the others passed him off as being paranoid. Scruggers said we were going to call tomorrow or Friday. Fine, get something definite. He said we were in New Hampshire. Fine, Broderick, you should arrange for some private men to track us down. Besides us, business had to go on as usual. And some business. The Frenchman referred to things only as "goods." And the goods either had a color or came from a place. It wasn't hard to figure out: they were unloading heroin. Lots.

They had black, brown, beige, and white. It came from Laos, Turkey, Iran, Mexico, and other places. In addition, they had number 14s—quaaludes. They had goo for the dens—opium. They had herb treated with goo—opium-treated reefer. Plus things for the medicine cabinets—codeine, Demerol, and other prescription drugs, I guess. Also, doctors' favorite painkiller—morphine. Everything was being stored in separate places. But they were moving them to one central location, a private island—we guessed Broderick's—

readying to make one shipment. A very risky move. Yet the Frenchman insisted, the apparatus to move all the different goods from different locations was too undependable. It was impossible to guess amounts. But every time the drugs passed hands, trickling down, they'd be stepped on; by the time the heroin reached the streets, the original amount would have tripled or more. The idea wasn't immediate profit. The idea was glutting, saturating the streets with heroin and opiate by-products. Heroin distribution is not the most organized and dependable chain, so goods had to move early. The Frenchman wanted people running up dime bags in shooting galleries as soon as possible. Because of us, Scruggers and Broderick tried, over and over, to delay things. Impossible.

I didn't sleep well. I kept waking from nightmares of wild dogs catching me in the warehouse, their teeth glowing in the dark as they went for my neck. I spent half the night staring into darkness, begging for sleep.

Heroin...

Everything they were moving oozed out from poppy plants. Pain killers. Nirvana. Heroin: a beautiful product—demand lasts until addicts overdose or go through withdrawals. And many times, death is easier than withdrawal. I remember Trip, strung out, hiding in one of our barns, trying to go through withdrawal alone, his eyes bulging, his skin creased with the lines of his bones, always shaking and sweating like he was being boiled in ice. I guessed the Frenchman— maybe an old guard from the French Connection —was trying to turn the streets around. In a muscle move he pirated cocaine. He probably wanted the streets dry and free. Then, when his heroin and opium goods seeped into people's pockets, they'd take it gladly; it'd be the only thing they could get. The black heroin was for truly initiated junkies, almost 100 percent pure, coming in from Mexico. The opium-treated reefer was for wary rookies, people scared of heroin. But I know opium-treated reefer—like nothing one's had before. And hey, what's wrong with a little codeine? Shit, even my dentist gives me that. Morphine, well, I don't know; but hey, doctors at Yale give it to patients. And sweet, sweet smack—two and a half times stronger than morphine—how could you ever get addicted if you only snort it? Or if you just smoke it? I remember Trip's promises. And then Trip had track marks over his body, his feet, legs, arms, crotch, and rump. I remember Trip showing up at a shooting party. He puffed his cheek hard so the veins in his neck swelled, and then he shot up through his neck. And then all the junkies showed off, shooting up their balls, behind their eyes, their noses, and women shooting up their breasts and vaginas. For the rookies, they pulled down their pants and slapped them and shot them up in the ass. It's a party of ghosts now: suicides, overdoses, murdered, disappeared. Somehow, Trip survived. This Frenchman made me sick: I never thought Trip's addiction had anything to do with someone's marketing strategy. Shit. I remember my parents wouldn't let me go to Woodstock. I was only eleven. But Trip went; what a blowout, he said. There they were, 400,000 hippies protesting pig-capitalist America with love and peace. And what were they? One of the most profitable consumer markets in America. Shit. I begged for sleep.

I woke after ten. The shower was running in Michele's room. I got out of bed and went into the kitchen, poured a tall glass of orange juice, then out onto the porch. I'd gone to bed around five. I don't know when I fell asleep.

The blue sky was streaked with wisps of white clouds. A wind blew through the trees. It was cool now; but when the sun rose above the ridges, it'd be hot. Michele came out with her hair shining black from wetness. She'd combed her hair so it slicked back from her face, smooth against her head. In the soft shaded porch her eyes shone a clear blue. The scent of shampoo and soap and baby oil melted me.

"Well," I said. "What's next?"

"I'm calling Hank. With the tape we got last night, I hope we can come up."

"I hope so, too." I felt like if we got the tapes to somebody, we'd still wind up dead. Yet innocent.

"I want to call Hank now."

"I want to go."

"Just hurry."

I took a quick shower, changed, and then we were on the road. Michele was nervous about always being around Cornwall, so we took Route 22 north through New York, then cut into Canaan. It was a small town and looked like a fading, forgotten postcard. It wasn't a retirement community, so there weren't gobs of restoration money. The center of town was a T intersection with a traffic light. There was a movie theater—I expected *Gone*

With the Wind—a clothes store, pharmacy, and hardware store. We parked in front of the only restored building in town besides the church—a shiny, art-deco diner with chrome and hot-pink trim. Outside were two phone booths.

I waited in the car as Michele phoned. She took twenty minutes. Her back was to me; I couldn't even get an idea of what she was saying. Finally, she hung up, closed the booth door, walked over, and got into the car.

"Well?" I asked.

"We'll meet tonight."

"What's he say about the tapes?"

"He has to hear them. They might be enough."

"He's pissed off at you."

She sighed, then looked at me. "Very."

"So where do we meet?"

"In Vermont. Around seven. He's secured a place."

"How many hideouts this guy have?"

"Anywhere. He picks tourist locations. As a stranger, he's never out of place. Always passing through."

"How about some breakfast?" She looked like she was going to collapse. The color had drained from her skin. She was pale like she'd been swimming in a chlorine pool for hours.

"Get it to go. I want to change cars. Again."

I went inside the diner and ordered a bran muffin, and a ham and egg and cheese on a hard roll. I got coffee for myself, tea for Michele. I drank my first cup of coffee while I waited for the high school kid to fix my food. It took him twice as long. Most of the time he talked to the high school waitress about why bloody movies were awesome. The waitress thought they were gross. He loved going into the details of the latest horror movies he'd

seen on video while his parents were out. He shut
up long enough to wrap my sandwich and muffin
in waxed paper and throw them in a bag with
napkins. I got a refill on the coffee. I saw a rack of
cigarettes, Old Golds even. But I'd made it through
the first day. Might as well try for day two. I got
three rolls of Life Savers, couple packs of gum, and
a handful of peppermint toothpicks. I threw them
all in the bag.

As I paid, I asked the cook if he'd ever seen *Texas
Chain Saw Massacre*. Oh yeah, he said. And he had
mental orgasms. He told the waitress about the
meathook scene. She giggled and shrilled—oh,
stop! It was so gross. He kept telling me it was his
favorite film; he wondered if it was my favorite,
too. Not bloody enough, I said. The real action
were triple-X slice-and-dice on 42nd Street. He decided then and there he'd have to go. He had a look
in his eyes—it'd be a religious mecca. He had to
go. Had to. And if he did, he'd be so grossed out
he'd never brag about loving violence again—I
hoped.

I left.

My God, kids these days. It was hard to believe
someone had as much trouble understanding me
as I had trouble understanding this horror movie
freak. The tip-off on the kid was he rented movies
when his parents weren't home. Something about
that command: Thou shall not eat that apple! And
then we drive ourselves crazy, finally chomping
into the apple, almost swallowing it whole. It was
too early in the morning to think. I tried to blank
my mind.

The sunlight hurt my eyes. I climbed in the car
and the seat was hot from the sun. The seatbelt
buckle burned on my back. I pulled out my stuff

and handed the bag to Michele. She had to fish
through Life Savers, gum, and toothpicks to get
her bran muffin and tea.

"What's all this?" she asked, raking through.

"Didn't you notice? I quit smoking yesterday."

"Oh. Well, today's going to be a long day."

"What? You don't think I can do it?"

"Probably not."

Now that burned my ass. Now I had something
to prove. I chomped into my sandwich. And grease
squirted out and dribbled down my chin. I was too
late with the napkin. Michele frowned—when
would I learn to eat?—and shook her head, eased
the car into reverse.

Chapter Forty

IIII IIII IIII IIII IIII

IN SPRINGFIELD WE changed cars and drove into
Vermont in a new white Thunderbird, complete
with digital speedometer. The modern world: im-
proving things that do nothing for anybody, leaving things that need changing untouched. All along
Route 91, state troopers were staked out. I guess
they were ordered to have lunch on the highway.
We saw nine radar traps: Massachusetts really enforces its laws. We took the first exit in Vermont,
followed Route 5 through Brattleboro and out to
Route 30.

As we followed the West River, everything was
wide open at first. The river stretched 100 yards
across, then blended into faded white rocks on the

banks. The banks rose into fields, and the fields spread to the base of small mountains. There were no clouds in the sky. The hot sun bleached the white riverbank rocks, making the rocks look blurred and soft enough to sleep on. The sky was deep blue fading into a white-blue along the horizon. A wind shuffled through the trees, and the trees were full and green, not wilted from summer heat and humidity. As we drove north, we wound into the mountains, the mountains rising on the left, falling off to the right toward the river. The road curved away from the river, then back to it. From a distance, the river looked black.

When we came to the intersection of routes 30 and 100, Michele flicked on her blinker to bring us down 100, toward Londonderry. It was only four o'clock. We had a few hours before we were supposed to meet Hank. I knew this part of Vermont well. Trip had a network of ski bums he sold drugs to, and I tagged along; I had a knack for skiing all day, sneaking through lift lines without paying for tickets.

"Hey," I said. "We got time. I know a great place for wine. Come on. Keep north."

"I don't want to drink before seeing Hank."

"Then watch me drink. Only a little. Come on. We have to eat. And let's throw a little romance into the day."

"Well, I guess." She turned off the blinker and kept heading north.

There were no cars in the lot for the River Cafe, but it was open. Inside, all the tables were empty. A waitress in black and white greeted us. Her hairdo looked like a tattered bird's nest.

"Well'p," she said. "Any table you like. It's yours."

"Can we sit on the porch?" I asked.

"That'd be fine. I'll be right out."

I led Michele through the dining room and out to the sun deck. Willow trees arched out from the deck—holes were cut in the slats of wood to let the trees grow through—and their stringy branches hung like a girl's long hair, shading the tables. The tables were white metal patio furniture with umbrellas advertising Italian vermouth. The deck was ten or more feet above the ground, overlooking the river. Large flat rocks, dried from low water and hot sun, were white like flour—nice place for getting naked and suntanning and other things. Except a restaurant overlooked the river. The water was low, but I could still hear water flowing through rock channels. The opposite bank was a snarl of scrub pines and vines.

We picked a nice table and waited. And here I was, again, with nothing to say, not wanting to talk about our predicament. The waitress brought out menus. She bubbled away about specials. I think we were her first customers in a week. I ordered a bottle of California Chardonnay and was surprised to see they had oysters and clams, fresh from Boston.

"You like oysters?"

"I never tried them," Michele said.

"Okay. Bring us a half-dozen oysters, half-dozen cherrystone clams. You like shrimp?"

"I love them."

"And bring her a shrimp cocktail in case she gags on the oysters and clams."

Ho-ho-ho! The waitress thought that was funny. She never thought she'd like those gross, slimy things. Nope. She for sure would gag. But now she loved them. Ho-ho-ho! I wished she'd shut up. Michele smiled politely.

"Well'p, guess I should bring on the wine." And she was off, chuckling.

She brought the wine back with glasses, ice bucket and towel. Afraid she'd talk our eardrums flat, I told her the wine was fine. I'd open it myself. I had her bring us some bread so the wine wouldn't go straight from our empty stomachs to our overused brains. I opened the wine and poured Michele's glass first, then mine.

She tasted it. "Oh, that's nice."

I clinked her glass in cheers, then tasted the wine. It was good. It was great. Or maybe it was the afternoon. The way the sun slanted through the mountains and shone on the river, lighting up the water to the bottom, turning the water a clean almond brown. The way the sun was hot on my back, yet the breeze kept my skin cool. The way the sound of rushing water blended with the sound of brushing wind. The way the cool glass of wine dripped moisture in my hand. The way Michele's blue eyes were just hidden under a crop of thick, brown-black hair. The way her hand pushed her hair back. She looked at me.

And we didn't speak.

The waitress brought our bread, shrimp, oysters, and clams. She left us alone, not stopping to talk. I forked an oyster out of its shell, dipped it into the cocktail sauce, and fed it to Michele with my hand underneath to catch the dripping sauce. I put it in her mouth, and she reeled back with a little cocktail sauce on her chin. I napped her chin clean. I watched her swallow. The wine was going to my head—she was beautiful when she swallowed oysters.

"These are good. I'm surprised."

And that was all we said. We fed each other

shrimp and oysters and clams. Broke off pieces of bread and buttered them for each other. Poured each other wine.

When we finished the sun had sunk below the mountains. Dusk was cool with a soft wind. I'd had more wine than Michele, but only two full glasses. Michele barely had one. But even my two glasses went right to my brain. I paid the check with cash, left an okay tip—I didn't want her to remember too much. But what the hell? So I threw down a great tip. And the wine changed my sympathies; I kind of liked our waitress. Or felt sorry for her.

Now I'd quit smoking for two days and had a worse habit—toothpicks. I'd gone through a handful. Plus a pack of gum. Plus a pack of Life Savers. Now I had a fresh toothpick already soggy in my mouth. I felt funny being slightly drunk with a soggy toothpick in my mouth. Oh well.

Outside, we climbed into the new rental car, the white machine. Michele drove. We headed south on Route 30, then took Route 100 east. I popped a piece of gum in my mouth. After a few minutes I noticed my head ached from chewing gum all day. I spat out the gum, went for another toothpick. I looked over at Michele. Our romantic interlude was gone. She was absorbed in something, her eyes fixed to the road, not very happy. My thoughts drifted. How, on such a beautiful day, could anybody want to kill us? And I remembered: Michele's boss was pissed off with her.

Chapter Forty-one

IIII IIII IIII IIII IIII

MICHELE TURNED INTO an access road for a ski mountain and followed it around a development of ski houses, some new, some old. We stopped at an old A-frame, gingerbread-style house. A new four-wheel drive Subaru was parked in the driveway. Both sides of the house had cords of stacked firewood. As we got out of the car, someone called to us from the upstairs balcony.

"Michele. Come on in. The downstairs is open."

"Okay." She waved to who I guess was Hank Stewer. All I saw was the back of him as he went inside. Downstairs we passed through the living room clustered with second-hand furniture, passed through the basement with a beer-stained Ping-Pong table and a wall covered with skis. We started up the stairs.

Hank Stewer opened the upstairs door and greeted us. "Michele..."

"Hank!" And she scooted up the stairs, opened her arms wide to hug him, hesitated, unsure of what he'd do. He opened his arms and wrapped them around her and pulled her out into the upstairs room. I followed, not quite sure I was welcome. She treated him like a little girl treats her weekend father, the father gone because of divorce. Or was I just squishy-headed from the wine? It'd been so long since I'd had a father. I stepped out from the basement door and was half in the dining room, half in the living room. Stewer was holding Michele, fixing her hair, grasping her shoulders, looking at her to see if she was still healthy.

He was over six feet tall, and his body was lean

and powerfully built, like a competitive swim-
mer's. With one graceful sweep, he'd combed his
thick, gray hair back to the side. He didn't tan—he
bronzed. And his blue eyes seemed bluer because
of his simple blue oxford shirt and blue jeans. He
wore Topsiders with no socks. More gorgeous than
movie stars, he'd spent his life with women going
goofy around him, like cats flipping on catnip. He
had an international air. He could tell me where to
get a great hamburger in Paris, or where to find
egg rolls in Rio. He'd tell me who his favorite
maître d' was in Palm Beach and which theater
manager in London would give complimentary
tickets when I dropped his name. I'm sure he knew
how to find Kentucky Fried Chicken in Finland.
Finally, he turned from Michele to me.

"Mr. Miles?"

It seemed I'd talked to him before.

"Oh, I'm sorry. This is Jocko Miles. Jocko, this is
Hank Stewer." Michele introduced us.

We shook hands. Nobody was not this man's
friend.

"Nice to meet you, Mr. Stewer."

"Please, call me Hank."

"Okay. Hank."

So, he said to both of us. "You two have been
quite busy. Surviving well, considering the odds."

"Please, listen to the tapes. See if we can break
cover?" Michele asked.

I hoped we could.

"Fine. Let's get comfortable, first. Something to
drink? Wine, beer, cocktail?"

"I could go for some coffee." It sounded crude.
I'd have to watch how I spoke.

"Fine. Michele?"

"Tea would be nice," Michele said. That's how I

should have answered, "Coffee would be nice."
Next time.

"No drinking on duty?" He teased Michele.

"Well, really, we already had some wine."

"Oh," and he drifted off into a chuckle.

Hank and Michele went into the kitchen. I followed. He filled a kettle with water from the sink, then set it on the stove to boil.

I said, "I'll get the tapes and recorder."

"Fine," Hank said without looking at me. Michele was washing out cups.

Well, I guessed I could go. I went back downstairs and out to the car. It felt good to be away from this man. I trusted him as much as I trusted a used-vacuum salesman. I had to stop. The wine—jealousy. It hurt after this afternoon. Hurt to see her have so much affection for someone else. He was part father, part mentor, part lover—maybe they weren't lovers. But I know it had come up. She'd transformed, like she'd been tucked under a blanket of security: all was well, nothing could sour. Jesus. I wanted out. Turn over the tapes. Go home. Back to the band. It must have been the wine making me want Michele. Shit.

I grabbed the tapes and recorder out of the car and went back upstairs. Michele and Hank were on the back porch. A coffee pot was on the patio table, resting on an antique iron hotplate. Michele had just finished steeping her tea, dipping the bag in and out of the water a few last times. She pulled the bag out and set it aside. I stepped out onto the porch and laid the recorder on the table and started threading the first tape. Hank was having a sweet vermouth on the rocks with a twist. He smoked a long, thin cigar. I bet Michele didn't give him shit about smoking. Hell, no—nothing he did could be wrong. I fixed my coffee. But I wanted a drink, a Snakebite—100 proof Yukon Jack with Rose's Lime. And I wanted a cigarette.

"Well," Hank said. "Let's hear what we've got."

I clicked the tape recorder to "play."

We listened to three hours of tapes: the tape of Eddy and me in the van, the ice cream truck tape, the warehouse tape, various tapes Michele had made at Scruggers's. When we finished, it was dark, and bugs swirled around the porch lights. Stewer wasn't emotional. He listened, meditated on his cigar, drink, and tapes. During each recording, Michele followed along with her notebook, watching the foot meter, pointing out things she thought were important. Hank made, I guess, mental notes, nodding his head. When the mosquitoes started bothering us, we decided to go inside. We set up around the dining room table. I was sick of coffee, had finished a whole pot, had caffeined my wine buzz out my bladder. I was bordering on hyper. This man was too calm for me. And I usually out-mellow anybody.

"So," I said. "We got enough, or what?"

"Maybe."

I thought so. They wanted to kill us, and said so. They were running drugs, and said so. They'd planted a bomb in my van, and said so. Hell, if we couldn't get them, I couldn't imagine what we'd need.

"But I'm not sure," Hank said. "Understand, evidence is vague with law. First problem: there are no positive identifications. Sure, one man refers to the other as Jack, and so forth; but there are millions of Jacks and Raymonds. Understand? But even more complicated, as evidence, they may not even be allowed in court. What you have done is illegal. As private citizens, you have invaded the privacy of others. That violation of privacy does not sit well with judges. Now, you have told me you have made tapes of Raymond Broderick and Jack Scruggers talking about alleged narcotic deals, and I believe you; but a jury is a different matter. Maybe the tapes are fabricated. You yourself, a musician, would surely be familiar with sound-recording procedures, manipulation techniques, and so forth. It's not—"

Why didn't he just say it was hopeless? I interrupted him. "Can't they match voice patterns or something?"

"To an extent, Jocko, yes. But someone knowledgeable could possibly replicate voice patterns. I am only pointing out, if the tapes were allowed in court, which is improbable, any good lawyer could call their accuracy and authenticity into considerable suspect. Furthermore, think of these tapes as a stranger, a juror. When you listen to them, you know what has happened, and you fill in blanks, bridge gaps. But those gaps can be filled in many ways. For instance: the ice cream truck recording. Allegedly, Jack Scruggers says, 'Are you crazy, they could have tapes.' Well, tapes of what? You fill in, 'Scruggers is afraid you have tapes of him talking with Raymond Broderick about your attempted assassination, or whatever.' But a jury? A good lawyer will manipulate the ambiguity of the tapes Scruggers is afraid you have. Why, they could be tapes of anything. Perhaps you have tapes of Jack Scruggers talking with a prostitute, and you are blackmailing him! Certainly possible, as even a bad lawyer knows. And I assure you, a man of Broderick's position will have only excellent lawyers."

It was hopeless.

Michele soaked everything in, taking notes as he spoke. This man was her mentor. And she'd worked with him seven days a week for three years. And she was still amazed at how much she could learn from him. Maybe I was wrong about her affection. And his. Maybe they just cared for each other, a bonding formed from constant work. He probably stroked her gently, glad to see she was alive. I had to be rational, I had to be. Which was probably hopeless. But no matter how they felt about each other or why, Michele and I were still outlaws. Hank got up and poured himself another vermouth over fresh ice. Michele flipped through the notes she'd taken. When Hank sat down he lit his third cigar. He didn't say anything until the cigar was well-lit, then he serenely, reflectively inhaled the cigar in peace.

"Understand," he continued, "this has been only one of the more complicated tangles. Michele was indirectly, through me, working for the FBI. But when Michele intervened and saved your life, she broke the law. Obstructed justice. Quite a mess, really. The FBI was furious and disengaged. They made it clear Michele was on her own. Michele knows how I feel about that."

He glanced over to Michele. And she shied away from his look, went back to her notepad.

"And she also knows how I feel about her making these other tapes when she was under strict orders to maintain a stationary hiding. But these tapes are excellent. And what is done, is done. True, I have mixed feelings: she broke an order, but in breaking my demands she produced excellent work. So, . . . we have to do what we have to do.

have been trying to secure amnesty for the two of you."

"So what's that mean?" I asked.

"Well," Hank took a languid draw off his cigar. "Let me ask you. Is life underground so bad?"

I knew what that meant. "I'm kind of sick of the same old clothes."

"Jocko!" Michele snapped, scolding; this was no time to be a wise guy.

"What I would like to do, because these tapes shed new light on the matter, is convince the FBI to allow you to work undercover for them. It would mean you would have to gather more evidence, but hopefully all the tapes could be sanctified with clearance from the FBI."

It was funny: as citizens, Michele and I had broken the law; but now the lawmakers could decide invading privacy was legal.

"What would we have to do?" Michele asked.

"More tapes. Possibly I could call other forces into play. Maybe arrange a wiretap. If we could pressure Scruggers into a deal agreement, then we would have something solid."

"The first chance they get, they're killing us," I said. Hank talked like we were tangling with real estate contracts.

"True. It is a risk. But I am confident I can neutralize the FBI's search force. And the police's search force. You would be free to roam, undetected. You would only have to worry about Scruggers and Broderick. And they feel you are in New Hampshire."

"But there's still a reward. $25,000." I wanted to quit. I'd try anything. Yet I had a sinking feeling—nothing would work.

"The chances of an average citizen identifying you are very remote."

"Shit."

"It would be best if you could identify the third party. He seems responsible. He also seems to have considerable clout. I hardly believe he would let you be. As soon as you went public, he would have contracts out on you. Probably just for pleasure."

"What would you like us to do?" Michele asked.

"Well, life underground is working well. You have defied a lot of people. Stick with it. See if you can find the date the shipments are to be made. And how. Gather hard evidence we can use to make arrests. Find where the drugs are stored."

"We don't have much time," Michele said.

"Well, then. Mr. Miles will not have to worry about wearing the same clothes for too much longer."

Chapter Forty-two

|||| |||| |||| |||| ||||

IN THE MORNING, over breakfast, we went through a detailed explanation of what we'd done so far. Michele told him about all the costumes. He wanted to know which ones we'd used, and when. Now he took notes. Did we go to the same place twice with the same costume? How had we handled the cars? Which ID's had Michele used? He complimented us on the ice cream truck tape and warehouse tape and tailing Scruggers. Then we mapped out a new approach. First, we'd try to find the drug stash. After sorting through costume options and proper motivations for cruising islands, Hank made his suggestions. Hank said if we found the drug stash, we should call Scruggers and tape the conversation. We also made arrangements for contacting Hank—how, when, and why. Then Hank withdrew into a makeshift office and spent hours on the phone.

When he came out, he announced the FBI was behind us, the state police search would be lifted; our excellent job gathering evidence had convinced them. Michele's hunch was right—they would've killed me. Hank could forgive her now and congratulate her on her bravery, on sticking to her convictions. So good-byes were happy. The FBI was behind us. The state police, too. We had a safe place for hiding. The local police wouldn't be informed of who we were or what we were doing— too risky. But they shouldn't pose a problem, Hank said. And the drugs were to move within three weeks, so we wouldn't have to stay underground much longer. I told myself I could see the light at the end of the tunnel. I fought the instinct that churned it was only the light of a train.

"Hell," Hank said, "we'd probably get Trip out of jail in no time." In a few weeks I'd be home, able to go lobstering with Trip. Able to play in the band, which I missed even if it was rockabilly topheavy. Able to sleep late and deep and peacefully. Oh yeah, I was feeling good. I'd also quit smoking for three days, now. I'm sure my new hair shoots would be bean sprouts.

After a four-hour drive, we pulled into camp, late afternoon. Exhausted, I stumbled into my room and flopped down into a deep afternoon nap. Michele went into her room. I guess she slept, too. When I woke after two hours, I padded around. Michele was gone. I took a long shower, letting hot water spread over me as I sudsed my body with soap. The steam cleansed and refreshed me.

Finished, I grabbed my saddle of harmonicas and sat out on the porch, just a towel wrapped around me. I cleaned all my harps. Then started with some practice riffs, warming the harmonicas, getting the reeds nice and juiced. Then I chose my E-flat harp for full wailing. And out came a honkey tonk, fast shuffle, going home and feeling good, country swinging blues. Oh yeah. Dance all night.

When the car door slammed, I'd been playing so long my throat was raw. Michele had a bag of groceries in each arm. She wore simple, nylon running shorts, a tee shirt, and tennis sneakers. When a woman looks beautiful no matter what, I know I've flipped. If her eyes were swollen and black and lumpy like a snapping turtle's, I would've thought she was beautiful, or cute when she was so tired. Hopeless.

She walked over with the groceries. She was beautiful when she carried groceries. I got up to help. If my towel had unwrapped and started to fall, it would've been held up magically, just below my waistline—look, Michele! No hands, and the towel stays up. I sat back down, acting like I was only brushing splinters from my rump.

"You sleep all right?" she asked.

"Yep. And you?"

"For a little. I feel rested, though."

"What you got in the bags?"

"Oh," blushing, looking in the bags. "I bought some things for a nice dinner."

"A celebration?"

"Sort of. I guess."

"It's a good idea. We made it."

"Well, not yet."

"You always act like a flat tire?"

"Stop . . ."

"Hey, so look. This is my third day of quitting smoking. How about some karate?"

"You're too out of shape."

"What? Look at this bod'." I leaned back, showing off my body.

"I know. It looks great. But it doesn't mean you're in shape."

"Course it does." I didn't tell her how religious I was about working out; I was in better shape than she thought, and she'd be impressed. Maybe she'd sexually assault me.

"Okay, big guy. I'll make a deal. We'll take a run for two, three miles. If you can make it without coughing out your lungs, I'll show you some karate."

"Deal." I thrust out my hand.

We shook.

True, I didn't look like an Olympic runner. I had leather tennis shoes, a pair of athletic socks, each a different color, both socks bunching down by my ankles, both socks doubling as leg warmers. I had on a pair of wild, extra-large boxer shorts, Hawaiian with colorful tropical flowers and jungle birds. We decided I shouldn't run on the road. I didn't want to because my sneakers couldn't take the pounding. Michele didn't want anyone to see

my shorts. She looked like the front cover of a runner's magazine—nylon shorts, sporty tank top,
$100 running shoes. I couldn't imagine her smell-
ing of sweat.

"Let's run through the pine forest."

Michele looked at her watch. "Fine. I'll time it.
We'll go three miles."

I pounded my chest, Tarzan style. "I can take it."

"Ready?"

"Yup."

And she was off.

I darted after her. My shoes were great for walking, but terrible for running. I felt like I was running in a pair of scuba-diving flippers. Michele ran
like she'd taken ballet track team lessons. Exag-
gerating things, I clodded up to her, my breathing
regular as a dying car. She breathed smoothly like
a sleeping cat.

"We done yet?" I asked, muffling my words with
gasping breath.

She giggled and shook her head no.

After five minutes I stopped faking that I didn't
know how to run. My legs were stiff, but warming
and stretching nicely. I eased into my normal six-
or seven-minute-mile pace. Now Michele was a
notch behind me in pace. We followed the road
through the pine forest. The road was quilted with
pine needles. As I breathed deeply, I was wrapped
with the scent of pine. The soft, needled road les-
sened the pounding on my back. After fifteen minutes we turned back.

When we came out onto the soccer field, Michele
asked: "Ready?"

"For what?"

"Try to keep up."

"Get off it."

And she bolted off, triple speed. Me and my big mouth. Now I understood why she had trouble with my pace—she was a sprinter, not used to long distances. I dug in and chased after her, my legs burning with exertion. After ten years of not working out for football, I could almost imagine I was back in the groove. I chased a breakaway receiver who'd score the winning touchdown. I was catching up. She had her head turned back, watching me, a fatal mistake in sprinting. I reached out to touch her. She reached back to touch and shake my hand, laughing. And then she buckled. Her legs tangled under her like rubber bands. She slammed onto her shoulder, and her face smudged through tall grass as she slid. I had to hurdle over her to avoid kicking her in the head. Then I stopped abruptly and scrambled back to her.

"What happened?"

"I fell in something." She gritted her teeth.

"How's your ankle?"

"It's my shoulder." She coughed, almost choked, forcing herself not to cry in pain.

"You okay?"

"I'll be fine."

I helped her, putting my hands under her armpits and hoisting her up to her feet. When she stood, she clutched her shoulder.

"I'll be fine." She was convincing herself.

She walked with a slight limp. We traced back from where she fell. Five yards back was an old fire pit, maybe two feet deep, filled with wet coals and ash. She shook her head, blaming herself.

"How could I be so stupid?"

"How could you know?"

She just shook her head.

We rested for the afternoon. I let Michele shower first. It felt good to have gotten exercise; my legs ached sweet pain. After showering I lay in bed and dozed off. When I woke I could hear Michele working in the kitchen. I thought about getting up and helping, but decided to just hang out. I'd do the dishes. After a bit, Michele looked through the door into my room.

"Dinner's ready."

"Great." I swirled out of bed and sauntered into the kitchen in another pair of Hawaiian print boxer shorts.

"How nice of you to dress for dinner," Michele said.

"I'd prefer to undress."

Michele still had to settle in with my humor.

She'd fixed a beautiful meal. Scallops in pesto sauce over linguini. A salad with splashes of colored vegetables. A bottle of white wine. Two frosted glasses were filled with wine. She motioned for me to sit. I did. After Michele sat, I held my glass up for a toast. She clinked her glass against mine.

"Cheers," I said. "We've made it."

"Not yet."

"Well, we're going to. The cavalry has come."

"I guess."

"So. When do we go back to work?" I started eating. It was excellent. Another sip of wine.

"Well," she said. "I think we should take tomorrow off. Then we'll start trying to find Broderick's island, if the island is his."

"Sounds good. There aren't many private islands out there."

"It'll probably be heavily guarded." She munched on salad. The vegetables crunched with freshness.

Heavily guarded. That I hadn't thought of. "I guess Hank can't do much for us out there."

"Nothing."

Shit...

I lost my appetite. The idea of going to an island packed full with drugs didn't settle my stomach. Drug dealers become delirious and do crazy, cruel things when their stash is threatened. A friend of Trip's sicked his three Dobermans on the police, letting the dogs bite for blood. The dogs had to be shot because Trip's friend wouldn't give the command for them to stop. And Trip's friend dealt only quarter ounces of coke.

"Hummm..." I had another sip of wine. How could I be so stupid? It never crossed my mind. I'd been ga-ga with the idea of "official" support. What the hell could they do for us?

Michele stared at me. "Jocko?"

"Nothing..." I shook my thoughts away.

"You sure?"

"No. But I'm okay."

"Well, all right. How do you think we should go about it?"

"Carefully."

I finished my dinner and poured us each some more wine. Michele finished, too. Before she could do anything, I cleared the dishes and turned the water on in the sink, waiting for it to warm.

"I'll do that," she said.

"Nah. You cooked." Besides, I wanted something mindless to blot my humming brain.

After I finished the dishes, we went out to the porch, bringing the rest of the wine. It was a nice night. The air was cool, not cold, and dry. The sky was black and dotted with stars. I played through my harmonicas, and Michele sat across from me sipping her wine, listening.

When I stopped playing, we sat in silence and listened to the sounds of late spring—tree frogs, crickets, and across the field a whippoorwill was singing, on and on and on and on. A fog covered the field, looking like a sheet of gray silk. I put my harmonicas away. I got up and sat behind Michele, my legs spread and pressed against hers, my chest flat to her back. I wrapped my arms around her. She nestled her back to my chest. I rested my chin on her shoulder. She buckled under me, softly.

"I'm sorry. Shoulder still hurt?"

"A little."

"Sorry."

"It's okay."

I rested my chin on her other shoulder. Then I started massaging her shoulders. I was glad she'd fallen. It gave me a natural reason to be gentle with her body with my hands. She shifted, getting deeper into the massage. I took my time, worked down her sides, then to her front and over her tight stomach, kneading over her breasts, gently. Her nipples were erect, firm. I kissed her ear with a moist tongue.

She whispered, "Jocko...no."

I stoped massaging and kissing.

She whispered softer, "I'm sorry."

"Anything the matter?"

"Nothing. It's ..."

"What?"

"Well ... I'm having my period."

First dates. Always a touchy subject.

Chapter Forty-three

IIII IIII IIII IIII IIII

WE DIDN'T TAKE the next day off. Instead, we
drove to South Norwalk and stopped at every
boat marina along the shore. We needed to find a
place to rent a boat. And we found the right
place, a used-boat lot, next to a car junkyard:
Eddy's Boat Lot. And Eddy was inside. Eddy had
thin arms and thin shoulders and a gut blubbing
over his belt like a dead seal. His legs were
skinny and covered with tufty blond hair that
looked like sun-dried seaweed. It was 8:30 in the
morning, and Eddy was having a liter of Pepsi
and Camel nonfilters and jelly doughnuts for
breakfast. It was like the breakfasts Trip used to
fix after our parents died. We told Eddy we
needed a boat.

"Sure, sure. Do me a favor, huh? Wreck it. Lose
it. Run off with it. I don't give two shits. I need an
insurance payoff for some cash. Pay off back child
support. I don't say nothing about yous, nothing."

We arranged to be back in the morning. Eddy'd
have the boat gassed and ready. We also bought
maps.

Back at camp, the only clouds were brush strokes of white over a pale blue sky. I set up by the pool, spreading the navigational maps out flat. There was a slight wind, so I pinned the map with my shoes. The sun was hot. I lounged in my boxer shorts, tanning, looking for a drug-runner's hideout. Michele was doing some last-minute adjustments with costumes.

It wasn't hard to narrow down the possibilities. All the islands in Long Island Sound were marked public or private. I figured because Broderick's family lived in Riverton, the family island would be close to there. Sometimes I'm so smart. Within ten minutes I had the private island marked off with corresponding landmarks. I'd been lobster fishing with Trip enough times to know how to get around the Sound. Far as I knew, Trip still had some traps out. Maybe we could pull some and have a lobster dinner. Michele came out and joined me. She laid her towel out, angled for optimum tanning. She had on running shorts and a bikini top.

"Costumes ready?"

She'd already closed her eyes. "Yes."

"I got the most likely spots."

"Guess we're ready."

"Seems so."

Not much else to say, just lie back and let the sun bronze my body. But I couldn't quite relax. I thought of everything that could go wrong. The dinky boat we'd rented couldn't top 15 mph. Whoever was on the island would be shocked. If they were armed. If they had a speedboat. If they chased us, it'd be like trying to outrun a Ferrari in a wheelchair. Suntanning and relaxing was out. I just remembered. I sat up.

"Michele?"

"What?" She was half-asleep.

"We've got to get another car."

She opened her eyes and shaded them with her hand. "What?"

"We can't go back to Eddy's tomorrow. We got to get another car and drop it off somewhere."

She sat up, too. "Shh—sugar."

So afternoon relaxing was out. We rented a car. Then, first thing in the morning, we dropped it off at a seaside restaurant. The bar overlooked a dock. Come happy hour, we'd be docking the boat forever, doing Eddy a favor, joining other couples for cocktails after a day's work. A little before nine we were at Eddy's. He'd gassed the boat and left gas in a can. He'd even thrown in a cooler with ice but not drinks. And he wanted the cooler back.

We tossed the duffle bags into the boat. It was a simple outboard with bench seats and a pull-start motor. I steered by angling the handle that stuck out from the Johnson motor. It took about fifty pulls to get the motor sputtering.

"Don't you worry," Eddy said. "She's just cold."

I noticed Eddy believed in conserving water; it seemed he only took a bath once a week.

The maps were wrapped in extra-large Ziploc bags. I pulled them out, got my bearings, then laid the maps flat on the floor by my feet. The plastic bag would protect the maps from water spray. A smeared map was useless. I clicked the boat out of neutral and into gear, and we were off into the channel with Eddy bidding us good-bye over the engine noise.

Of course, Michele didn't trust my driving. She was in the bow looking out for things. She kept pointing right and left. And she kept yelling over the engine—watch out for this, watch out for that. Her arms swangled like fly-swatting cow tails. I felt like walking up and pushing her over. But I didn't.

Out of the channel and in the open water, the ocean was calm. A raisin-textured surface was splintered by sunlight. The ocean was deep blue, and Long Island looked a dark, hard blue; and the sky was pale blue with flat, white clouds. It was calm enough to run full throttle. We were going maybe ten mph. It was relaxing to feel salt spray misting over my face with the sun hot on my back. But Michele started barking. We were going too fast for her.

First we stopped at a public island. The tide was high, and we coasted in close to the beach. I put the engine in neutral, not wanting it to get cold, and threw the anchor—a large cinderblock with yellow nylon rope—down into four feet of water. Time to change into the costumes.

"We wading to shore from here?"

"No," I said. "Change right here."

"Here? Everyone will see."

"Everyone?" I looked around: no one on the beach, a couple of sailboats miles out, New York and Long Island miles away, too. Women, no matter how old, are always so shy; someone told me it was because they grew up with stalls in their public bathrooms.

"So who's everyone?" I asked.

She looked around and frowned—I was right. "Okay. But turn your back."

Shipwrecked with a Girl Scout. Last night we were so close, yet Michele was still shy. She didn't want to undress in front of me. Intimacy develops as fast as rocks are worn smooth by the sea. I turned my back and waited.

"All right. I'm finished."

I turned around and reached into the bag, pulled out my costume, and started changing. It didn't take long. I got out of my clothes and shoes, then slipped into the brown-rice-colored robe made of rough cotton. I also slipped into a pair of sandals. I looked at Michele. She looked at me: we were a pair of Hare Krishnas. I gave her a paper flower to pin on her robe. I pinned one on myself. I handed her a few sticks of incense.

I said: "May the oneness be with you," and closed my eyes and bowed.

"This will never work."

I pointed upward, saying, "Our protection will come from Him."

"It's stupid."

Now I was pissed. "Hey, it's *your* boss who suggested this rig."

"I know."

"It'll work. But you should take your bra off."

"No. I'll show right through this."

"Well, that's the point."

She crossed her arms over her breasts, to keep my X-ray vision from seeing through, I suppose.

"Look, I don't want to be a pig. But, probably, a couple of macho dicks'll be guarding this hoop-la. I don't want them looking at my face. I don't want them looking at your face. If they stare at your chest, all they'll remember is some religious nut with beautiful tits."

She frowned. "Do you have to use that word?"

"It's only in the line of duty. I'm sorry."

"Let's go." She hated it when I had a good point. She turned around and faced forward, taking off her bra with her back to me. I pulled the anchor, clicked us into gear and headed us out to sea.

It took us an hour to check three islands, none of

them likely prospects. They only convinced Michele I didn't know how to read maps. The fourth island was promising. There was a new dock with a speedboat tied to it. Away from the beach, 100 yards inland, was a large canvas tent. Someone was sitting outside reading a newspaper in a comfortable lawn chair. The beach was groomed—raked sand, no rocks or seaweed or debris. As we docked, the guy looked away from his paper at us, then back to his paper, unconcerned. I tied us to the dock and helped Michele out of the boat.

"I hope this works," Michele said.

I said, "Ommm..."

I led the way down the twenty-five yards of dock. When the guy realized we were a couple of Hare Krishnas, he stopped reading his paper and watched us come toward him. I lit our incense.

He stood and stretched. He was about six foot eight, about 300 pounds. His blond hair was cropped free-style and short—six-dollar special. He had to be in his thirties, but he had a baby face, making him look like he was thirty-five going on sixteen. He wore a white undershirt and green gym shorts. Wrapped around his neck was a padded brace—that's what happens to you when you skid through oil patches and crack into trees. I walked right up to him and pinned a red paper flower on his shirt. He stared at me in disbelief.

"What can I do for ya'll?"

A good ol' boy, maybe from Texas. Trip said a southern oaf. I wished I were strong enough to jump him and choke him until he confessed. Instead I handed him a stick of incense. Michele stood off to my right.

I spoke softly, calmly, meditatively like even my

vitamins had nirvana in them. "Do you own this parcel of serene, beautiful land?"

"Well'p, can't say I do." It was working. When I spoke he'd look at me then answer by staring at Michele's chest. Michele kept her head bowed in respectful, religious observance, her arms folded over her stomach.

"Our community is very interested in this land. For a religious retreat," I said. "How might we speak with the owner?"

"Well," he said to Michele. "Usually speak to homeland every half-hour or so. Just had 'em on the horn a minute ago." He jerked his thumb over to the canvas tent.

The tent was the size of a one-car garage. Canvas was wrapped around a wooden frame made out of two-by-fours. The floor, wooden also, was raised above the ground, resting on stilts. A metal pipe stuck out, probably from a wood-burning stove. Off to one side was a wooden house for a generator.

"Would it be possible to speak with the proper people?"

"Who? The Brodericks? Sure can. Try the phone book. But I don't reckon they're lookin' to sell."

"We're able to offer several million. Understand?"

"Yeah? Hot damn," he said, looking at Michele. "Now that's a price tag anyone'd be interested in hearing 'bout, huh?"

Michele nodded her head yes.

Being humble and respectful of universal beings, I asked, "Could you possibly show us around this island?"

"Well, maybe. Maybe. Come on, step inside here. Let me give the boys homeland a holler. Then I'll take ya around."

He led us into the tent. In one corner, by the
wood stove, was a small kitchenette, all gas fixtures. There were two bunks, one on each side of
the tent, a small card table and lanterns. *Hustler*
pin-ups checkered the wall. The place smelled of
canvas dampened by salt water. One wall had a
gun rack with six shotguns, mean barrels, the kind
that could blow a Greyhound into confetti. Michele looked at me; she was nervous, yet she felt
things were going okay. This guy was having a
hoot of a time—imagine that! he'd tell his bud-
dies, a couple of religious fiends cruising the island.

"Yo!" He was talking on the shortwave radio.
"Yeah, me. Look, I'm going to be out and about for
a bit." He looked at Michele. "Uh-huh...yep. Got
me a couple of religious hounds looking to buy
some beach front...uh-huh, couple of Hare
Krishnas. Imagine that!"

After he shot the bull he signed off. He pulled a
pack of True Blues off the top of the radio and lit
one.

"Okay, ya'll ready?"

I said, "Please."

He led us outside. He had a funny walk, like he
was readying to crouch down on the defensive line,
ready to bolt through soon as the ball was hiked—
walking with his chest and stomach pitched forward, in front of his legs. He led us down the
beach. When he looked at us, he had to turn his
chest forty-five degrees so he wouldn't strain his
neck.

"Tell me now. What's a pretty young gal like you
doing with a hound of religious goofs, huh?"

"I'm connecting with the universal soul," Michele said.

Good going, I thought. After today I'd have Michele working airports. Our guide shook his head in disbelief—with this story, he'd have the guys in stitches for weeks. He flicked his cigarette out into the ocean.

"By the way, name's Randy."

He stuck out his hand. It was the size of a roasting chicken. We shook.

I said, "I'm Rashna."

Michele said, "I'm Hana."

"Them your real names?"

"Observed, religious callings."

"Figured."

After shaking hands with Michele, he angled his head down to me and whispered, "Tell me, man to man, ya'll get into any wild hay romping or what?"

I was getting cocky because this guy was so dumb. Or so it seemed. I put on my best Buddha smile. "When the moon is in its proper season, rituals with a sacred cow are common."

"A cow?!" He blurted out, laughing. "Hot damn. I thought only Oakies were that dumb." He lit another cigarette.

Chapter Forty-four

IIII IIII IIII IIII IIII

IT TOOK ABOUT twenty minutes to walk to the end of the island. Then we followed a worn path, winding through scruffs of young hardwoods being strangled by tangles of vines. Tufts of wild, overgrown weeds and prickers walled us in.

"I want ya'll to meet my partner. Helps me overlook the place."

We came into a clearing with a cinderblock
house; it was the size of a two-car garage. The
front was squared off with a screened porch. I
could hear a pack of dogs barking off to the side.
Randy led us into the screened porch, holding the
door for both of us.

Inside, an Hispanic man was playing solitaire,
using an old telephone wire spool for the card
table. His ghetto blaster was tuned to a Spanish
station. His brush mustache looked like the tail
of a black squirrel. He looked at me, then stared
at Michele, obviously undressing her in his mind.
It seemed he was applying for a job at Mount
Rushmore: he had an unbreakable stone face. He
casually lit a Marlboro, kept staring at Michele.

"Albert," Randy said. "Meet my friends, Rashna
and Hana."

A man of many words, Albert said, "Ello."

Behind Albert a shotgun leaned against the
cinderblock wall. A Browning automatic rested
on another chair. Under his left armpit was an
ivory-handled .45. I looked out at the dog pen. It
was the friendly home of four German shepherds,
each the size of a 1000cc motorcycle. It seemed
they were fed shark meat. They kept barking and
throwing themselves against the fence in a pro-
tective frenzy.

"They you friends?" Albert asked, going back to
his cards, then looking at Michele. He shifted in his
chair and stuck his leg out; his ankle was wrapped
in a plaster cast. He must have broken it in the car
crash.

"Well, not exactly. They're looking to buy this

strip of beach for a few million. Think Mr. Broderick'll be interested?"

Albert said, "No." His long, shiny black hair
hung down to his shoulders like an Indian's. He
kept it in place with a white bandana. He stopped
playing cards and leaned back in his chair, pulling
his arms back, splitting open his unbuttoned shirt
further. A gold cross hung from his neck, shining.

"I don't believe in you religion."

Time for some PR work. "We accept all religions.
Anyone who believes in God is a friend. Jesus
Christ was a holy man."

"What you think of them dogs?" Randy asked,
pointing over to the pen.

"They seem filled with hate," I said.

"Just like we like 'em," Randy said. "Hate everybody but me and Albert. Ol' Albert just presses
that gismo and bingo! The door raises on up and
sets 'em free. They'll have for dinner anyone they
don't like. Mostly you. Think we'll save Hana for
ourselves."

Things turned. Our cover was blown. They'd
been expecting us. The only reason these dumb
costumes worked was because Randy had played
along, letting us think we'd fooled him. And after
we'd sent their car into a tree, and them into the
hospital and out with a sprained neck and broken
ankle, they weren't happy with us. And they'd
enjoy the chance to be alone with us. I acted like I
hadn't heard what he'd said.

"I believe we've seen enough."

"Not so sure 'bout that." Randy was grinning at
Albert. Albert grinned back.

"I want to thank you so much," I said.

And Michele was right on cue. All her religious
humbleness left her. She whirled her leg and

kicked Randy in the balls. Albert, staring at Michele in shock, went for his gun. But I grabbed the ghetto blaster and swung it into his head. The left speaker cracked off, and Albert slapped hard onto the dirt floor. Randy was trying to get up. Michele kicked him in the balls again, then kicked him in his stomach. He choked on a gust of air. Even though he was only semiconscious, Albert thrashed instinctively. He pulled out his .45 and shot wildly. The sound hammered into my ears, and I couldn't hear what Michele was yelling. I knocked Albert on the head again with the ghetto blaster. This time he blacked out. I kicked the gun out of his hand.

I took off my robe and ripped it into shreds two inches wide. With the first strips, I tied Randy's feet, real tight—I wanted his toes to turn blue. With the next shreds, I tied his hands behind his back. Then I took a shred and tied his bound hands and feet together. I did the same with Albert. The dogs were thrashing against the fence. My ears were still ringing. Spanish music squeaked out of the radio; for the hell of it, I busted the other speaker over Randy's head. He groaned. And the radio went dead. Now it was only the dogs, thrashing against the fence, their saliva balling like caterpillars' nests around their mouths. I couldn't calm down. Adrenaline was shaking me violently. Michele didn't look any better.

"Inside," Michele said.

I reached down and took the keys from Albert's belt. The metal door into the cinder-block building was sealed with three locks. After fumbling through key and lock combinations, I got the door open. We went inside. Dark. I found the lights and clicked them on. A checkering of fluorescent lights

shivered on. It was cool inside, and there was the
steady hummm of refrigeration. Also, the steady
rumble of a generator somewhere. The walls were
flecked metal, and the back of the door was flecked
metal, too. Black garbage bags, like sackfuls of cement, were stacked on the right and left walls. The
back wall was covered with stacks of boxes. Michele pulled out a small Olympus 35mm camera.
The electronic mechanisms working—flash rising,
her taking pictures, film being wound automatically.

I stared at the right wall. I grabbed random bags
and ripped them open. I dipped my fingers into
one bag and took a snort—cocaine. My nasal pas-
sages and throat went numb. Then my front teeth
started numbing. And I started trembling. The
coke was clean, not stepped on many times at all. I
took another quick snort for the other nostril. So
long since such sweet coke. And once I have it, I
can't stop. I wanted the whole bag. A kilo at least.

I moved to the back wall and ripped open one of
the boxes. It was filled with gallon-sized jars of
mayonnaise, no mayo inside. Each plastic con-
tainer was filled with pills the size of 1000 mgs of
vitamin C. I unscrewed the jar top and broke the
tinfoil seal. My guess, quaaludes. The number 14
was clearly indented on each tablet. Michele kept
taking pictures. I ripped open the other boxes.
Red, pink, and white capsules—Seconal, codeine,
Demerol. And yellow Valium. The good and fruity
candy man was hitting the streets, singing everybody into dreams.

I moved to the left wall, ripped open a bag. On
top was an ounce sample bag. I dipped my finger
in, took a quick snort. And the jitters started softening. A dream of tranquility. A soft setting sun in

Bali. Heroin. The smack was sealed in wax bricks,
kilo size. Each wax brick was stamped with an insignia: an Oriental dragon swirled after its tail,
flames flaring from its nostrils. I knew that snow.
Trip had dealt it, was strung out on it for years—a
cherished dream among junkies. Beige and sweet
and clean. Shipped in from the golden triangle,
mostly Laos. I knew the source. Michele kept clicking. I ripped open other bags. All smack. White,
black, beige, brown. I ripped open another bag and
found a sugar-caked kilo of reefer; I peeled off a
bud, would try the hoochy later. But the heroin
was softening my look on life. I went back to the
right wall. I breathed on my thumb and index
finger, and dug my moistened hand into the open
bag of coke. My finger and thumb were white to
the knuckle. I snorted both clean. The cocaine
started kicking in and over the heroin. Now I was
an encrazed, scared shitless man. Like I wanted.
Michele kept taking pictures. Now I was rattling
from a too-pure cocaine buzz—this shit could bust
open my heart. Was I an asshole?

"Got everything?" I yelled to Michele.

She was right behind me. "Almost."

She took shots of the whole room.

"Come on." I grabbed her by the arm and led her
out. Randy was struggling, trying to break free. Albert was half-conscious.

"You little peckers," Randy said.

"You fucking bastard," I said.

And I grabbed him, one hand under his chin, one
hand on top of his head. I cranked his sprained
neck hard, to the right. He screamed in pain, his
face flushing red. He tried to bite my thumb. I
slapped him across the face with the back of my
hand. Then I yanked his head hard to the left. The

drugs made me crazy. This fucking asshole burned my brother. And I wanted to feel his neck crack in my hands. I yanked his head again. And he screamed and bucked.

Michele grabbed me. "Jocko! Stop!"

I flung his head to the ground then. I walked over to Albert, shaking free from Michele's clutches. He stared at me with glassy, half-awake eyes. I wanted him fully awake. I grabbed his tied legs, down by the ankles. Then I lifted his legs by the ankles, lifting him until he rested on the ground with his shoulders only. Then I slammed his ankles down, hurling them against the dirt floor. The plaster cast cracked open. He screamed. The pain burned him awake.

"Jocko!" Michele grabbed my arm. I ripped out of her grip and turned to her. Instinctively she slashed her arms into a karate fighting stance.

"Don't make me." Her voice trembled.

"Take their pictures."

I grabbed the shotgun. I'd used one plenty of times skeet shooting with my grandfather. So long ago. This looked about the same—all shotguns do —but it housed more than a double round. A riot gun. Michele took their pictures.

"We gonna slash your ass yet." Randy said.

I pumped the shotgun and shoved it into Randy's mouth. "You'd better, asshole. Next time, I'm not leaving you talking."

"Jocko, stop. Come on. Let's go."

I made one last shove with the nozzle of the gun then ripped it out.

We went out the screen door and were off, the door slapping shut behind us. We jogged down the path through the tangle of growth and out to the beach. At the beach we broke into a full run. When we rounded a corner and sloped down a hill, I could see the dock, the boat. I couldn't breathe well; the cocaine and heroin clogged the tops of my lungs. My lungs felt like a brittle paper bag, brittle from dried bacon grease.

Then I could hear the dogs. And now they were different. They were getting closer. I couldn't believe it—we'd forgotten the electronic kennel opener. I remember Randy pointing it out: a plastic case like an electric garage opener. Albert or Randy must have squirmed over and let the dogs out.

"Michele!"

She yelled back, "I know."

My legs were tight and burning. I looked over my shoulder. The four German shepherds crested over the hill in single file, then fanned out, four abreast, running full speed. We got to the dock.

"Untie the boat."

And Michele hopped down into the boat. I stayed in the middle of the dock, crouched and ready to fire. I tracked the lead dog in the gun sight. The dogs were close to the dock. I fired at the lead dog. My shoulder almost ripped off. I couldn't hear anything but ringing, always ringing. My eyes went black. Then I was looking again. The first dog was down and hurt and bleeding. But the other three were past him, one of them cresting the sand mound leading to the dock. I pumped and fired. The dog buckled and rolled over its front legs. The other two passed it. Their claws clacked over the wooden dock as they ran full speed toward me.

Michele screamed, "Jocko!"

I ran backward and pumped and fired and somehow missed both dogs. I turned and jumped into the boat. And my ankle buckled under me. Pain scorched through my leg. Yet I forced myself through the pain, forced myself up, and pushed the bow away from the dock as Michele pushed the stern. With our mutual thrust, we shoved ourselves about five yards from the dock. Not far enough.

In a running leap the first dog flew out for the boat. It overshot and butted into the bow, its front legs in the water, its back legs into the boat. I grabbed its hind legs and flung its ass into the water. Then, in a scrambling dog paddle, it tried to claw into the boat.

The other dog jumped and landed in the boat. I pumped and fired, and it exploded into shreds, the tattered carcass gusting into the water. A spray of blood and flesh splattered over Michele. Her screams were choked. I scrambled to the back of the boat and started yanking the pull-start. The last dog had its front legs over the bow, its hind legs scraping frantically against the hull as it tried to claw into the boat.

The engine turned over. I rammed into gear at full throttle. We turned at such a hard angle that the gunwale dug into the water and water poured over the side. Michele slapped onto the deck. We almost dumped. But then I had the boat straight. The dog lost its grip and folded under the bow. And then the propeller thudded into hardness, almost stopping, then dug in, shredding, then let free. I looked behind me. I'd run over the last dog. It was swimming in delirious circles, crying in pain as salt water seared into its shredded side.

Chapter Forty-five

|||| |||| |||| |||| ||||

COCAINE AND FEAR and adrenaline and the only speed that felt normal was full throttle. The engine whined, overcranked. And the water was choppy now. So we hammered over small waves and slapped down on the back sides. As shore came into view, I realized I was wailing to happy hour in boxer shorts and sandals. I cut the engine. Our swells wrapped around us, pushing the boat forward. And the waves gently pushed us back.

"We have to change," I said.

I didn't wait for an answer. I dug into the duffle bag, pulled out my clothes, and slipped into khaki pants and a blue, pin-point oxford. Now I was a normal preppy, out motoring for gin and tonics. I took the shotgun and dropped it over the side. It sank. Shyness was a luxury when one had time to think—Michele stripped out of her robe, unconcerned. She swished it around in the ocean to wet it, then used the damp robe to wash the blood from the dog off her arms and neck. Her body was supple, her breasts full, firm. Her nipples erect from the chill in the wind. Her skin soft and smooth and unscarred. I wanted to wrap close to her nakedness and be buried under a stack of blankets, our bodies glazed with oil, and be swallowed by warmth. She was dressed. Another preppy motoring about for gin and tonics after yachting or before a day of tennis. I cranked the engine into gear.

It took less than ten minutes to reach the dock by the restaurant where we'd parked. I hoisted myself onto the dock and tied the boat. People were out on the patio, the lunch crowd filling the inside and outside. I took the duffle bag as Michele handed it to me, then helped her out of the boat. As we walked along the dock, we passed under the patio. People were enjoying shrimp cocktails and white wine and talking about the horrors of the office: broken Xerox machines, crabby bosses, asshole co-workers. We walked past, and quips of conversation drifted down like fat, wet leaves; I wished I could go back and deal with the nightmare of a broken copy machine.

In the parking lot Michele fumbled through the duffle bag, pulled out the keys, and let us in the car. I collapsed in the front seat. I shook uncontrollably. Like standing in a sleet storm, naked. My teeth chattered. I grabbed Michele and pulled her close, hugged her deeply. I never wanted to let go. She was shaking, too.

When we got back to camp, I'd come down from the cocaine and heroin. Now I was depressed. And nothing would do. My sinuses were clogged. I was getting a migraine. The tops of my lungs were congested. I hack coughed. And the coughing made my head pound. Pounding, the pounding; someone who knows a lot ...

We took showers, The steam almost helped. Then I lay in the sun, trying not to move fast. Michele joined me. It was good not to think. But I couldn't stop. The thoughts rushed my head, making the pounding worse. And I was pissed off at Michele. And I was thinking of heroin.

Way back, when Trip was strung out, he used to steal smack, like a lot of junkies, for his head. He'd get a quarter ounce and cut it into nickel bags for a shooting gallery and sell it off. His profit was free

heroin. He got excellent stuff. He started dealing
more and more to feed his habit. Then he got an
offer: if he'd go straight, he could start cutting
pounds. Lots of money. The offer was made by a
Chinese woman. But she wouldn't have no junky
moving pounds, because junkies are too skittish
And they made lousy businessmen. So Trip went
straight, at my parents' expense, $300 a day, and
started working for the woman. It was more than
money; it was also love. Her husband was killed
shot seventeen times, his kneecaps broken, his ribs
splintered, his head scalped—the police claimed it
was suicide. Yet she knew better. The French mafia
explained things clearly: she could unload her
cache, then she'd have to pull out unless she
wanted to join her husband. That's when Trip was
hired, to help unload the warehouse. And after
they finished, Trip and his Chinese lover, Tai
eloped. We didn't know what happened to him
until we got a postcard from Costa Rica: "Living
happy ever after. I'm married! Wish me luck and
come visit!" Only there was no return address
only a picture of the Costa Rican shore. The Costa
Rican banking system, similar to the Swiss, was a
haven for people with lots of unexplainable cash
But banking was the only haven. Trip had a pony
tail, braided, reaching down to his ass, and he wa
always being slapped around and hassled about
being a drug dealer. And then he got a crew cu
and still got hassled for carrying a backpack o
wearing sandals or wearing cut-off jeans. And h
couldn't buy drugs, too risky. And they had to
much money, so working was silly. So they spen
their days basking in the sun, then lying tan an
naked at night in a beachside cottage, the sur
pounding, they going crazy. Trip started drinkin

fruit and rum punches. His wife turned to tequila
and food, and swelled on central American rice
and bean dishes. At first Trip thought she was
pregnant, she'd said so. Then Trip found out she
was just getting fat, huge. And their love became
soaked with the raunchy stench of alcoholic's
sweat. One morning I was getting ready for school
—my mother acted like my schooling was important—and I passed Trip's room. He was sleeping
on his bed. Nobody knew he'd come home. I shook
him awake. He was skinny, his arms and legs
shriveled like old string beans. He woke. So glad to
see me; hey, would I get him a drink? I knew how
he liked them. I fixed him a screwdriver with three
shots of vodka and one shot of orange juice. I
handed him the tall, moist, and cool glass, and he
downed it, his hands trembling, slops of drink
drooling out the corner of his mouth. I was a great
brother, he said. How about another drink?

Chapter Forty-six

IIII IIII IIII IIII IIII

AND I WAS pissed off at Michele. Mostly Hank.
Mostly myself: how could I be so stupid to go to a
drug dealer's stash in a Hare Krishna robe? And it
was Hank's idea. The asshole. It sounded so plausi-
ble when he explained it. And how'd they know we
were coming? Michele didn't let me blame anybody: they were being cautious, and they'd
guessed we were poking around in disguises; so
they were looking for anybody funny coming to the

island. I had no interest in being dead. The next
time we saw Hank, he'd have to work harder; I
was convinced he'd set us up, for some reason. But
then it'd be his fault, not mine. And I was stupid to
listen to him instead of thinking it through myself.

Anyway, later that night, after ten, we drove to
Tai's Hunan Garden, a Chinese diner stuck in the
north end of Riverton, squeezed between a Subaru
dealer and Oil City Gas, not the most valued property; from the outside it looked like a used-auto-
parts store with thick, orange curtains. Inside was
a skinny room crammed with glossy-topped tables
for two and four. A cheap, nicotine-stained wallpaper, with swirling dragons, covered the wall.
The place was dank with the feeling of overfried
egg rolls.

We seated ourselves. After a bit, a Chinese man
stopped cleaning and came over, took our order.
He was well-practiced in not speaking English. I
had Chinese beer and egg rolls. Michele ordered
stir-fried vegetables.

Tai was in front, behind a cash register. She was
obese, maybe three hundred pounds on a five-foot-
two frame. Her arms were soft and thick with fat.
She was going over the night's checks, wearing
cheap, drugstore reading glasses. The cash register
was set behind a wood and glass booth; the glass
was bulletproof. And most of her waiters had black
belts; they muscled people, whacking them around
with karate and screaming violently in Chinese. I
scared the shit out of people. After Trip left Costa
Rica, Tai followed and opened her restaurant, then
opened her heroin business after the crumbling of
the French Connection in the early seventies. The
heroin she moved came from the golden triangle

usually kilos cased in wax bricks, the wax indented with a fire-breathing dragon.

The meal came all at once, and tasted a few
notches better than cold TV dinners. I didn't finish
mine, neither did Michele. The waiter didn't care.
He just wanted to get the hell home. He dropped
the check before he cleared the dishes. I took a pen
out and scribbled a note on the back: Tai—Jocko
—have to talk—please. It was risky. I told Michele
to be ready if things went bad. But Tai always
loved Trip and forgave him; I know they'd seen
each other off and on over the years—it's hard to
break from past lovers. I didn't know if they were
officially divorced, yet. Also, she'd always liked me.
We walked over to the cash register and I handed
the check to Tai. She looked it over, not looking at
me, staring down her nose through her glasses.
She looked behind me, yelling in Chinese. I could
feel Michele tense her muscles. Our waiter scurried to the front. Tai stepped out from the cashier's
booth, breathing a steady wheeze like reedy paper
was stuck in her nose. The waiter took her place in
the booth. She nodded her head for us to follow.

A flower print shirt ballooned over her, hiding
her rolls of fat. As she walked, she fell heavy on her
right side like she was going to buckle and fall; she
crept along like a VW Beetle with a flat tire. Passing the kitchen, the sound of clanking dishes and
babbling Chinese spilled out from an open door.
Tai stopped at the office, fiddled through a set of
keys and opened the door, letting us in first, closing the door behind her. The light flickered on and
glared off bare linoleum floors. The walls were
brown with water stains, with almost every inch of
the shackled, tea-colored Sheetrock covered with
male pin-ups; a sad old woman with pelvic thrusts

for young, muscle-rippled studs, yet she'd feel
shitty because she was too old and fat, and she
could never have one—unless she paid for it. But
then she'd feel worse about herself than if she just
accepted that she couldn't make love to young
men. She motioned for us to sit. She sat behind a
gray metal desk.

"Jocko, you big trouble." She lit a More. The
long skinny brown cigarette looked like a thin cin-
namon stick. She pulled out a bottle of Glenlivet
Scotch and three brandy glasses. She poured and
smoked, squinting her eyes as the smoke stung
them.

"I didn't know you. You probably didn't know
me. Right?" She motioned to her breast and body
blobbed with fat.

"I knew you."

"Well, you big trouble. Messy business." She
fanned out the glasses of Scotch. I picked up mine;
Michele left hers. Tai and I toasted.

Tai nodded toward Michele. "Who she, wife?"

"No. This is Michele. Michele, Tai."

Tai nodded. "Nice to meet you."

Michele nodded back.

"Tai, you don't have to say anything."

"I won't."

"But let me tell you what I know."

"Shoot." She always tried to speak with slang,
but she always overemphasized it, making sure
people knew what she was saying, making sure
they knew she was using street talk.

"We're beating around and found your heroin
warehoused on Broderick's island."

"He buy me out for months. Good price. Easy
Street for me, know?" She shrugged her shoulders.

"What's he holding it for?"

She didn't know. "Maybe New York. Who know? I only sell. No questions. Money talks."

"We also found cocaine. Lots."

She shook her head with disbelief. "Crazy. They say they burn Colombians. Then don't dump on the streets."

"So they're holding the coke?"

She guessed so. "People say they give heroin to people they burn coke from."

"What?" Now things didn't make sense. They, whoever "they" might be, were pirating cocaine, holding it, buying out heroin, holding it, and planning to give the heroin to the dealers they pirated the cocaine from.

"Who know. I hear so much. I even hear they give cocaine back after heroin shipped."

"What?" Pirate cocaine. Set up my brother and me as cocaine pirates. Stock-pile heroin. Give the heroin to the people whose cocaine you pirated. Then, after they move the heroin and other goods, give the cocaine back.

"Jocko, it all gooo in one car and out the other. Who know? I know for sure—big money for you."

"Yeah, I know. $25,000."

"No, no. I mean blood money. $50,000 if you alive. $75,000 if you dead. Plus goods."

That sinking feeling—street money was on my head, lots. I looked at Michele. She swallowed deep and repositioned herself in the chair.

"Thanks for the warning," I said. I wondered if she didn't think about cashing in on us. We'd never get out of the restaurant.

"How Trip?"

"Well, it's cancer. It's hard to tell how long he'll be around." Around...I referred to his dying like he might get a corporate transfer.

"He good man. Make me happy when I sing the blue."

"He's in the prison hospital, you know."

"I should visit," she said. Knowing she probably never would. She drifted into her past, maybe when she was thin, back when she and Trip were lovers, the first few months in Costa Rica—plenty of money, good loving, tropical sun. And now she's back in industrial Riverton running a greasy diner, pushing heroin.

"We should get going," I said.

Tai came out of her daydream. "Jocko, I never see you face. You never see mine. Nothing. Okay? Don't want to sleep with my husband. All I know is old lady, cackling hen gossip."

"I know." I finished my drink, then had Michele's. I stood up and leaned over and kissed Tai on the cheek.

"Thanks for everything," I said.

"Dinner on me," she said.

"Thanks for that, too."

"Hey," she said, as I stood with my hand on the doorknob. "Take it easy for sure."

Chapter Forty-seven

IIII IIII IIII IIII IIII

BACK AT CAMP the early morning sun edged over the foothills, only a smear, blotted out by gray rain clouds. The snarled forest across the field seemed dull green, making the earth darker. I'd put on clean clothes after brushing my teeth. We were going to call Hank. Waiting for Michele, I stood looking out the window, across the field, staring blankly into the cool darkness of the green forest. I felt like a cigarette. Maybe some drugs. Some more cocaine. I should've grabbed a kilo. Maybe some more euphoric heroin to send me sweet dreaming.

But I wasn't on drugs. And I wasn't dreaming. I saw a bush move. Then it moved again. Then a few behind it moved. Somebody with expert camouflage was coming in after us. I stared out the window. I knew they couldn't see me—the thick, wire mesh would turn the window into a black square from the outside.

"Michele," I grumbled in my loudest whisper.

"What?" She snapped right in my ear. I almost flew out the window.

"Shhh!"

"What?" she whispered, curious. She thought maybe there was an exotic wild animal in the field.

"Look. Someone's coming in."

We stared out the window. Some of the bushes moved.

"What'd you think?" I asked.

"Probably a hometown SWAT team."

I scanned the woods. I counted seven, maybe. "Do we have enough lunch for everybody?"

Michele ignored me. "I'll pack. Keep watch."

Shit. I'd had it with Hank. "I thought he was going to take care of these things."

"He said he couldn't do anything about the locals."

"So what do we do?"

"Try the backdoor. I guess."

Michele left. I stood watch.

The bushes were about three hundred yards off,

on the edge of the field. A couple of them headed to the right, a couple headed to the left. I lost the ones on the left as they went behind a field house. They were by the pool. I pressed my face hard against the screen. Up the dirt road, toward the soccer field, along the high edge of the road, crouched in tall, brown grass, two men shuffled toward us like beetles; the brown grass parted as they moved closer on their hands and knees. The team was closing in fast. To the left, the two who'd gone behind the field house and around the pool were scurrying toward us. The team was too close. I had to stop them. I pushed open the screen door, stepped halfway out, then let the door slam shut. Back at the window I looked out—everyone had stopped moving, and I could almost feel the tautness of their muscle tension.

"Jocko?" Michele whispered from behind a corner.

"It's only me. They're right on our ass. You ready?"

"All packed."

"Okay. When I step out on the porch, give me a second, then call me back in for a shower."

"Okay."

I took a deep breath and swung the front door open, stepped outside. The air was still and cool with the feeling of rain coming. My whole body was tense—I was probably centered in seven gun sights. My neck started trembling uncontrollably. I poked my head out from under the porch, looking at the sky.

Michele called out. "Jocko? Come on. Let's take a shower."

"Shower? I already took one."

"Well, so. Take another with me."

"Ahh, all right."

"What?" she yelped.

"All right," I said. "Just a second."

I acted like taking a shower was the biggest burden of the day. Because nobody had shot me, I figured they wanted us alive. I hoped they were licking their lips, thinking—soon as those suckers hit the shower, we're busting in. I wanted their cue for moving in to be the starting of the shower. We'd never turn it on.

I went back inside. Michele was in my room, and we ran back to her room. She handed me a duffle bag, filled and heavy. I motioned to her feet, and we both took our shoes off—sock feet are quieter. I raised my eyebrows asking, "Ready?" She nodded her head, yes. I opened the backdoor, and we stepped out in our sock feet. I didn't look around. If any of them saw us, they'd let us know.

I grabbed Michele's hand and led us through the thicket of an embankment. After ten yards we were on an old dirt road, now covered with patches of tall grass. We ran down river, away from camp. I turned and ran backward. One man rounded the corner of the bunk house, his head cocked away from us, intent on closing off our back exit. The road curved. I turned around.

And we broke into a full sprint. The road was damp with dew, and my feet were getting wet and muddy. Young maples and birches arched into tangles over us like sprigs of parsley. The green grass, green leaves—we sprinted through a natural tunnel, the smell of wet, lush growth filling my lungs. We made it to the old Grumman canoes. I turned around and kept watch as Michele readied a boat. She climbed in first.

"Jocko. Come on."

No one had followed us. I turned and threw the duffle bag into the middle of the boat then climbed halfway in, shoving us out into the river with my other leg. The current pulled us gently downstream. After a hundred yards of floating, the river bent sharply to the left. I grabbed my paddle; Michele grabbed hers. We dug in hard and paddled around the bend.

Around the corner and through a thin fan of trees, we could see the main road. Two state troopers zipped by, their blue lights swirling, yet no sounds of sirens. An ambulance followed. Someone figured people would be hurt. Also, every vigilante with a police band radio would know we were loose; time for every sicko with a shotgun to go man-hunting for $25,000. When would this be over? I felt like floating over to the bank, walking up, hitchhiking away, hoping someone would arrest me.

"Jocko! Watch the rock!"

I had to backpaddle hard, almost stopping the boat so Michele could gently push us away from the boulder. I had to pay attention. On our left were spreads of unused corn fields with deep brown, waist-high grass. A soft, steady wind was picking up; it would rain sooner than I thought. The current was stronger now, and there were no big rocks. We stopped paddling, letting the river pull our canoe.

"Michele. What'd you get?"

"I got all the tapes. Tape player, microphone. Cash. My set of fake ID's and credit cards. Some clothes."

"You get my harmonicas?" Panic streaked my voice, like I was scared I was going to be locked in a closet as a child. Michele looked at me, confused, scared I'd yell and never forgive her—she'd forgotten. Damn it. We started paddling again. In silence.

After going about a mile I pulled us over. The water was swift and shallow, and scuttled us over cantaloupe-sized rocks. As we bounced and jawed to a stop, Michele blurted: "What're you doing?"

"Getting lost."

"What?"

"We got to. First place they'll look is the river. The road. We got to head into the boondocks and hope for the best."

The canoe jarred to a complete stop. Michele didn't say anything. She stepped out of the canoe and onto the shore. I grabbed the duffle and scrambled to shore. Then pushed the canoe out into the river. The current pulled it away.

A soft rain started to fall. Not really rain, but a fine mist. We bullied our way through a tangle of young poplar trees and raspberry bushes and out onto an unused field. The mist blurred the landscape. The field spread into the forest like a water stain. We headed for the forest. As we walked through the drenched grass our legs got wet. My hair was already wet and sheened black.

Chapter Forty-eight

IIII IIII IIII IIII IIII

I DIDN'T KNOW if this would work. I'd been here before, with Trip, of course, backpacking. And I'd seen the two backpackers at the country store. The Appalachian Trail was around here. Also, a network of smaller trails for local backpackers carved

through the woods. I wanted to intersect with one
of these trails, any one, and hike north.

"Michele. You bring the radio?"

"It's in there."

Well, we could hike at night if we had to, listening to the AM stations, keeping track of our news
progress, if any. Halfway through the field the
grass parted and was flattened by an old road. The
road was dirt, only two grooved tire tracks. We followed the road. Puddles blotched the dirt road and
got bigger with more rain, the puddles broken by
ringlets from falling rain. Off by the river an ancient willow blurred into the gray mist and gray
sky.

The rain made the world so calm. Except I was
freezing. My clothes wrapped around me like a
soaked sock. My teeth chattered; I was jangled. I
kept imagining little green bushmen springing out
of nowhere. Bush blurred men ramming machine
guns down my throat, giving me diarrhea. When I
was a kid, Trip locked me in a toy chest, and I
thought he'd never let me out. I pounded and
screamed and cried until my throat was raw and
my eyes were bloodshot. I could feel myself as a
child now, locked in a toy chest. But no fun and
games. Only life and death. My feet were soaked—
I was walking in my socks. I stopped.

"I think we got time to put on our shoes."

I sat down and put my sneakers on. Michele
chattered with cold. Her face looked blue, like she
was bruising. She sat down and put on her shoes.
Then, back to walking. At first the sound was muffled by distance and rain. But it kept getting closer
and louder. Some kind of vehicle was ramming
down the dirt road toward us. I turned and looked,

couldn't see anything. We could've jumped out in
the field and laid low; but if they found us, that'd
be it. If they were looking for us. They had to be.

"Come on," I said.

And I grabbed Michele's arm and pulled her into
a full run. A hundred yards and we'd be shielded
by woods. The vehicle was closing in; it sounded
like a dump truck. I looked over my shoulder: in
the waist-high grass was a trail of semidried grass,
dried from our running through. Two black lines
traced our path. We still had fifty yards to the
woods, fifty yards with a black tail etching the
path to our hiding. Then we heard it. It was muffled by rain-heavy air. A puffing explosion—shotguns being blasted aimlessly into the sky.

There were three. They must have belonged to a
4-wheel-drive-in-black club. A black Toyota truck
bucked over a fallen tree. A black C–J7 swirled into
a skid on the road, rammed into a lower gear and
started shredding through the field. Then, a huge
pickup truck—needing a stepladder to climb into
the cab—mangled through a grove of saplings,
kicked into a lower gear, whined, then kicked back
to a higher gear. Each machine was powerful
enough to shred over a Volkswagen; the truck
looked big enough to maul over a school bus. They
were filled with groups of men in down vests and
flannel shirts and Budweiser and Mack truck hats.
Shotguns blasted off. The men hooted and hollered
like their favorite linebacker had broken the neck
of a hated quarterback. Michele and I were
$25,000—a lifetime of Coors beer, a lifetime of Jets
football.

We scrambled into the forest, a tangle of young
swamp maples. I didn't know how long the woods
would stop them. I looked back. The three ma-

chines fanned out. The Toyota went to the left and stopped, and the group of guys in back jumped out, with shotguns, and ran forward. The Jeep went right, stopped; guys jumped out, running forward. Everybody was running ahead of us, hoping we'd pop out of the woods on the other side, in the swamp.

The Ford truck bullied through the middle of the swamp maples. The guys in back jumped out and spread out, closing off the rear. This patch of trees was 100 yards wide, 50 yards thick; now it was surrounded on all sides. Everyone expected us to come out the other end. We kept scrambling forward. In splotches the forest turned into swamp. The Ford truck was a dark shadow behind us. The driver couldn't see us. So I lined us up directly with the path of the Ford. This guy could've cared less about catching us—he was having too much hooting and hollering fun ripping his awesome 4-wheel-drive machine through the forest. He shredded and plowed, going a steady five mph.

I pulled Michele down with me, and we crouched behind a felled tree, an older swamp maple now brown with rot. I set us up five yards behind the tree, lying flat. We hovered in the swamp bog. The grinding of the Ford drowned everything but the muffled spurts of shotgun blasts.

Michele begged: "What are we doing?"

"He'll come right over us. When he gets past, run up and karate the hell out of him. Then the truck is ours."

She didn't think it would work. I didn't either. But the truck was moving slowly. And our only hope was to overtake it. The Ford hit a stretch of cleared forest and ground into second gear. I looked over the tree to get the truck's line. I rolled

Michele over and lay on top of her, the duffle bag sandwiched between us. The truck slammed into the log. And the log spat forward, then splintered backward as the truck tore over it. The front wheels bucked over and slammed to the ground, two feet from our heads; the front wheels shredded swamp, dragging the back wheels over the rotten tree. The bog slowed the truck. Between us and driveshaft was maybe a four-foot clearance. As the truck lugged forward, we clawed out the rear. And Michele leaped up and ran to the driver's side.

His face reflected in the huge rearview mirror, half his tongue hanging out, his hand clenched around the steering wheel. Michele jumped onto the running board. She cocked her arm back and thrust a straight punch to his neck. The driver sprawled out flat into the cab. The truck kept going. I jumped into the back with the duffle, then got into the cab through the passenger's door. The driver was in the footwell, fading in and out of consciousness. Somehow he had his foot twisted and pinned against the gas pedal. I swatted the shift into neutral. The engine whined with over rpms, then settled. I pulled the driver out of the cab, ripped off his orange hat, orange down vest, and flannel shirt. I took off my clothes and got into his. I dragged him, a scrawny runt, away from the truck and left him, bare-chested, in the bog. I grabbed the duffle from the back and tossed it into the cab. Then I ran around the front and climbed in. Michele slid into the passenger's seat. The truck was deluxe. Individual bucket seats with X-crossing seatbelts; the driver hadn't bothered with his, which is why he sprawled flat into the wheelwell, unconscious. This rig was duded for Baja country. We strapped ourselves in with the seatbelts. I rammed into reverse. Michele grabbed a shotgun off the gun rack. On the floor was a case of shotgun shells. She loaded the double barrel, keeping the box of shells in her lap. The CB's squelch was turned full volume. It seemed like a riot was going on. Nobody could see us; we were hidden by woods. I grabbed the CB handle and started screaming.

"I flushed 'em. I flushed 'em. Dead center. Middle of the swamp."

The voices from the Jeep and Toyota squelched through in hysterics. I stomped the monster truck into gear and pulled out to the left. When we cleared the swamp maples, I rode the edge of the swamp, the harder ground firm under the left wheels, the softer bog squishy under my right wheels. I got the truck up to 30 mph. The Toyota rounded the edge of the trees. I kept barreling straight for it.

The panicked driver screamed over the CB, "What the fuck you doing?"

I answered him.

He tried to turn around. Didn't make it. He faced me broadside. And my front tire tore into the rear, pulling the weight of the truck over and through the back. We bucked left, off angle. The Toyota mushed into the water-soft earth. My rear wheel spat the truck away from us. I pulled hard into the woods, slammed into reverse, backed around and started off. The Toyota's back end was mangled and smashed flat into the bog; it looked like a tuna fish can scrunched by a garbage disposal. I yanked my truck into second gear and ran over the Toyota another time, pressing it deeper into the bog. The driver struggled to get out of the window. He held his CB handle in his hand.

His voice started to come through the CB, "Hey!..."

But Michele broke open the rear window with the butt of the shotgun. Then she stuck the barrel out of the opening and blasted in the Toyota's direction. The driver leaped out his window, dropping the CB handle. Michele fired again. And the driver scurried to the front of his truck for cover. He couldn't warn the Jeep. Michele reloaded and kept firing, keeping him from getting his CB.

I followed the swamp's edge and got into an overcranked third gear, a steady 40 mph. As soon as the Toyota was out of sight, the driver's voice came yelling through the CB: "They got Ricky's truck! They got him!"

We rounded a bluff of trees. The C–J7 was scurrying, trying to turn around and get away. The driver lost control and shot out into the the bog as he turned too sharply. The jeep humped over a wad of swamp moss and dirt, digging its nose into guck, its back poking straight out like the tail of a duck bobbing for food. Two guys leaped out. One went waist-deep into the swamp and half-swam, half-ran away; the other landed on firmer ground and made it to the woods. They both had guns. Michele leaned out and started blowing off her shotgun; it was loud enough to be an avalanche cannon.

In third gear I bounded over a swamp mound. We splashed in muck and sank to our bumper, our headlights under the tail of the Jeep. I muscled into second gear and popped the clutch, my foot punching the gas to the floor. The truck lurched like a hooked and fighting shark, water and mud spraying and splattering over the windshield. The left bumper slammed into the butt of the Jeep, crushing the metal like tinfoil. We scraped and

shredded over the Jeep, the rear wheel spitting out
scraps of metal and canvas top.

The swamp bog covered half the tires, slowing
us down. I swept out further into the swamp and
followed the line of the woods. Michele leaned out
of her window, shotgun ready. As men showed
themselves, she pumped and fired like she was
picking off carnival targets. After she fired both
rounds she ducked in and reloaded. Shotgun fire
splurted out from the woods in flashes; buckshot
sprayed the truck like sudden, violent gusts of hail.

All four tires shredded at the swamp like blood-
drunk sharks. The mud and water and swamp
grass thinned out. And we were on firm ground
again. I cranked the truck into fourth gear in the
open field, then snarled through sprigs of young
trees, the cleated tires gnawing the trees like a
wood chipper. The truck's cab was so high off the
ground that branches kept lashing through my
open window. After we got out of the trees we
pulled onto the dirt road. In the rearview mirror, I
could see a group of guys running behind us,
crouching and firing. Michele fired back, and the
group scattered and panicked and took cover. The
flashes from their guns were harmless as Bic
lighters, anyway. The image of them rattled in the
rearview mirror as the truck vibrated violently. I
followed the bending road and their image was
gone.

Chapter Forty-nine

|||| |||| |||| |||| ||||

THE TRUCK DROVE like a school bus. We followed the dirt road up river, away from the beer-crazed, 4-wheel-drive club. I had to stop. The rain fell hard. The windshield wipers flickered on top speed and still couldn't keep the steady sheet of water clear. The rain chattered on the roof. I fixed the heat and defroster, cranked it high, so hot air blasted out like a blow-dryer. I spun through the CB's dial until I found the police band.

The airwaves were alive with our position. Dangerous, armed, frothing to kill, merciless: no private citizen was to try to pull us in, no matter what the reward. Everybody headed south because there was no place to cross the flooding river except on a covered bridge. Information came in patches. Apparently, the local police chief had maintained a volunteer SWAT team for years, even though he never used the team, except with us. And now the state police were joking about the team's inability.

"Well," I said, "they're coming from the south."

Michele cupped her hands in front of a heater vent. "I guess we go north."

"Back to camp?"

She rubbed her hands. "I don't like it either."

"Okay."

I ground the truck into first gear—the rain had softened—and started off. Michele reloaded the shotgun. As I went faster, the engine noise drowned out the CB, so I turned the volume higher. The state police called in the National

Guard. A flock of helicopters from Albany was on
its way. Someone crossed the bridge ten miles
south of us. Others were headed north to cross another bridge. They wanted to sandwich us in on
the dirt road. Ambulances were instructed to cross
the bridge, head down the dirt road, and tend to
the vigilantes. The vigilantes did us one favor: they
told nobody they'd found us, wanting to keep the
glory, and money, for themselves. The state
troopers cussed their tongues limp at those jibber
fools—cussed the dinky police chief and his home-
stewed SWAT team. According to the state police,
the police chief's male parts were ridiculously
small.

Across the water from camp, I swung the truck
into the river. If the truck didn't make it, we'd
swim. The river bed was soft like clay. We sank
about five feet. And the current plowed broadside
against the truck, forcing me to drive at an angle
downstream. The truck churned through the
muck-bottomed river. We jagged and jolted over
hidden boulders. I pulled the truck into the canoe
launch, clanging and flattening over rusted boats.
I followed the tree-tunneled, grass-splotched road
we'd run down this morning. With luck, nobody
would be waiting for us at camp. I didn't try to
sneak into camp; it'd be easier to sneak a bulldozer
into a chess tournament. We bucked out onto the
field by the pool. It seemed nobody was at camp. I
stopped the truck.

"Get the car," I said. "And grab anything you
missed."

"Right." And Michele leaped out, ran over to our
cabins.

I swung the truck around, squared off, and
drove through the shallow end of the pool, into

the deep end, pressing the bumper against the tiled wall. I grabbed the shotgun and boxes of shells. I hopped out onto the hood and walked out on the diving board. Under the board was a tattered pool cover, bunched up. I sheeted the cover over the pool, draping the truck, semihidden—I didn't want helicopters to find out we'd ditched the truck. I ran across the field to Michele who was waiting in the car. I pulled open my door, tossed the shotgun in back. Michele had the heater and defroster cranked to ten. Her hair was matted in thick clumps. She chattered from the cold, chattered from the overdose fear-spiked adrenaline electrocutes one with. I wasn't any better. We left, saying good-bye with chattering teeth, to camp.

As Michele drove, I changed clothes. Then she pulled over, and I drove and she changed clothes —again, preppies just driving about for the scenery. We headed west into New York, into Poughkeepsie where we changed cars, leaving the shotgun and wet clothes locked in the trunk, throwing away the trunk key—of course, mam, we left the keys in the ignition—and we headed to where we were least expected: Riverton. We checked into a Holiday Inn. The room was sterile—flower-print bedspreads, thick light-blocking curtains, pastel wallpaper with a picture of a quaint New England fishing village, and the white bathroom with the toilet seat wrapped in paper, ensuring it'd been cleaned. All the room needed was elevator music.

I undressed and flopped onto the bed. It felt like I was ending a no-sleep, three-day bout with bad speed. My body had the dead weight of a mud-sunk, 100-year-old snapping turtle; my mind raced like a rat on 100,000 milligrams of caffeine, running endlessly on a rotating, squeaking wheel, going nowhere.

I got up and emptied the duffle bag on the second bed. Michele was still in the shower. All the tapes were unharmed, thanks to her wrapping job. The roll of film seemed intact. The tape recorder was fine. Our evidence was in good shape. But she'd forgotten my harmonicas, again. Shit: "I feel like walking, mama,...but I don't know which way to go..." Thank you, Leadbelly, thank you so. I lay back down. Thoughts started rushing. I didn't want to think. Please. In between the two beds was a control panel; lying down, I could control the lights, open the curtains, turn on the air conditioning, the heat. I turned on the TV and spun through the channels, settled on a rerun of "The Brady Bunch." I didn't need to see the beginning because I'd seen the show before, many times. As a kid I loved "The Brady Bunch," knew every episode. Their family life was so neat, orderly; everything resolved like a perfect love song. I watched it every night, thriving on reruns. Then my dad would turn off the TV for dinner, and I'd be back in the junkyard of my family.

Between commercials there was a news flash: "The mystery drug-world couple were unearthed at their hideout but escaped officials. More details on the nightly news. Tonight at seven." I rolled out of bed, walked over and knocked on the bathroom door.

Michele called out from the shower. "Jocko?"

"Hurry up. We're on the news."

"Okay."

I flopped back onto the bed, face down. I only heard the voices of "The Brady Bunch," but I could still see their faces in my mind, their gestures. Of course the strife ended, another happy conclusion. Then a solemn message: "Have you hugged your child today?" I remember my mother. Every night while she fixed dinner, she'd hear that message and then chase after me, catching me, then smother me in gin-reeking kisses, hugging me as I squirmed, smudging my face with thick, red lipstick, leaving me with the scent of tobacco and booze.

Michele came out of the bathroom and sat on the end of my bed. She'd wrapped herself with the hotel's white terrycloth robe. A towel spiraled up from her head. And she'd used another one to dry her feet and legs. The scent of soap, shampoo, and baby oil wafted over me. I wanted to bury myself next to her skin, the soft terrycloth warming me, the scents stroking me. But the news came on. I rolled over, propped my head with pillows.

We were the main story. There were aerial shots of the camp, the dirt road, the river. And they interviewed everybody: police, SWAT team members, National Guard, people from the calm community, vigilantes, the man we stole the truck from. There was footage of the swamp and the crushed Jeep and Toyota and the truck in the pool. Pictures of our camp, inside the cabin. Everyone interviewed speculated on what kind of people we were: ruthless, scared, killers, innocent. The state police commended the efforts of the local SWAT team; the SWAT team had acted on a tip from unrevealed sources. And the reporter put our lives together with scraps and bits, impressions left on those who tried to catch us. The reporter went through our cabins, the camera sweeping through racks of clothes, over the book *Crime and Punishment*, over Hawaiian boxer shorts, health food. Who were we? Underworld drug dons? Spies? Or just scared, innocent people? Whoever, they've hit hard times with no way to sing the blues—they left the harmonicas behind. And there was a shot of my saddle of harmonicas.

In a related story, another report had news of Trip. The reporter stood outside the prison hospital. The man who got this whole thing rolling, Trip Miles, died of liver cancer this morning. Trip told the priest, "Father, if there's a God, I hope He forgives me because I can't wait to die and leave this shithole. And when Jocko gets back, tell him I love him. I wish he was here." The reporter said Trip hadn't eaten in ten days. All he did was drink apple juice brought from home by his brother's girlfriend, Nicky. There was a shot of Nicky, trying to talk. But all she could do was cry and sob—"Trip was innocent," she said.

I turned off the TV.

Michele turned and looked at me.

I clenched my teeth hard, trying not to cry. But I could feel my face bending into a frown-smile. My eyes teared. My breathing shallowed. I clenched my teeth and face so hard I shook. The fucking idiot. Why'd I love him? Asshole. And now he's dead. Maybe it was just a coma. Maybe Please? Trip? I shook. And it felt like the earth was turning to sand and opening under me. No bottom. Nothing solid. Just falling. Emptiness And me scratching onto crumbling sand, trying not to be swallowed by dark. I let myself cry— why the fuck did I try to stop crying? I let my self. I cupped my hands over my eyes. Gasped for air and choked on tears. Michele wrapped around me. I pressed hard against her chest. I drowned in her warmth. My eyes bloodshot and burning. My throat raw from crying. My head pounding. Thank God he's dead. And why the hell did I think that? I'm a fucking asshole. Why did that thought come to me? Why? I wailed and wailed like I'd just been spanked on the ass and brought into this hell-hole world....

Chapter Fifty

|||| |||| |||| |||| ||||

> half asleep   half awake
> I'm talking to Trip
> you're dead   I say
> he says   I know
> are you okay
> I'm fine   he says
> when you die you're supposed to be gone   but you're still with me
> memories are ghosts   he says
> they have fortune cookies in heaven
> fuck off   he says   why you think I'm in heaven
> you're too good
> right   only a sobbing junkie
> I'm all alone   I say
> you are   the last of the family
> if I die the family's gone
> well hurry and knock someone up   he says
> fuck off

hey   a little respect for the dead

Trip eats green peppers   his hair is long again   his
beard is grown   he sits in a field of poppies   the
poppies are red and orange and yellow and blue and
purple   they are bulbous   and Trip slits them   the
ooze drips   Trip covers his green pepper with poppy
ooze and eats   he drinks apple juice   he calms   I
sit next to him poppy dust drifts in the wind

Trip says   I'm happy here

I guess   I say

the sky is blue   the sun is warm   Trip and I walk
through fields

we see grandpa drinking   grandma has just
died   grandpa drinks and drinks   he goes through
horse stables and chases horses into fields   they run
free under the moonlight silvered shadows   the
shotgun blasts   the horses panic   but grandfather
is too drunk to kill horses   but this is true   this
happened   I'm a little kid   father fights with
grandpa   and Trip and I run   trying to catch horses

I can't breathe

see grandpa was a junkie too

grandpa drinks   grandma shoots morphine   we
fix gin and tonics with slices of orange for mom who
lies in sheeted hospital beds hung over   we play the
blues with dad and drink Jack Daniels

see   they're all drunks   I say

it's no excuse   Trip says

it doesn't help   I say

and I feel rhythm   it's dark   the moon rises   the
sun sets   the tides   breathing dark water surrounds
me   womb warm   drunk hungover   strung
out   withdrawals   I feel so good when I got the
flow in me   I'm field hollering and I feel so bad
when the juice's flowed out of me   I'm field

hollering   life so simple   got the juice or don't
  heat from flames   they grow bigger
  Trip
  yes
  where are you
  here
  Trip's on his lobster boat   sitting cross-
legged   flames wrap around him   he melts into
flames   smiling   he turns to ashes   so happy
  I'm glad to be gone   he says   his voice mists out
from ashes and I love you
  and I wake

I wake staring at the floor. Light from the moon
spills through cracks in the curtains. Seeps through,
turning the room into a blend of light and dark—so
many gray tones—shapes. Michele's breathing. Her
breath rhythm lulls me to sleep.

I slept off and on for three days and three nights.
Only getting out of bed to go to the bathroom. Hoping each time I dove back into sleep the world would
go away. Yet the time came when I couldn't sleep—
it hurt to lie down. And the world hadn't gone away.
So I forced myself out of bed.

Michele was out of the room. She'd been busy
while I slept, tracking our story in newspapers.
Clipped shreds tattered the room. I went into the
bathroom and took a long, hot shower. I simply
stood under the steaming water and massaged my
neck and shoulders, arched my head back under the
water. I felt I had Trip's blessing: He'd wanted to die.
In my dreams he told me to enjoy the relief of his
being dead. He was happier. It still didn't seem real.
I hadn't seen him in six or more weeks. I guess it

would have been real if I held him in my arms and heard his last words. But even then, I don't know. There's no way to know about death. A lot of things can be imagined. Not death. And Trip is gone, forever. My mother and father—gone. I'm alone now. Yet I want to live.

I turned off the shower and walked out in the room. I didn't know what time it was. I pulled back the curtains. I couldn't see where the sun was; the clouds, spread flat and gray, blocked it. It could be morning or afternoon. All I know—it wasn't night. Naked, I did my exercises: 100 sit-ups, 100 push-ups, 100 deep knee bends, 100 side crunches. There was no chin-up bar. Instead, I did handstand push-ups. My blood pumped hard. That felt good. I decided I'd fast, drink only water for a few days, then start eating again, slowly. After working out, I was damp with sweat. I went back into the bathroom and started the shower. Stood under the hot water until it cooled, then toweled dry and went back out into the room. Alone. I needed to fast. To cleanse my liver. To cleanse my intestines. To cleanse. I'm starting over. My past can't be a blanket that suffocates. I must move on. I'll be 30 soon. I can't hide from the past. I must grow out of it, shed its skin like a snake, move on. I felt spiritual; Trip would say I read too many fortune cookies.

I slipped into a pair of Hawaiian boxer shorts and sat cross-legged in bed. Like I'd last seen Trip in my dream, sitting cross-legged with flames wrapped around him. I closed my eyes and rubbed my temples. A key slid into the outside doorknob.

"Jocko?" Michele shut the door behind her.

I opened my eyes. "Yeah."

She sat next to me, placing the back of her hand against my forehead like she was feeling my temperature. "You been up long?"

"About an hour—hour and a half."

"How do you feel?"

"Like I slept too much."

"You did. You kept talking in your sleep."

"What'd I say?"

"I couldn't tell. But you were talking to someone."

"My brother."

"I got some lunch." She pulled sandwiches out of a bag.

"What time is it?"

"About four."

"Oh."

"You want to eat?" She unwrapped a sandwich for me. It was a work of art: turkey with lettuce and tomato on rye bread. I started salivating. Well, maybe I could fast at another time. No sense in becoming a Yogi; I didn't even know how to stretch before running.

"That looks pretty good."

"Here." She handed me the sandwich then pulled one out for herself: Swiss cheese and tomato and lettuce. She also pulled out a half-gallon of apple juice, oranges, plums, and sliced watermelon.

"You feel okay?" She sat across from me, crossing her legs, too.

"Not bad. It's hard. But Trip was never happy. And really, it's a relief. Never knowing if he'd be alive or dead. Maybe he would have lived longer. Maybe not. I mean I feel guilty, but in a way, I'm glad he died."

"I guess."

I started eating my sandwich. I was starved. "Have you done anything?"

"No. I wanted to wait until you were awake."

"Well, I know what I'm going to do."

"What?"

"I'm coming up. I have a friend who's an editor of a newspaper. I'm calling him. Giving him the whole story. My side, anyway."

"Jocko, you can't."

"I can't go on."

"Let me talk to Hank first."

"No. After."

Russ Beardon originally convinced me to publish "Skateboard Blues" in his paper. He had a thing about artistic insight, feeling artists were canaries in coal mines. Soon as the bird topples over dead, miners know gasses are being released, and it's time to clear out. He said it wasn't his own analogy. But artists were warnings of bad times coming. Instead of being the canary, I'd rather watch the canary go limp— then I'd be able to get out alive. Russel said I had no choice in the matter. Artists are chosen. I never really thought of myself as an artist, though. Yet Russel insisted I was a poet; I felt "Skateboard Blues" was just another unfinished song, words with no music. I let him publish it anyway. Also, he was a friend of Trip's from way back. Maybe I called him just to be with someone who knew Trip.

Russel arrived just after getting his yearly haircut. Every June he got a crew cut, not getting another haircut until the following year. He never shaved his beard, and it hung down to the middle of his chest. He was on a macrobiotic diet—Trip got all his diet tips from Russel—but he still chain-smoked Pall Malls and drank cup after cup of coffee from his thermos. He fixed his coffee with goat's milk and raw sugar. Russel was a hangover from the radical sixties, still fighting wars against injustice. As the editor of his free weekly magazine, he'd take on the Mafia, politicians, big business, exploitative doctors, oppressive governments—people who're infuriated with the wrongs of the world will always have something to do.

Michele and I played him all the tapes. He recorded them onto his machine directly. We gave him the roll of film; the newspaper's lab would develop them. It took over six hours. But we told him everything. And he just sat there furiously sucking Pall Malls, scribbling notes, his cassette recorder running nonstop. When Russel smoked, he pulled at his beard like he was milking a cow, or a goat.

"Well," Russel said. "This'll be my paper Wednesday. My mouth'll be shut. And I'll be in jail Thursday." He smoked and milked his beard.

It took some doing, but on Wednesday we finally found a copy of Russel's paper in a punk-rock clothing store. He was right: our story was the paper. The cover was a collage of our pictures taken on the island. There were also stock photos of Scruggers and Broderick. Russel wrote a narrative account of our story with actual inserts of our recorded conversation. He transcribed the tape recordings in full. He had pictures of our camp. Of Cove Beach. Of the private yacht builders. Of Trip.

That night we were on the news, local and national. Scruggers was too. A group of reporters surrounded him at the police station, shoving microphones at him like swords. He scuffled with one reporter and started swinging wildly, knocking the woman on the head, swatting the camera onto the ground, the last picture being a breaking lens, the image shattering into blackness. They had shots of Broderick coming out of one of his restaurants, who said, "It's a hoax. The reporter should write fiction." When reporters persisted, he said, "Careful. You might ruin my suit. And I know none of you can afford to buy me a new one." And he climbed into his Cadillac limo, the door held open by Francis. And there were shots of Russel: he was handcuffed and dipping into the backseat of a police car. He'd refused to reveal sources. Refused to hand over tapes and notes and photographs. He was arrested and charged with a dictionary of terms.

And by Friday we were a national story. A stampede of journalists rumbled into Riverton throwing microphones in front of everybody, interviewing anybody who had a "real anecdote" that offered insight. I told Michele I wanted to call Mike Stills and give him everything. A lot had been found out. But I still didn't have answers. Before we called Mike Stills, Michele wanted to call Hank.

Chapter Fifty-one

|||| |||| |||| |||| ||||

WE CALLED HANK Saturday morning. Michele kep talking to him. Or trying. She stuttered, trying to say something; all she could get in were half-sen tences, half-words. The steady pumping of Hank' voice came through the receiver, a muffled squelch spitting through the ear piece.

I grabbed the phone from Michele. "Look, Hank. What's done is done. It was my idea. Not hers. I wasn't going to risk my life for you. Now, I'm taking everything to Mike Stills. If you want to see us first, just tell me when and where."

The phone hissed with dead air.

"I'll explain to Michele," he said.

I handed the phone to Michele. Hank's voice came through, steady, resolute, explaining when and where to meet.

We didn't talk all day. Michele sat around flipping through papers. I started a spy novel I'd bought in the lobby, got halfway through it, put it down, probably never finish it. I took a long bath, soaking in hot water until it cooled. Took a nap. Called for room service. Watched an old Tarzan movie. All day we didn't talk.

And as we drove to meet Hank, we still didn't talk. After ten o'clock we pulled into a South Riverton marina. The parking lot was empty except for glaring street lamps. The clubhouse was a thin-walled, square building, with fake wood paneling covering the outside.

"Wait for him here?" I asked.

Michele got out of her door. "No. He's inside. The backdoor is supposed to be open."

I got out and followed Michele around back. The kitchen door was open. No lights were on inside. But enough light spilled in from windows—moonlight and streetlight—so we could see. We walked out of the kitchen and into the dining room and bar.

Hank was sitting at a table in front of a picture

window. This wasn't a rich man's club. Tied to the docks were cheap motorboats, probably bought secondhand. Bare bulbs glared bald light over the fiberglass boats. Hank was only a shadow, the only light spilling in from outside. He drank from a snifter, then the tip of his cigar flared red as he inhaled. He stood to greet us but said nothing. He offered us chairs with a silent sweep of his arm.

"Anything to drink?" he asked.

I said, "I'll have a brandy."

"Michele?"

"White wine, please."

Hank went behind the bar. Old refrigerators and rusting plumbing clicked and hummed in the dark silence. Hank made drinks—ice into glasses, lifting and returning bottles—behind the bar. Just for something to do, I opened the duffle bag; Hank told Michele to bring everything so he could make copies. I fiddled with the tape recorder. Then sifted through the boxes of tapes. After we played them for Russel, Michele had resealed them. We still had some blank tapes and camera film.

Michele choked a whisper, "Jocko."

Something was wrong.

I looked. Hank swung out from behind the bar and stopped by the kitchen door. Behind him were two men, just shadows. All three walked toward us. As they neared the light spilling in from the picture window, their images sharpened— Broderick and Scruggers. I threaded a blank tape into the recorder—what did I have to lose if they caught me? I clicked the player to record, hoping the internal microphone would get something They stood in the dim light, no guns.

Scruggers looked the same, only older. He hadn't aged well. His face was creased with wrinkles. His pinstriped suit was matted and ratty. Scruggers couldn't stop fidgeting: he'd stretch his neck, clear his throat, run his fingers through his gray hair. He kept squeezing his wrists like he was doing forearm exercises. Broderick looked bored. He was dressed in crisp linen pants and an oyster-white, silk shirt. He lazily pulled out a Dunhill cigarette, lit it, and exhaled slowly. Michele looked at me. The gig was up. I knew why we were expected at the island. I knew how the rookie SWAT team got its tip-off. Hank spoke to Broderick in fluent French. Then Broderick called back to the kitchen. Francis, the driver, walked out clutching a Browning 9mm in his left hand, his right hand still wrapped in a cast. I got up. Scruggers grabbed under his arm. Francis jerked his gun at my chest.

I said, "Take it easy, guys." And walked over, taking the drinks from Hank's hands, then went back to the table. I gave Michele her drink. She didn't say anything. She just stared at Hank. Everything she'd fought for dissolved like moth wings over a candle flame. I knew the feeling. Everything lost. Nothing, nobody to turn to. Anxiety searing through your insides. Waking, and my parents were dead. Waking, and Trip had died. Michele's dreams and dedications were nothing, only useless yearnings she'd feel stupid over. She'd been tricked, used like a whore. Michele sipped her wine, then looked away from everybody. Hank gave some orders to Broderick in French.

"Time to leave," Broderick said.

"Yo," I said. "Tell the Frenchman to obligate a dying man. I want to know what's going down."

Broderick looked to Hank. Hank nodded yes. And pulled out a .38 revolver, holding it on me. Francis led Michele out, motioning with the gun that she was to move. Broderick and Scruggers followed.

When the kitchen door slammed shut, Hank said, "Well, what would you like to know?"

I didn't know where to start. "How about Trip?"

"You may wish to adjust the volume on the recorder. I am not concerned."

Oh well, I wasn't as smooth as I thought. I pulled the recorder out of the bag and pointed the microphone at Hank.

"Look," I said. "Let Michele go. Just off me."

"I am afraid I cannot. She simply knows too much. I feel bad for her."

"I feel bad for you."

"Why is that?"

"Soon as we get done with these jerks, you're next."

He laughed, leaning his head back slightly. "You are a funny man, Jocko. Go ahead. Ask me anything you would like."

Chapter Fifty-two

|||| |||| |||| |||| ||||

WE TALKED FOR an hour or so. He answered everything I asked and told me more. Then he led me out to the Cadillac where Michele, Scruggers, Broderick, and Francis waited. Broderick sat in the driver's seat with Scruggers across from him

Francis was in the backseat, facing Michele, his gun locked in at her chest. Hank opened the door for me. I climbed in with the duffle bag of evidence; Hank assured me Broderick and Scruggers knew what to do with the duffle. I got the keys from Michele for the rental car and gave them to Hank. He jingled them as he waved good-bye. We pulled out of the parking lot, leaving Hank alone, letting himself in the car.

"Broderick, got a cigarette?"

"Have the pack." He handed me a pack of Dunhills with matches. I lit one. The first drag gave my head a spin.

I started rambling. "Can't believe I quit smoking for nothing. Here I am, going to die anyway."

Michele wasn't well. She stared blankly out the window.

"Yo, Broderick. Obligate a dying man. Got any blow?"

Broderick reached over into the glove compartment, pulled out and handed me a vial. It was gold, the size of a film canister. But the top was skinny, like an aspirin bottle. I unscrewed the top. Connected to the top, like a rubber-cement brush, was a gold coke spoon, able to reach all the way to the bottom. I didn't have to dig that far. The vial was full. I did two snorts.

Within seconds my throat numbed. I couldn't tell if I was swallowing. My front teeth numbed. My eyes watered. My head was fresh and clear and crisp as subzero weather. I did two more snorts. This just might work. Simple plan: coke myself hysterical. Coke myself until I vibrated like a chainsaw. Coke myself into maniac jitters so I'd have one last encrazed whirlwind of exploding energy. One last resistance. I didn't want to die; hell,

I'm almost thirty, too old to die. I only hoped Michele snapped at the right time. This toot was fine. Just a little pleasure; hell if I'm going to die. They'd have to fight an encrazed coke fiend—overdosed—who was scared shitless of dying. And ready to die fighting, clawing, scratching, biting—anything. Crazy coke fiends are big jobs for anybody.

Broderick didn't take chances. He drove the speed limit on every road. It took almost forty-five minutes to get to North Riverton. I guessed I'd done about a gram of coke already. But I figured the gig was close to over so I kept snorting cocaine. My heartbeat thudded around 160. My teeth chattered. My hands shook like I was on a roller coaster. On top of the cocaine I chain-smoked. My body was in hysterics. My mind, too.

We stopped outside the gates of a private, small yacht club. Broderick got out of the car, went through a set of keys, then unlocked the gates and swung them open. He got back into the car, drove through, stopped just past the gates, got out, and locked the gates behind us. He got back into the car and drove to the docks, parking behind a club house leaving the car in the shadows.

With the machine gun, Francis motioned for us to get out of the car first. The air was thick with humidity, sticky. Across the water, bald bulbs shone hot over the docks. About 100 boats were docked—new, sleek powerboats and racing sail boats. In the deeper water, $100,000 yachts were moored.

"How come nobody gives you shit about coming in here?" I asked.

"I own the place," Broderick said. Money has its advantages.

Michele and I had the honor of leading the way. Our shoes clacked over the wooden dock. The moon half sphered in the sky, almost full. Across the sound, Long Island looked like a skinny, rotten, and purple eggplant—coke does odd things to my vision. So I did some more.

We stopped next to a powerboat; it was the size of a Buick. Broderick took the machine gun from Francis. Then Francis scurried about, undoing the tarp that covered the boat. After, he folded the tarp neatly and placed it in a rear compartment. There was no cabin in the boat. It had one large, double seat in the middle. Three people could sit with the driver; three people could sit with their backs to the driver. Francis got back onto the dock and took the machine gun from Broderick. Then Broderick climbed into the boat and started it. The engine turned over instantly, quietly, like an electric-start motorcycle. Scruggers stumbled in and sat next to Broderick, facing forward. Michele and I sat with our backs to Scruggers and Broderick. Francis undid the lines, then pushed us away from the dock and hopped in, sitting on the casing above the inboard motor. I lit another cigarette. I did double snorts of cocaine. It was going down soon. Too soon.

Good citizen that he was, Broderick observed the channel's speed limit. In open water he steadily eased the boat to higher speeds. It felt like we were skimming over glass. My hair that had grown back after Michele's butch wrapped around the side of my head. Francis squinted his eyes as the wind blew in his face, his hair pushed back by the wind. He looked like an advertisement: "Gay Men

Can Enjoy Windsurfing, Too." The machine gun
suggested gay men had better enjoy windsurfing.
Or else.

I lowered my head between my legs, sheltered
from the wind, and did aspirin-sized snorts of
coke. I lit another cigarette from the end of the last
one. Michele was huddled into herself, trying to
fight the chill wind, her head tilted so her chin
rested flat on her upper chest. What was she thinking? Had she decided, Fuck it, I'll just die? Or was
she still in shock? I didn't know. And couldn't
begin to imagine.

I wrapped my arm around her and pulled her
close for warmth. She pressed hard against me. I
nestled my head behind her ear, tried to say something. The wind drowned my words. I didn't want
to yell. I kissed her ear. She bunched her
shoulders. The kiss tickled. So I kissed her again.
She pulled away, a soft giggle puffing out, "Stop." I
kissed her on the neck. Hell of a time to get romantic.

Broderick slowed down, and we edged around
the tip of an island. The dock where the dogs had
lurched out at us looked skeletal as the moon
shone behind it. A seventy-foot sailboat was tied
up at the end of the dock. The cabin light was on.

Broderick eased to the dock. The shadows of
two men came out from the sailboat's cabin and
helped tie the motorboat to the dock. I didn't
need light to see who they were: Randy and Albert. They looked like an odd pair of twins. Albert now had a removable neckbrace, probably
from when I smacked him with his radio. And
Randy limped, probably from when Michele
kicked him. They both limped and hobbled and
turned their upper bodies with stiff necks when

they needed to look left or right. They'd be happy
to see us. Yet I doubted the reasons were social.
Broderick cut the engine. A soft wind ruffled the
water. Little waves, like thousands of eyebrows,
slapped lightly against the wood beams of the
dock. Broderick, Scruggers, and Francis got out
of the boat, leaving us inside. Francis sat on the
dock, dangling his feet over, swishing them back
and forth like a lovesick schoolgirl, angling the
machine gun at our heads. Broderick talked with
Randy. Then Randy went back to the cabin of the
sailboat, Albert followed. When they came back
out, Randy had a shotgun and three or four
cinder blocks. Albert carried an extra-large,
canvas duffle bag.

"Please, your duffle," Francis said, pointing with
his machine gun.

Albert walked over. I handed him the duffle
bag of evidence. He laid it flat on the dock and
pulled out a butterfly knife, the same one he
sliced Nicky with, I'm sure. With the knife he
made minute, razor incisions all over the bag.
With little holes, the bag would fill with water
faster. And sink easier. Then Albert placed our
duffle into the large canvas bag. Randy had filled
the canvas bag with cinderblocks. Albert continued with the knife work, jabbing the canvas duffle with holes. He handed the duffle back to me.
With the cinderblocks it was heavy enough to
pull out my shoulder.

Scruggers paced and smoked and coughed, unable to stand still. Broderick supervised like a
museum curator, making sure things were just
so. Francis dangled his legs, curled his toes. Broderick spoke to Randy, their backs angled away
from us.

"Fine, fine," Randy blurted. "Albert, let's be off."

Randy climbed in first, and the boat bobbed with his weight. Albert undid the lines, then hopped in.

"How ya'll doing?" Randy asked.

"Fine, fine," I said, mimicking his southern accent.

After laying his shotgun on the front seat, Randy started the boat. Albert sat in the backseat, making us sit on the deck. His chest was bare except for the shoulder holster. The ivory-handled .45 rested under his left shoulder. He'd also taken the machine gun from Francis.

Randy slipped into gear and gently pulled away. Ten yards out, he worked into high gear. We turned in a sweeping arch and headed out for the point of Long Island, out for open ocean. Michele and I sat over the engine. The vibrations gave me super cocaine jangles. I felt like a high-speed dentist drill. But I kept doing more cocaine. I was strung out on cocaine. On adrenaline rushes. Soon as I overdosed on fear of death, I'd be crazy. I kept smoking, hoping the nicotine would pump my heartbeat higher.

"Ya'll got nothing to fret about," Randy called out over the engine noise. "Well just set you afloat. Say there's a great white feeding on a darn whale. Hell if I know. We damn near spent all day fishing by that whale, still didn't catch no great white. A lot of other sharks, though. I heard if ya'll don't kick around much, they won't bother you none. Ya'll can let us know."

I leaned against a life preserver. It was harder than a rock; I wouldn't want anyone throwing it at me. A steady spray misted over the sides of the boat. Now I was cold. I chattered. It was hard to

smoke. Michele bunched close to me. Last chance,
soon.

We passed the tip of Long Island, about 1000
yards out. Now there was nothing but ocean and
sky and the almost-full moon shining. Randy
flicked on a flashlight and checked his nautical
charts, hoping the currents hadn't swept the dead
whale too far.

Chapter Fifty-three

|||| |||| |||| |||| ||||

THE DEAD WHALE floated belly up, its white stomach gleaming under a sheet of moonlight. Blood
pooled around the carcass like an oil spill. There
was a steady churning under the whale; the
sharks fed on its underside. Occasionally, a shark
slashed through the surface and thrust its jaws
into the side of the whale, taking a chunk of rotting flesh the size of a lamb, then knifing back
underwater. Randy eased the boat next to the
whale. Sometimes a frenzied shark slapped
against the hull. We couldn't see the sharks. But
we heard the churning, the ocean frothing
around the rotting whale. And the blood pooled.

"Be with ya'll in just a sec," Randy said.

He flicked off his flip-flops and slipped into a
pair of metal baseball cleats. He carefully stepped
out of the boat and onto the whale's belly, the
cleats giving him firm footing. Then he strolled
about thirty feet up to the whale's head and took a
leak off the other side, whistling to himself. As he

walked back, the cleats made a biting, squishing sound as they spiked into the whale's blubber. Randy hopped back into the boat, took off the shoes.

"Now, ya'll have to be naked," Randy said. "Put your clothes in the duffle. Come on, don't be shy."

The moonlight made it easy to see. Our skin was milky white. I looked at Michele. Randy pumped his shotgun.

"Go on, boy. Strip."

I stood up and undressed. I started shaking with cold and fear. I felt my teeth would break as easy as icicles.

"Go on, put your clothes in the duffle."

I did.

"Now, honey," Randy said. "I'll help you with your clothes. Come on up here. Albert, make sure he stays put."

Albert laughed. "Sure."

"We'll just make him watch, nice and helpless."

Albert chuckled. "Maybe we watch them."

"Come on up, honey."

Michele clung to me, trembling. She didn't move.

"Now, Albert, don't you know—I love 'em when they fight and scratch. Nothing like a little blood."

Randy walked to the back of the boat. He grabbed Michele by the arm and yanked her up. Michele tried to tear away, but Randy's hand leeched too tight around her arm. He squeezed her and yanked her to the front like she was a bag of toilet paper. He slapped her down on the bench seat. Then sat on her stomach. Michele groaned under his weight.

"Honey," Randy said. "I tell you, you ain't never

seen a pecker like mine. Sure ain't no string bean like your dink boyfriend's."

Albert laughed. "How you know? Maybe his grow more. You two friendly maricóns, huh?" He kept laughing.

"Just taking a learned guess," Randy said.

Randy arched his ass off Michele, keeping her pinned with his left arm. With his right hand he pulled off his shorts and underpants, then sat back on her.

"See what I'm saying," Randy said. "Now. Stroke it nice with your teensy hand."

He grabbed Michele's hand and placed it over his crotch. Michele yanked, hard.

He screamed, "You bitch!"

And he stood up and ripped Michele's shirt off. Michele screamed and tried to bite his arm. He pulled his arm back and swatted her across the face.

"Now I'm nice. Ol' Albert likes your mouth. But just one teensy, weensy scratch. And he blows your ears with his .45."

These two had been this route before. Albert was having too much fun watching his buddy struggle with Michele. And Michele was putting up a hell of a fight.

Albert blurted out, "Hey, I think you gay boy. Can't pork no little chick, huh?"

"God damn it," Randy said. Michele had bit him or something.

It's good Albert had fun, because he wasn't watching me. He didn't notice. I lit another cigarette. Then another. And another, until I had six lighted cigarettes. I put two between each finger. I made a fist, the cigarettes poking out, flaming spikes. I waited for Michele to get a good one in.

And she did—jabbing Randy in the balls—and Albert lost it, laughing. This would hurt me, too. But it'd hurt Albert more—he wasn't expecting anything.

I rammed my fist into the side of Albert's head. Two cigarettes crammed into his ear. Two cigarettes crammed into his cheek. Two cigarettes crammed into his moist eye. He screamed as 1600 degrees of burning tobacco seared his ear and flesh and blinded his eye. My hand burned. I released my fist, and the cigarettes singed into Albert's flesh. He swatted them away, lighted tobacco spraying like sparks. Albert clutched his face, screaming. And I pounded him again and again. On the side of his face. On his stomach. He buckled over and threw up, choking on his puke. I kicked him in the ribs. Kicked him in the back, hoping to feel cracking spine. Randy stood up. I grabbed the rock-hard life preserver and hurled myself wildly at Randy. The life preserver slammed into his neck. He choked on his scream and slapped onto the deck. And I blundered into him. But it was all or nothing. His hand grabbed for me. I tore myself apart and clutched at the hard life ring like it was an ax, and started hacking at Randy. Over and over. His top leg kicked me, his bottom leg scraped the deck, trying to push himself away. Michele got up and grabbed me by the shoulders, yanking me away. I stood up, shaking so hard I couldn't calm my arms.

I dropped my face into my hands, trying to get calm. I wanted to kill them both. Brutally. Slowly. So I could feel life breaking, bleeding out of them. Maybe crack their necks. Break their legs. Tear out their hearts. I'd lost it. My mind, gone. I had to stop. I lifted my face from my hands.

And Albert—the side of his face burned and bloody with open sores—leaped at me. He knocked the wind out of me. And we toppled over into the water.

Michele screamed, "Jocko!"

And she reached over, her hands stretched out for me. The water churned, a circular motion like a hot tub, the water warm with pooled blood. Albert screamed as salt water seared his burned face. But he fought. To kill. He swatted my head, pushing me under. Into the darkness of moonlit water—did I see the shadows of sharks, or was I hallucinating? I yanked his hand off my head. And grabbed his head and butted it against the boat's hull. He went limp. Long enough for me to grab desperately on the side and haul myself out of the water. My eyes burned with salt water. I rubbed them. And opened them—Randy was half-standing on the opposite side, the shotgun ready.

"Michele! Behind you!"

She turned, instinctively sensing danger. She swirled and hammered a kick, heel first, into Randy's knee. His bones crushed like Styrofoam. The shotgun blasted off, drowning Randy's scream. Buckshot clouded into the air, then pelted down on the boat and water. Michele kicked Randy again. His collarbone cracked. And she was going to kick him again. But I wrapped myself around her, my dead weight forcing her to stop. Then we heard the screaming. I turned to the side of the boat. Albert was bobbing up and down like a spastic epileptic. I reached out to him—I had to save him. He reached back. I clutched his arm and pulled. But I was almost torn into the water. Then a shark shredded his first leg off, then his second. Albert went light. And I yanked him up. His legs were gone, only stubs with veins and arteries dangling like tentacles. His eyes rolled up in shock, frozen. I dropped him in the water and threw up over the side. And a shark arched in front of my eyes, pulling Albert down, its mouth open, eyes glinting, crunching its jaws into Albert's chest. Down into darkness. I pushed myself into the deck of the boat and burst with dry heaves. My head and arms and legs and body shook violently. I huddled into myself. Brought my knees up to my chin, pressed my stomach against my thighs. Wrapped my arms around my folded legs and hugged them tighter. I closed my eyes and tried to stop the tears. Tried to stop the shaking. My head jittered against the deck. I needed darkness and warm fluid surrounding me and the rhythm of heartbeats and breathing.

Chapter Fifty-four

IIII IIII IIII IIII IIII

I BLACKED OUT. But I was awake now. Driving the boat full speed, salt water mist spraying over my face. Michele wanted to dump Randy—anywhere —and clear the hell out. Randy was tied, hands and feet, with yellow nylon rope. I didn't want to clear out. I couldn't. I had things to do. I offered to drop Michele off. She stayed with me.

I eased around Broderick's island; the sailboat

was still docked. I idled the boat and pulled along the sailboat's side, parallel. Michele hopped onto the front deck and got down on her stomach. I put the speedboat in neutral and hovered in the water. I pumped the shotgun.

Francis came out, curious and confused—he knew it was the right boat, but why hadn't they just docked? I took the pivoting spotlight and pointed it toward him, turning it on and scorching his eyes with 1000 watts. He covered his eyes with his arms.

"Hey, please."

He knew something was wrong. He pulled out another machine gun. I kept my aim low, rested the butt of the shotgun against my love handle. I pulled the trigger. The gun exploded and bucked into my flesh. Francis ballooned in the middle like a flying squirrel and flew back across the deck, the shotgun blast drowning his scream. My ears rang.

Below, in the cabin, the shadows of Broderick and Scruggers scrambled, sure they were caught. Michele was still flat on the front of the deck, her body yellowed by the cabin light seeping out of the portholes. I cut the speedboat's engine, pocketed the keys, and hopped on board. I pumped the shotgun. The teak floor was slick with a thin film of blood. I reached down and pulled away the machine gun from Francis; his hand wrapped around it soft and fleshy and lifeless, limply letting go to my yank.

"Michele," I called out. "You see them?"

"No." She kept looking in the portholes, trying to find them.

"Here," I tossed her the second machine gun. She clasped it. I looked in the cabin. Where the

hell could Scruggers and Broderick go? I guessed
they holed out up front. Armed, ready to die.

"Michele?"

"What?" she hissed back.

"Stand back."

I peered into the cabin—empty, still. They had
to be all the way in front. Time for some flushing. I
pointed the shotgun into the cabin and fired. It
blew off and kicked my shoulder like a donkey—a
hell of a gun.

Michele yelled, "What are you doing?"

"Flushing the slimes," I yelled back. Then I
yelled into the boat, "Come on Scruggers. You
don't come out, I'm going to blow this cannon into
the hull and sink this mother."

I waited. No answer.

I pumped and fired. Buckshot sprayed the cabin,
tattering everything into confetti.

"Michele! Shoot it from the front."

Michele broke open a porthole and stuck the
nozzle into the opening. There was a dull spattering as she fired with quick, spastic bursts.

Silence.

"All right," a muffled voice came from the front.
"Stop shooting. We're coming out."

Michele yelled back: "One at a time. Hands
wrapped around the backs of your heads."

Scruggers came forward first, his fingers laced
around the back of his head. Then Broderick followed.

Michele yelled: "Lie facedown on the floor."

I was losing control. If I ever had it. The shotgun shook in my hands like a runaway jackham-
mer. When they noticed how calm, cool, and
collected I was, Broderick and Scruggers started

cooing, scared for their lives—"Jocko, please. Take it easy."

"Flatten your faces," I screamed. They lay flat on their stomachs and tilted their heads into the deck.

Michele came around and went down the cabin stairs first. I was about to follow. All I heard was the grunting of a painful leap. The mass of weight fell on me like bags of wet tennis clay. Breath burst out of me. My shotgun went off. A mass of flesh wrapped around me—fucking Randy. Two arms, long as elephant trunks, clawed at my face and gut and tried to strip the shotgun away.

Michele yelled, "Jocko!"

Randy tried to strangle me. I bit his hand and tasted blood—how had he untied himself? His scream pierced my ear. I knew his weak spots. His neck, leg, and collarbone. I shook and thrashed, jabbed. I squirmed away. And a huge wrap of flesh gripped around my leg. I thought my shin would splinter. I pumped the shotgun and blasted Randy. He was crouched on one knee. The force of the gun smashed him into the rudder wheel, breaking the fiberglass casing. I screamed. But no sound came out. I screamed and screamed to myself—who was I? Three dead. Killed by me. Kill or be killed, I know. But it didn't help. How was I a murderer?

"Jocko?!"

Michele's yell snapped me back, for how long, I didn't know. I went into the cabin. I tried pointing the shotgun at Scruggers and Broderick. But it jittered like a seismograph needle reading a 7.8 earthquake.

"All right," I yelled. Deranged. "Broderick, up! Now! Strip this joint and spill the drugs."

Broderick carefully got up on his feet. Then I followed him as he tore open everything—cupboards, floor boards, engine box, front bunks, tool drawers, wall panels, bed cushions, seat cushions, fake life jackets: a custom-built yacht, built for stashing drugs. Bags of heroin and reefer and opium and quaaludes and pills fell out like dead pigeons.

When we finished, I made him lie back down next to Scruggers. Then I took all the sails, went up on deck and threw them in the water. On the main mast I unfastened the mainsail and blew it apart with the shotgun. I found the uninflated rubber dinghy and tossed it overboard. Then I pulled the spark plugs out of the engine and tossed them in the water. All the real lifejackets I tossed overboard. Then I untied the sailboat from the dock. And took two lines from the bow of the sailboat and tied them to the stern of the speedboat, fastening the lines on cleats. Now we were ready for towing.

Michele towed the sailboat with the speedboat as I sat below deck, shotgun in one hand, machine gun in the other, watching over Scruggers and Broderick. It took about an hour and a half to tow the boat south in the sound. When Michele stopped, we were two miles, north and south, from the Long Island and Connecticut shores. We were in direct line with the Port Jefferson Ferry route. I clicked the shortwave radio onto the emergency band.

I screamed, "Emergency! May Day! Long Island

sound. Marooned boat in the middle of the Port
Jefferson Ferry route. Help!"

An official, bored voice came back, asking for a
formal explanation.

I screamed back, "Get the fuck out here, asshole.
There's been a shootout. People are dead. The
boat's sinking with heroin, reefer, quaaludes—you
name it. It's a sailboat, asshole. Direct line to Port
Jefferson."

The voice cracked in panic. I shut off the radio.
Michele came below. I grabbed a dishtowel from
the sink and furiously rubbed the shotgun down,
over and over. I emptied the cartridges and shoved
the gun into Scruggers's hands.

"Touch it," I yelled.

He did, at first tentatively. Then I screamed in
his face, "Touch it all over, understand?"

He did. He smeared his fingerprints all over the
gun. I took it back from him, gripping it with the
towel, and laid it away. Michele took the towel and
wiped her machine gun clean, practically sterile.
She unclipped the magazine and handed the gun
to Broderick. He didn't need instructions. He
swirled his hands around the gun like he was
finger painting. Michele took the body from him
and handed him the clean magazine; he smeared
his fingerprints all over it. She took the magazine
and clipped it back on.

Then I went into the rear cabin and pulled out a
wooden paddle that was for the dinghy. Back in
the main cabin I made Broderick and Scruggers
crouch on their knees. I pulled the paddle back and
swung it full force—like a baseball bat—into the
base of Scruggers's skull. He sprawled flat onto the
deck, unconscious, gargling noises coming from
his throat. I did the same to Broderick; he slapped

onto the deck, next to Scruggers, out cold. They'd wake up to the Coast Guard's questions. I took the paddle with us.

When we went onto the deck, the Coast Guard's boat was cruising toward us, its spotlights sweeping the water in front of it. The speedboat had drifted out from the sailboat. Michele and I dove into the water and swam out to the speedboat, hauled ourselves on board, turned on the engine, curved out into the open water with no lights, glided away, the rushing air slashing through our wet clothes, both of us freezing, our teeth chattering.

Chapter Fifty-five

|||| |||| |||| |||| ||||

WE LEFT THE speedboat at a public dock; no one saw us. In the predawn light—a soft, washed-out pink—we walked to the main road of a small town restored to postcard perfection. Souvenir shops and seafood restaurants cluttered the quaint main street. At the end, we found a colonial inn. Inside, the night clerk commented on our wet clothes. I told him we tried to skinny dip but forgot we had clothes on. He chuckled—kids, he said. Anybody under sixty would be a kid to him.

In the room I stashed the duffle bag under the double bed. I stripped, laying my clothes over the chairs and desk so they'd dry. I climbed in under the blankets while Michele showered.

When she finished, I took a shower, a quick one, because most of the hot water was gone. After, I climbed back into bed, under a mound of covers, curling with my back to Michele, coming down from a cocaine overdose. My body was battered, tired. I felt old. My heart sputtered arhythmically. My mind raced as fast as the speedboat, images washing over and over. I didn't sleep much. If at all. Only half-asleep. Half-awake. I kept seeing and feeling the shotgun blasts into Francis and Randy. Kept wiping the gun clean of my prints—I washed away the prints, but I'd never wash out the images. Kept walking through pools of blood, hearing a squishing sound. Blood on my sneakers. Blood on my pants. Still a ringing in my ears from the shotgun blasts.

When I woke, a steady pounding pulsed at my temples. I shivered. My lungs ached, clogged, and I coughed in fits, with nothing coming up. And the coughing slapped my head into more pounding. I crawled into the bathroom, hugged cold porcelain, and had a bout of the dry heaves. My stomach retched painfully. Hot light glared off white tiles. Then I crawled back into bed. Michele tried to help. Her face was scallop white; she was in worse shape. She tried to knead my shoulders, but her fingers trembled in spasms, her massage useless. It takes so long to build health, and only one night to destroy it. It'd be the last.

Late afternoon I called Mike Stills. A woman from the secretarial pool answered.

"Hello," she said. "Riverton Police, may I help you?"

"I want to talk to Mike Stills."

"He's not in right now. May I ask who's calling?"

"Sure. Jocko Miles. The guy everyone's looking for. Find Stills. Tell him I'll call back in one hour. And he should be there."

She lost her composure, "But, but ..."

I hung up.

And at 5:07, exactly one hour later, I called back.

He answered, "Mike Stills."

"Mike, it's Jocko. I want to turn everything over. But I need a favor."

"Well, I'm not sure."

"Make sure. I want Trip's ashes. And I need time before I show up for anything official."

"I'll see what I can do."

"Just make sure," I said.

"Where can we meet?"

Mike Stills came to the motel. He hadn't changed. He wore a cheap, dark blue suit and white shirt. His dark blue tie had little American flags on it. We played him all the tapes. The only break we took was for the evening news newsreel footage of the Coast Guard and police on the sailboat at dawn. Broderick and Scruggers were in a minimum security hospital, both arrested on murder charges, possession of narcotics with the intent to sell. The anchorman said this was the biggest drug bust in northeastern history possibly American. The mystery tip-off man was still being sought. The undergound duo was still missing. The motel had cable, so we turned the volume low and switched to a 24-hour-a-day news station. Later we found bail had been set $1,000,000 for Broderick, and $750,000 for Scruggers. The last tape I played for Mike was the tape of my conversation with Hank Stewer. Mike Stills popped a Life Saver in his mouth; I'd asked him not to smoke in the room.

"Well," Mike Stills said. "If we can find the guy, that'll pretty much wrap it up. If we can find him. Any ideas?"

Michele shook her head. "None."

We turned everything over to Mike Stills. And we made statements of what happened to us from the beginning. He gathered everything and put it in an oversized carry-on bag he'd brought with him.

"And this," he said, "is for you."

He felt awkward and embarrassed. Well, leave it to Trip to make a joke out of his death. Mike Stills handed me a Skippy Peanut Butter jar, filled with Trip's ashes.

"It was his request," Mike Stills said, looking at the obscene jar.

"I believe it." I took the jar from him.

"I'll give you a week. Then someone'll bring you in if you don't come in yourself."

"You know where I'll be."

"I know," he said.

After Mike Stills left, I sat on the bed. My fucking brother. He'd finally cracked a dying joke I could laugh at. I held the peanut butter jar in my hands. I shook my head and started laughing. I laughed and laughed until my stomach hurt. I laughed so hard I cried. And cried. And kept crying. Salty tears dripped in my mouth. Crying until my eyes were sore and red. Crying. A grin-like expression stretching across my face. I couldn't stop crying.

Michele wrapped around me. "Jocko," she whispered. "Don't worry. It's all over."

I wiped my eyes with her tee shirt. But couldn't stop the tears.

She whispered, again. "Jocko,...it's all over."

Chapter Fifty-six

|||| |||| |||| |||| ||||

IT'S ALL OVER...

Those words echo. And it's been all over, for maybe two months now. Maybe longer. I don't know. Days drift like smoke. I try not to think. Sometimes I have to try so hard. Michele tries not to think, too. She's been living with me, all moved in. She runs ten miles a day, then practices karate. With physical exhaustion, she blots her mind dull.

I sing the blues. I bought a new set of harmonicas, from the bass-tuned G to the soprano-tuned F. I've worked them slow, not wanting to sour the reeds flat; harmonicas need to be broken in carefully. I spend my days singing, stretching my voice beyond its comfortable range. When my voice is sore, I play my father's piano. It helps some. Yet I still wake at three or four in the morning. Some nights I fall off to sleep again. Others I can't. I'll try my stomach, my back, my sides; I'll listen to the clock ticking, look at its glowing face. I listen to Michele's breathing. After forty-five minutes, I know it's useless. I'll get up and make soup or something. Play my acoustic guitar. Or stare out the window at the moon over the field. But mostly I write. I pull out a spiral bound notebook and write as fast as my hand can move. Later, during the day, I'll copy it over. I write until dawn, until exhaustion drains me. Then I'll sleep until ten or eleven. And wake confused, disoriented as insomniacs always are. After breakfast, I warm my fingers at the piano. Then I work my voice—scales, arpeggios, intervals, songs—for three hours. I drink herbal tea while I sing; Michele bought it for me. It soothes my throat. I used to drink coffee and always finished my singing wired on caffeine. After singing, I lay my harmonicas in a row on top of the baby grand piano and work through each one. Maybe I'll get a chromatic. At night Michele and I don't do much. She reads or watches TV. I listen to music and pore through music history books—a new repertoire is forming. I don't rush it. The Armadillo's Armpit wants me to lead the band again. Not yet. Maybe soon.

I keep telling myself, it's all over.

But it all comes back, somehow. On hot days I think of Broderick and Scruggers. Their bail was paid in full, in cash. And then it was three days before security guards called the police. The chief of security knew it was Broderick's Cadillac because Broderick was a principal owner of the Riverton Mall. So security let the car stay on the top parking level, unbothered. But after three days the stench got worse. The car had to be opened. Inside, Broderick and Scruggers were dead. Both had been shot in the middle of the forehead, the bullet hole centered like a Hindu's third eye. Death drained their feces and urine out, and the smell mixed with rotting flesh as they baked in the metal car, the heat scalding the days into the hundreds.

Most of what I know I've pieced together from my talk with Hank Stewer. And what happened after. Broderick knew what he was doing; he was the principal financier and wanted to route drug traffic through Riverton. I almost felt sorry for Scruggers. Almost. He'd been blackmailed. So long ago, Trip and I used to play a honkey, stomping blues at the Arctic Bird, the whore-house in Riverton. Trip played a boogie piano, and I played harmonica and sang. The madame wanted a down-home, New Orleans feel. The music had to be upbeat with lots of references to crawfish and Mardi Gras. I had to wear sun-glasses and act blind so none of the patrons would complain about a kid musician. I drank Boone Farms strawberry wine and Trip drank screwdrivers. Drinks on the house. And got our choice of women. They all wanted me, being an easy trick. I'd never guessed the only reason the whorehouse wasn't raided was because of Scrug-gers—he was the madame's friend. Good friends.

And fifteen years later a Frenchman shows up and knows all about it and plans to ruin Scrug-gers. And Broderick refused to put money up for the next election unless Scruggers went along. Scruggers had to cooperate. All he had to do was pick a fall guy and promise no police would snoop around too deeply. A fall guy and a rookie narc—Trip and Mike Stills. But Scruggers didn't find out things until after. No one told him two black men were going to be killed. And Scruggers goofed: he never told anyone his fall guy, Trip,

had a brother, me. That wouldn't do. So the
bomb threat scheme was concocted, with the
guise of a special security force. That's when
Scruggers got a call from Hank Stewer. Mr.
Stewer had a woman who needed field experience. Scruggers didn't want anything to do with
a professional. But the Frenchman and Broderick
convinced him it was an excellent cover. Besides,
she was a rookie. And Hank needed Michele taping Scruggers, finding out if Scruggers was turning or flipping or what. Michele thought she was
working for the FBI, gathering evidence on a
crooked cop. And nobody told Scruggers the plan
was simply to blow me up. And who was this
woman—a rookie—running off with Jocko
Miles? Hank didn't care about us; he figured Michele would obey orders and not do anything.
His energy went to calming Scruggers. He converted Scruggers, letting him know what was
"really" going on. And then Scruggers became an
ideological agent, a zealot—he couldn't do
enough for the Frenchman, even if it meant
murder and drugs. The end justified the means.

But the drugs never hit the streets. And race
riots broke out. The South Bronx policemen accused of killing the Snowman and the Coalman
were acquitted. "Skateboard Blues." Riots
scalded the city. And street wars broke out—
homemade bombs, random shootings, looting,
muggings, fires. For three days the South Bronx
was a war zone, worse than the 1980 Miami
riots. Encrazed crowds were clouded with tear
gas. Fire trucks hosed people to the ground. The
National Guard was called in. And tanks rolled
through the city. And men with machine guns

and gas masks and riot sticks and German shepherds raked the streets night and day.

When Hank first approached the South Bronx
dealers, they laughed. So he hired two Haitians
to burn the Colombians for high stakes cocaine.
Showing off, he set up Trip as the cocaine pirate.
When he went back to the dealers, he claimed to
have police support—how else could he set up
such a flimsy murder cover and get away with
it? He offered them the cocaine back if they
dumped his goods first. Hank wanted the streets
saturated with heroin, opium, quaaludes,
downers, reefer—any kind of sedative. People
blowing their noses out with coke and ripping
their minds with crack and wiring their nerves
with speed were too hyper. They excited too easily. But people running smack up their arms
could care less; if the South Bronx was dreaming
on heroin, they'd never notice if policemen were
acquitted. Drugs pacifying the masses. Big
Brother spoon-feeding nirvana. But Hank claimed
to work by himself, for nobody. And Scruggers
believed the slanderous commie press was responsible for creating unrest over the trial;
Scruggers would've done anything for his fellow
policemen.

After the riots, Hank Stewer was the big story.
Who was he? Technically, on paper, he didn't exist.
No cancelled checks. No phone numbers. No
school records. No Social Security number. No
birth certificate. No employment history. On
paper, the Institute for Undercover Training didn't
exist. It seemed he'd vanished. A man in Honduras
was shot and killed—maybe Hank Stewer. A man
was blown up in Lebanon—maybe Stewer. A man
was arrested crossing East German lines—maybe

Hank. And one man confessed to being Hank Stewer; he was drunk, had been for days, probably years.

But Hank showed up. Dead.

He'd told me the only concession he made to the South Bronx dealers was an agreement to move the drugs with one shipment. They didn't trust him. After all, he burned them for cocaine, then came back with a screwy offer. Real screwy. One shipment made inventory tracking easier. Hank wanted things distributed piecemeal; they wouldn't hear of it. So he agreed. I guess after he last saw us, he went down to the South Bronx— somewhere—and waited for the drugs to sail in. They never did.

Hank Stewer was found in an abandoned building in Harlem. The brick was charred from fire. Hank weighed less than a hundred pounds. His skin wrapped around his bones like melting waxed paper. The autopsy confirmed Hank was addicted to heroin at the time of death. Cause of death: starvation and heroin withdrawal. I'm sure the South Bronx dealers took perverse plea-sure in getting Hank strung out on smack, then watching him die with no food or water or her-in. He'd cost them drugs and money, and caused too many headaches. They never wanted to see him again. And made sure. Sometimes in my dreams I see and hear Trip screaming as he goes through withdrawals. The image blurs into Hank Stewer begging me for help. And it scares me. In my dreams I could care less if Hank's in pain.

So it'll never be all over.

But I tried to wrap things up. I took six hundred dollars and went to see Len, from Tasty Treats. I gave him the cash, it's what we took in the day of

the recording. I hoped he'd keep it for himself. But
he put it in the Tasty Treats cash box—too honest
He showed me the truck we'd used. Only one small
dent. He was proud his trucks were so tough. He
offered me a cigarette. I didn't take it. He though
it was good—if I played football I shouldn'
smoke. I almost told him it had nothing to do with
football. But didn't. I stood with him while he
smoked, then left.

I've seen Nicky a few times. She came around
making sure my feelings weren't hurt. She was
dating one of my friends, Eddy, the mad Puerto
Rican drummer. Eddy could've cared less abou
my feelings. He sauntered in one day, unan
nounced, tequila, lemons, salt, playing the drums
insisting I get hammered with him. A celebration
He sang all about it. He'd gotten out of the hospi
tal, his skin splotchy white from the burns.
kicked him out, told him I'd call him when I pu
together another band. I went down in history as
being a major pin-head for not drinking with him
He swore when he became a famous movie star al
he'd do was spit on me. After being on TV news, he
decided to become a screen star. I'll live withou
his affection.

I don't know how long Nicky's been with him
After I vanished, she started taking care of Trip
Trip didn't give a fuck—it was her gig if she
wanted to fall for a dying man. And he neede
someone to bring him apple juice from home. S
she did, every day. She couldn't figure how ther
was always a fresh supply of apple juice, whe
he was in the hospital. Who put the apple juic
there? A friend, Trip said. One day she was late
so she just picked up apple juice at a Gran
Union in Danbury. Trip screamed at her an

made her go back to his house. Later, after Trip died, Nicky was arrested for smuggling drugs into the prison hospital; the apple juice was treated with heroin. Judiciously rationed, Trip was able to dose himself with heroin throughout the day. They had it on videotape: every one or two hours he'd take a measured swig. Trip's autopsy determined he was a heroin addict. But Nicky had no idea what she was doing; she was acquitted. I had no idea Trip was strung out on heroin, again.

Tai did. I had dinner one night at her Chinese place. She told me. She'd been giving Trip free heroin for over a year. It was the only way he could tolerate the pain of cancer. A year. That's when he first started his macrobiotic diet, when he was dismissed from the hospital. In the prison hospital he couldn't smoke the smack. Couldn't snort it. Couldn't shoot it up. Tai came up with the solution. And, unknowingly, Nicky brought Trip his relief until he died. It eased the pain. Tai said he couldn't stand the pain. Mostly, he didn't want me to watch him die slowly, and wretchedly. He wanted to spend the end of life with me, hanging out like brothers and friends. Like things were normal.

Sometimes I talk to Trip in dreams.

I played publicly once. I drove to Chaz's place, on Thursday. It was after seven weeks of stretching and working and conditioning my voice, flexing it into shape for three hours a day. It had been so long since I played, it felt like the first time. But better. I had eighteen years of experience. And all of it seemed fresh, new. Feeling the pulse of the crowd. The heat. Sweat on my head. Sweat soaking my back. I wore my tee shirt from

Blind Pig records. I'd sing, then solo on my harmonica, then solo with my voice—blues scat
singing. Something I'd worked on for years but
never used. The crowd loved it. Chaz gave me the
spotlight, only backing me with his mean baritone sax as I sang. And the bass player, guitarist,
pianist, drummer all took backseats. My show.
For the last two numbers I did "Blues with a
Feeling," a slow, wailing blues, one of Paul But-
terfield's numbers. I finished with a stomping
version of "Everybody's Fishing," something I got
from Walter Horton. When I finished, the crowd
yelped and whooped and hollered and stomped
their feet. More! More! More! Sweat soaked my
hair. My shirt was soaked too. My skin started to
chill. I lifted my arm and waved, my harmonica
between my first two fingers. The crowd
whooped, More! I'd give them more. But not tonight. I'd be back.

Upstairs, Chaz was ecstatic. He'd always said
my real talent was my voice. Always gave me shit
saying I just coasted on natural gifts. Always rattled off incongruous examples: How did Michelangelo become a great sculptor? And how did Walter
Payton become a great running back? They had
talent. And they worked their butts off. You got talent, and all you do is use your butt for a cushion
Like Michelangelo toodling around with balsa
wood. But tonight, upstairs, he kept slapping me
on the back, saying my honkey ass was wising up
He carved beautiful lines of cocaine on a slab o
pink marble. I didn't snort any. "That's good," he
said. "Cocaine ruins the nose. And a ruined nose is
a ruined voice. My, my," he said. "Your honkey as
sure is smartin' up."

I couldn't sleep after playing, the pulse of the

music in me, throbbing. So I wrote all night in my journal. In the basement of my barn, I have ten stolen milk crates from Marcus Dairy. They're filled with spiral bound notebooks. About five to ten thousand pages, I'd guess. I started keeping a journal after my parents died. Thirteen years now. Filling the pages, hoping to catch a breath for a poem. Then it turned into just journal writing. I skipped the hope for poems. Each notebook is marked on the cover, showing which months of which year are included. Anyway, Russel Beardon, the newspaper editor, found out I was obsessed with keeping a journal. It's a habit. I start feeling disoriented if I go too long without writing. The longest lapse I had was while I was underground with Michele. Russel convinced me to write down what happened. Just as I remembered. So that's how these words came to be put onto paper. Every night images soak my dreams and I wake, sweating. If I don't fall off to sleep again, I pull myself out of bed and write until dawn. Write until sunlight washes away darkness. I hope by writing—always the same hope —that things will make more sense. Russel serializes my writing. It's all true. Of course names and places and so on have been changed, to protect the innocent. If there is such a thing.

My first entry was about Trip ...

Chapter Fifty-seven

‖‖ ‖‖ ‖‖ ‖‖ ‖‖

6/21/86

It takes all day to hike to the top of Bald Mountain.
We are above the tree line, mostly. Only scrub
pines, like Bonsai trees, snarl the rocks. Michele
and I set up in a pine lean-to, in a small ravine
covered with scrub pines and aqua-colored moss.
The floor is covered with soft, brown pine needles.
The smell of pine wraps around us in darkness.
But I can't sleep.

I walk out, naked, onto the mountain top of rock.
The sky is smeared with stars. The moon is full.
There is a puddle of rain water, a dark stain on the
silvered rock at night.

A soft wind blows.

I stand naked.

I stand with my back to the wind. The rain
puddle spreads before me like a small spring lake.

I kneel. I take the top off the Skippy Peanut
Butter jar—only Trip. And tilt the ashes into the
wind.

The ashes spread through the puddle like blood.
I stir the water with my hand, blending Trip's
ashes with rain water.

I kneel farther and drink the water, wanting
nourishment from the dead.

I drink.

A thin silt is filtered by my teeth—the dust of
rock or the dust of ash? I drink and drink.

Then I crawl into the puddle and bathe in the
water of ashes, splashing water over my chest and
legs and arms and back and face and hair.

Out of the water I lie next to the puddle. The wind dries me. I shiver to sleep.

I wake.

It's morning. A soft rain falls from one flat cloud over me. Yet in all directions the sky is blue.

The sun rises, a flat, dull orange disk; opposite the sun, the full moon sets, a pale white like mother's milk.

Sunlight shines through rain. A rainbow arches over the valley, blessing from a sun shower.

I go back to the lean-to. Michele zipped our sleeping bags together.

I climb in with her, cold. She wraps around me and rubs me until the heat from her rubbing palms warms me. I wrap around her.

Our arms around each other.

Our tongues, moist, warm, meeting.

The heat blends us.

She is ready. A sweet parting to the wetness and warmth between her thighs—I'm throbbing.

I'm alive.

She's alive.

We are among the living.

I pull her on top of me. Heat from our bodies. We melt with love and warmth.

Our blood dances.

Please, may our child be conceived ...

The End?

The end of a book is never really *the end* for a person who reads. He or she can always open another. And another.

Every page holds possibilities.

But millions of kids don't see them. Don't know they're there. Millions of kids can't read, or won't.

That's why there's RIF. Reading is Fundamental (RIF) is a national nonprofit program that works with thousands of community organizations to help young people discover the fun—and the importance—of reading.

RIF motivates kids so that they *want* to read. And RIF works directly with parents to help them encourage their children's reading. RIF gets books to children and children into books, so they grow up reading and become adults who can read. Adults like you.

For more information on how to start a RIF program in your neighborhood, or help your own child grow up reading, write to:

RIF
Dept. BK-1
Box 23444
Washington, D.C.
20026

Founded in 1966, RIF is a national non-profit organization with local projects run by volunteers in every state of the union.

A NOVEL OF PURE TERROR!

BLOOD FARM

by

SAM SICILIANO

From a stolen hour of feverish passion to a
narrowing dance with the emissaries of evil,
Mike and Angela are driven through a storm-
tossed night into the yawning maw of
hell! What terrifying evil lurks in the unspeak-
able needs and insatiable passions of the
undead? What ghastly savagery awaits them
when they accept the chilling hospitality of
Blut Farm?

0-517-00660-X $3.95

ON SALE NOW
FROM PAGEANT BOOKS!